I0623772

THESE
BODIES
BETWEEN
US

ALSO BY SARAH VAN NAME

THE GOODBYE SUMMER
ANY PLACE BUT HERE

THESE BODIES BETWEEN US

SARAH VAN NAME

DELACORTE PRESS

This is a work of fiction. Names, characters, places, and incidents either are the product of the author's imagination or are used fictitiously. Any resemblance to actual persons, living or dead, events, or locales is entirely coincidental.

Text copyright © 2024 by Sarah Van Name
Jacket art copyright © 2024 by Hokyoung Kim

All rights reserved. Published in the United States by Delacorte Press, an imprint of Random House Children's Books, a division of Penguin Random House LLC, New York.

Delacorte Press is a registered trademark and the colophon is a trademark of Penguin Random House LLC.

Visit us on the Web! GetUnderlined.com

Educators and librarians, for a variety of teaching tools, visit us at RHTeachersLibrarians.com

Library of Congress Cataloging-in-Publication Data
Names: Van Name, Sarah, author.
Title: These bodies between us / Sarah Van Name.
Description: First edition. | New York : Delacorte Press, 2024. | Audience: Ages 12 and up. | Audience: Grades 10–12. | Summary: In their familiar North Carolina beach town, Callie and her friends, Talia and Cleo, are joined by the enigmatic Polly, who introduces the idea of learning how to make themselves invisible, a plan that initially seems impossible but eventually works, leading to a recklessness that makes it increasingly difficult for the girls to return to their former selves.
Identifiers: LCCN 2023045708 (print) | LCCN 2023045709 (ebook) | ISBN 978-0-593-64617-5 (hardcover) | ISBN 978-0-593-64618-2 (lib. bdg.) | ISBN 978-0-593-64619-9 (ebook) | ISBN 978-0-593-81045-3 (int'l ed.)
Subjects: CYAC: Friendship—Fiction. | Invisibility—Fiction. | Summer—Fiction. | LGBTQ+ people—Fiction. | LCGFT: Novels.
Classification: LCC PZ7.1.V353 2024 (print) | LCC PZ7.1.V353 (ebook) | DDC [Fic]—dc23

The text of this book is set in 11.5-point Joanna MT Pro.
Editor: Hannah Hill
Cover Designer: Trisha Previte
Interior Designer: Megan Shortt
Copy Editor: Colleen Fellingham
Managing Editor: Tamar Schwartz
Production Editor: Natalia Dextre

Printed in the United States of America
10 9 8 7 6 5 4 3 2 1
First Edition

Random House Children's Books supports the First Amendment and celebrates the right to read.

Penguin Random House LLC supports copyright. Copyright fuels creativity, encourages diverse voices, promotes free speech, and creates a vibrant culture. Thank you for buying an authorized edition of this book and for complying with copyright laws by not reproducing, scanning, or distributing any part in any form without permission. You are supporting writers and allowing Penguin Random House to publish books for every reader.

FOR CHLOE,
THE ORIGINAL
SUMMER GIRL

PROLOGUE

I

1   THE START OF SUMMER
2   CLEO'S PLAN
3   LAST SKATER STANDING
4   DAYTIMES IN JUNE
5   MEDITATION PRACTICE
6   THE DAWN OF JULY
7   THE BASEMENT
8   GRADUATION MORNING
9   THE NEW MOON
10 RITUAL

II

11 THE DAY AFTER
12 CLEANING UP
13 REAL LIFE
14 FIRST
15 THE POLTERGEISTS

16   MARCO POLO
17   LIGHTNING
18   SUNRISE
19   RUNAWAY
20   TOO MUCH

III

21   RUNNING ON SAND
22   MIAMI PARTY
23   HUMMINGBIRD
24   POURING RAIN
25   THE BIRTH OF VENUS
26   THE END
27   THE END, PART II
28   AFTER

PROLOGUE

Four girls. Four girls skating home on four-wheel skates, both sides of the road, fearless, their hair in tangles around their faces, the sun crystallizing on their skin. Four girls at the mouth of an infinite ocean, sugared and salted with sand and seawater, the tide licking their sunburned feet, twirling blindly and laughing in the black of a new moon. Four girls in two pairs, four girls alone, absent-minded at dinner tables with parents and grandparents, falling asleep with their windows open, feeling the breath of the wind.

Four girls together again in the morning, lowering themselves onto their towels. Paperback books and cheap sunglasses, water bottles and cold coffee and pretzels, fighting over the playlist on the Bluetooth speaker as the beach fills up with families. Four girls like kites, twisting and colorful, visible from space.

Four girls who could be anyone, anywhere, four girls timeless in their careless and unbounded youth. But we aren't lost in time, and we know exactly where we are. It's June in Little Beach, North Carolina, and we're about to disappear.

I

1

THE START OF SUMMER

You can measure the start of summer in a lot of different ways. You could call it the day after the last day of school. You could use Memorial Day, or the solstice, or the first day the temperature tiptoes over a hundred. If you're in Little Beach, where I'm from, you could say it's begun when the percentage of people in the grocery store is more tourist than local, or when the skating rink opens for seven-days-a-week service. But for me, the beginning of summer was always the day that Cleo arrived.

That year, it was June 16. School had ended only one day before, and I could taste the emotion of that ending on my tongue—the release, the excitement, the exhilarating knowledge that this was our second-to-last last day ever. My best friend Talia and I were seniors now, if, like us, you thought of the start of the summer as the real start of the next year. We sat at the top of the wooden steps of Cleo's grandparents' house, waiting. We could have come over after Cleo arrived, but that would have meant missing ten minutes with her. Like every year, we had skated over as soon as she'd texted us saying their car had passed the exit for Wilmington. Between us were a box of cupcakes (chocolate, melting) and my phone (playing Sylvan Esso, bopping through my earbuds). The left earbud was in my ear. The right was in Talia's, until she took it out, untangling it from a curl of dark hair.

"I don't think I get this song," she said, scrunching up her face.

I was ready for this objection. "Is it the lyrics?" I asked. "Because I know they don't make sense per se, but—"

"This is just random bleeps and bloops and— Is that a banjo in the background?"

"No, I think that's just a different kind of bleep. But it's great running music. And they actually do get more melodic in the chorus, like, here, listen . . ."

"Okay, but more I'm just saying, like, this is not a pretty song, you know? This is not a song that I *enjoy* listening to."

"Not every song has to be—" I started, but then the little green station wagon pulled in, crunching on the gravel, and we both jumped up. Talia started waving her hands, like she was guiding a ship in from sea.

Cleo tumbled out of the car before it had stopped moving and shrieked as she ran up the stairs to us. In the few months since I'd seen her, she'd cut her hair short and she was wearing new clothes—white sandals and a yellow dress that glowed like the sun on her dark brown skin. But as she catapulted herself up the final stair to hug me and Talia, she was the same as ever. Same strong arms, same orange-body-wash smell, same voice in our ears.

"I swear the drive's never taken so long, there was a crash on highway seventeen, and then we had to stop for Grandpa to use the bathroom— *God*, it's so good to see you."

"We missed you," Talia said.

I echoed her. "So much," I said. "So, so much."

"I missed you too, I have so many things to— Oh, where is Polly?" She pulled away from us. I readied myself for our first break from routine. This part—this girl, Polly—was new.

"Polly, where are you?" Cleo called.

Below us, the car doors were opening. I peered down at three figures climbing out: Cleo's grandmother and grandfather and a thin, pale girl with a low yellow ponytail, large blue eyes, a face like a doll, and no presence whatsoever. Polly. We had met her a handful of times in the background of video chats, grainy and quiet; at the time, I hadn't understood her appeal. The same was true in person.

She raised a hand. "Hi," she said.

"Hi," I said.

"Hi!" Talia exclaimed, enthusiastic. "It's so great to meet you for real! Finally! Can I help you with your bags?"

This was why Talia had more friends than I did.

"What are we, chopped liver?" Cleo's grandma gestured to herself and her husband as we followed Cleo down the stairs to the car.

"It's nice to see you again, Mrs. Haynes," I said as she embraced me. "Hi, Mr. Haynes. Thank you for bringing us Cleo."

"It's our pleasure," Mrs. Haynes said. "Without you two there's no way my granddaughter would visit for the whole summer."

"We're too boring," Mr. Haynes added.

"*You're* boring," his wife corrected. "I'm cool. Now, who is going to carry this luggage upstairs?"

We got everything up in one trip: the bags the girls had checked on the plane from Washington, DC, to Raleigh and their two carry-ons, Polly's plain black duffel and Cleo's backpack bursting with rainbow pins and patches. We set them in the guest room with the two twin beds before convening in the kitchen. Cleo started telling a story: "There was this woman on the flight who could not *believe* that Polly and I were flying alone"—while Mr. Haynes asked Talia how the first week of summer hours at the rink had gone, and Mrs. Haynes bustled around unboxing the cupcakes and setting out glasses of sweet tea.

I sat down at the kitchen table, my back to the windows and the ocean, and let myself settle into the noise and laughter. This was how it always was when Cleo came: the kitchen, the tea, the voices talking over each other. I felt the summer shifting into place.

With one snag. I glanced at Polly, who was sitting to my right.

"So is this your first time ever visiting North Carolina?" I asked as Talia burst into laughter at Cleo's story.

Polly turned, looking startled as a deer. "What?"

I exhaled. "Nothing."

Cleo finished her story, sighed happily, and sank into a chair. A lull settled over the room. In the background, the ocean murmured.

Mrs. Haynes broke the silence by asking, "So, girls, what's your project going to be this summer?"

Cleo's eyes lit up. "I have something in mind."

"Really?" Talia leaned in. "You haven't said anything."

"It's a secret," Cleo said, a smile curving across her face.

Polly was staring out the window, not reacting. She seemed transfixed by the waves. I assumed this was because she was secretly a robot, but Cleo's grandma must have thought poor Polly was getting left out, because she explained, "These girls always have a project for their summer. I find it quite industrious. All I did in my summer breaks was work and chase after boys, but these girls . . ." She chuckled. "What did you do last summer again?"

"We learned how to make ice cream." Talia smiled at the memory.

"Goodness me, was that just last summer?" Mr. Haynes exclaimed. "I still think about that cherry chocolate swirl. Best ice cream I've ever had."

Our summer projects have always worked out perfectly. The summer we were thirteen, our goal was to learn to skate, and now we had the best jobs on the island. Two summers ago, when we were fifteen, we got into scrapbooking—which, okay, sounds like an old-lady thing to do, but it was great, going to the drugstore to get pictures printed and then pasting them into books alongside old journal entries and newspaper headlines.

I had an idea for this summer. I hadn't told Talia because I knew that she wouldn't like it, but I hoped Cleo might be interested, and Polly was a wild card. My dad had a friend of a friend at the alternative radio station a few towns over, and he'd mentioned they might be looking for DJs for the less popular shifts. No one listened to the radio, but . . . surely some people still listened to the radio, right? We could get in contact with the guy, learn how to work with the software, memorize whatever arcane rules governed radio broadcasting, make playlists. I had a vision of us sitting in a recording booth together as the music that mattered so much to me drifted out over the airwaves to unknown cars and kitchens.

But the glint in Cleo's eye told a different story. In our phone conversations and texts and postcards over the last few months, she had been unusually quiet about summer plans. I never thought she had forgotten about them, but she had been so excited talking about Polly joining us—showing her the sights of Little Beach, working with her at the rink—that I thought maybe Polly *was* the project. It seemed I was wrong. That was good, at least.

"Speaking of ice cream," Mrs. Haynes said, standing up, "anyone hungry for dinner?"

It was only four, but my and Cleo's hands shot up. I was always hungry. Besides, Talia and I had to be at work in an hour, so it was either dinner now or much later.

"I thought I'd pick up pizza and salad from Island Italian. That sound good to everyone?"

"Yes please," Cleo said, beaming. "God, Island Italian. My second favorite pizza in the world."

"Rude," Talia said.

"Favorite in North Carolina. That's not nothing."

"We'll go pick it up," Mr. Haynes said. "You girls stay here and get settled in. We'll be back in half an hour, okay?"

"Thank you," we chorused.

They got their things and went out the door, and we sat in

silence at the kitchen table. Polly kept looking out at the ocean. Talia glanced between me and Cleo. I unwrapped a cupcake and waited for the sound of their car pulling away.

"Now," said Cleo. She leaned into the light. "Here's what we're going to do."

2 CLEO'S PLAN

I can't remember a time without Talia. I mean that literally: In my earliest memory, she's there beside me, the two of us digging our pudgy three-year-old hands into the sand. We were each other's favorite friends in day care; our parents would pass us off on alternating Saturday nights so they could go to Island Italian or to Wilmington for a movie. There are whole photo albums filled with pictures of just us together on the beach, her olive skin and my sunburned freckles, my frizzy brown pigtails and her dark curls. We went to the same elementary, middle, and high schools. Her house was a mile from mine. When I was too serious, she made me laugh; when she cried, I calmed her down. We made each other better. We called each other sisters.

Cleo came to us later. Talia and I met her on the beach a few days before the Fourth of July, the year we were all eleven. We had floated far down the beach on the tide and were walking back. In front of a house the color of orange juice, a short Black girl was building an elaborate sandcastle. It had a moat and a tower almost three feet high. The girl was walking around the edge, placing shells at even intervals on the moat's wall. Sand covered every inch of her. She had been at it for some time.

As Talia and I drew closer to her, we slowed. Growing up at the beach, I had seen a lot of sandcastles, from the childish to the ambitious, and this was impressive. Still, I probably would've kept walking but for Talia, who stepped forward and said, "That's beautiful."

"Thanks," the girl said. She drew a hand across her forehead, leaving a swipe of sand there. "It's taken me a really long time."

"Can we help?" Talia asked. We had another hour before we were supposed to be back for lunch.

"I promise we won't mess anything up," I added.

The girl looked at us warily. "I have a plan," she said.

"We'll follow it," Talia said.

After a beat, the girl nodded. "Okay. I'm Cleo."

"I'm Talia."

"I'm Callie."

"Nice to meet you." She crouched by a nearby towel, consulted a sandy notebook, and straightened up again. Her dark brown eyes were alert, excited. "So the next step is to build guard towers. Four of them. Here, I'll show you . . ."

By lunchtime, we had learned that Cleo lived in Washington, DC; that the little orange house belonged to her grandparents; that she was right smack in the middle of three sisters and three brothers, but she was her grandparents' favorite; and that she wanted to read one hundred books that year. Her family often spent a week here in July. In her grandparents' two-bedroom house, it was chaos: seven kids laughing, fighting, playing games, gossiping, crying, scheming. Some of her siblings thought the beach was too boring, too hot, or both.

But Cleo loved it. She loved the mint chip at the ice cream shop, and the colors of the sunset, and playing in the sand. Most of all she liked being in the ocean—the briny scent of it and the endless white noise—and she liked that when she was floating, she couldn't babysit or be babied. She was just herself, a small creature in a big blue sea.

After the last summer, when her grandfather had told her she could stay longer if she wanted to, she had spent the year begging her parents, who finally acquiesced. She was here for the whole month. And she was already planning her campaign to spend the entire summer at Little Beach—a campaign that would be successful the next year, and the next, and the next.

We hadn't known we needed Cleo until she arrived. At eleven, we were still children, but we finally had permission to swim by ourselves and walk to the grocery store or the skating rink, as long as we were back for dinner. Left to our own devices, Talia and I would not have taken advantage of this new freedom. Nor would we have fully taken advantage of what we already had. We would've read books and watched movies and swam in the ocean, and that would have been enough.

Cleo helped us go further. We ran races from my house to Talia's and back, built a fort in the abandoned lot behind the rink. We explored the park by the sound, pretending we were witches gathering ingredients for potions, until a couple of older boys started following us around and calling us names that made us uncomfortable. We wrote and illustrated stories in blank books and made covers for them out of wrapping paper, then hid them among the real books on our shelves and waited for our parents to notice. We walked halfway across the bridge to the mainland on the narrow sidewalk, which our parents always said was too dangerous, and watched the sun set on the sound while cars whooshed by just feet behind us. We played hide-and-seek with all the lights turned out. The seeker pretended to be a ghost.

That month was the most fun I had ever had. By the time Cleo left on August 1—all of us sobbing together, holding hands so tightly our parents had to tug us apart—Talia and I were two parts of a three-piece band. Cleo was an alchemist: We were grains of sand and she made us glass, tied together at a molecular level.

She came back every summer, and even after she went home, she had a presence. Talia and I texted her and called her, tagged her in posts of the ocean, spent long late nights at our sleepovers with her on video chat. Cleo came out to us as gay in eighth grade, and after two churning, confusing weeks where I thought about what she had said and how I felt when I looked at Clara Richards on the track team, I called Cleo and Talia at midnight, and they helped me figure out I was bi. We sent Cleo postcards, beach trinkets, and homemade cookies, and she ordered books to be delivered to our houses. When we turned fifteen, Talia and I applied to the skating rink job together; the rink, stuck somewhere in the seventies technologically, required paper applications, so we mailed Cleo hers.

It's not that Talia and I didn't have other friends. We did. There were girls at school, from the playground when we were younger and our favorite classes when we were older. With each successive year, Talia got prettier and more outgoing while I got taller and shier, so she was friendly with a lot of people, while I basically only had the track and cross-country teams. And

Cleo had tons of friends in DC, endless rotations of people with whom she went to movies and cardio kickboxing classes, got tacos, walked along the waterfront in Georgetown.

Each year, all of our lives grew busier, and though we texted every day, our phone calls got less frequent. But that was okay with me. Because at the end of the day, in the summer, we always came back to each other. We understood each other as well as three people could, and even knowing all that softness and ugliness and messiness, we still liked each other more than anyone else in the world.

I tried to remember that as Cleo pulled her laptop out of her backpack, angling it toward us and gesturing for me, Talia, and Polly to scoot closer. She opened tab after tab as she hummed to herself. She was clearly preparing for a presentation of some kind, but I caught glimpses as each of the pages loaded. They were news articles, some from local papers all over the country, others from big national publications. Threads from Reddit and other more obscure discussion boards, some archived newsletters, a handful of PDFs that looked like scientific papers, videos. I didn't understand. It seemed to boil down to—

"There's a way to make yourself invisible," she said. Her eyes were bright, her skin luminous.

The words hung in the air for a second, and then I laughed. Talia did, too. Cleo didn't.

"Come on," I said.

"Did the plane scramble your senses?" Talia asked with another laugh.

Polly said nothing. She had looked at the laptop with the rest of us as Cleo was pulling up all the documents, but now she turned back to the ocean. She squinted into the late-afternoon sun, slowly smoothing her hands over her thin, pale thighs. The light turned her hair translucent.

She must have sensed me looking, because she turned a little and met my gaze. I expected her to look down, but she didn't. Instead, her jaw sharp and her pupils like pinpricks, she raised her eyebrows in a movement so tiny I might have imagined it. A small, subtle challenge.

Cleo had already told her, then. It just made me resent her more. New to us, but somehow ahead of the game, closer than we were to the thing that was approaching.

"I'm not making it up," Cleo continued, and I tried to set aside my thoughts of Polly, turning back to the screen. "This is real. It's something you can learn. Or possibly something inherent, like some people have it, some people don't. All these articles"—she waved her hand at her laptop, as if casting a spell— "they're talking about girls who have gone missing. Most of the time they come back a few days later, like they're runaways. But in some of them, there were witnesses to the girl disappearing. Like, they saw the girl in front of them, and then she was gone." She clicked to a new page. "And this scientist is saying some things about epigenetics, and camouflage instincts in lizards—"

"Humans aren't lizards," I said.

"That's what I said at first," Polly interjected, giving me a slight, almost pitying smile. It reminded me of a teacher consoling me for getting a math problem wrong, trying to make me feel better about the incorrect line of thinking that had led me to my mistake. I did not respond.

"Wait, is a chameleon a lizard?" Talia wondered aloud. "Aren't lizards different?"

"Whatever, look at this." Cleo tabbed over to a blog entry, ads for sports bras and skincare products cluttering the sides of the screen. She read aloud: " 'I wouldn't have believed it myself, but I swear to God, it was just a matter of learning. Once I figured out how to tap into that part of myself, it was easy. It can be easy for you, too. I want all the girls out there to be able to do this. I think it would make the world a better place. Safer for us.' "

Cleo looked up at us. I glanced at Talia, who looked like she was fighting a smile.

Cleo said, "Okay, maybe people make up stuff on the internet sometimes, but how about this?" She scrolled through one of the Reddit threads. "It's a lot of girls talking about their experiences. All our age or a little older. They call it *learned invisibility*. This one girl says she's been able to do it for six months now. And"—her eyes met mine—"there's a YouTube video. We can watch."

"Okay, Cleo, this is very funny," Talia said, "but we get it, there's some weird shit on the internet. Do you want us to help you unpack?"

"I'm serious," Cleo said, and I had never heard her sound more so. I shared a glance with Talia—*Is our best friend insane?*—and Cleo said, "Y'all, come on, please. Just watch."

Talia and I didn't look away from each other, and I was about to double down, when Polly coughed. She pulled her hair up in a ponytail, her eyes fixed somewhere in the middle distance. "You should watch," she said mildly.

"I really—" I started, but Talia said, "Okay," and that was that.

Cleo sat up a little straighter and nodded. She clicked to the last tab in her browser, something on YouTube. "It's private," she told us. "Only if you have the URL. You can't find it just by searching."

She pressed play.

On-screen, a girl sat at her desk, her bedroom behind her. Sixteen or seventeen, maybe, curly dark hair, medium-dark skin, freckles, brown eyes. Pretty. She looked like one of the girls in the makeup tutorial videos Talia liked.

"Hey, y'all, it's Amy, and, um, I've been posting in the *Collective Space* comment section—"

"That's the name of one of the blogs that talk about this," Cleo interrupted, pausing the video for a moment and then starting it again.

"—for, I guess, six months now, and this is my first video, but, um, yeah, I just wanted to film this to kind of show y'all what I can do. Since we've talked about it a lot." She had a deep Southern drawl, edged with nervousness. Her shoulders were tense. She forced a laugh. "I guess it'll probably look like I'm faking it. But I promise you, I'm not. Okay, here goes."

She closed her eyes. Slowly, her shoulders relaxed. We watched her chest rise and fall.

Again. And again.

There was a long silence as we watched the girl breathe. Beside me, Talia fidgeted with her hair tie. I waited thirty seconds, maybe longer, before I said, "Cleo, honestly, this is—"

"Just wait," she said. She stared intently at the screen, and I sat back.

We waited another thirty seconds.

And then the girl on the screen started to fade.

All three of us, even Polly, leaned forward. "Holy shit," Talia murmured.

At first, you could see a little of her room behind her, as if you were looking through translucent glass. Then it was as if the glass were getting clearer, and then you could barely see her, and then she was gone. It looked like an effect, like something out of a movie. Which was what I had expected, because of course, it was an effect.

"So, yeah," came Amy's voice on-screen, and I startled. I had assumed the video would end after she applied whatever editing trick she was using. Instead, her voice sounded exactly the same, but the camera was pointed at an empty room. Cleo pressed pause. She spun the chair around to face us.

"You see?" she demanded.

"It's real," Polly said quietly. There was no doubt in her voice.

"It's just good editing," I said, trying to sound like I knew anything about videos. I had barely even edited videos for social media, though in fairness, I had seen plenty of movies.

"Yeah," Talia said, but she sounded a lot less certain than before.

"Okay, you have to admit it didn't look like editing," Cleo said, turning back to the computer, "but if you don't believe me, there are more. More just like this."

Together, we watched four more YouTube videos of girls disappearing, including one where the girl reappeared at the end, all accessed via private links. The videos were basically the same as the first one, with slight differences depending on the person. One girl disappeared a lot faster, one much slower. In another, there was a moment when I thought I could see the girl's skeleton, fine, thin bones, but I must have been imagining it.

The last video ended. Talia tugged at a curl of her hair.

"See?" Cleo said. She sounded like she was pleading.

"Cleo," I said, trying to be gentle, and the door opened.

"Pizza's here!" Mrs. Haynes called. "Girls? Come help us carry this upstairs!"

"Coming," Cleo yelled back. She shut her computer and launched herself out of the chair. Polly rose and followed her.

I looked at Talia.

"This is bananas," I said.

She bit her lip, opened her mouth to answer.

"Callie? Talia?" Mr. Haynes appeared at the top of the stairs with a box of pepperoni. "Get the plates, I know y'all have to leave soon."

"We can come with you to work tonight, you know," Cleo reminded us as she, too, made it up the stairs, balancing a salad on top of some breadsticks.

"Absolutely not," Talia said, finally standing up, shaking her head as if she was clearing away a thought. "You get settled in, and we'll see you tomorrow."

"Right," I said, and got up. As we were filling glasses of water for everyone, I looked to Talia again, but she didn't meet my eyes.

Cleo didn't convince us that evening that invisibility was even possible, much less that it would make a good summer project. She didn't have a chance. After we ate, Talia and I skated to the rink and did our jobs, handed out socks, made sno-cones, yelled at kids for jumping. I got home just before eleven, said good night to my parents, and retreated to my room. I put on my headphones and the playlist I was working on for Talia. But I could still hear Cleo in my head, whispering to us as we got ready to leave: *Think of everything we could do. We could . . . I don't know, we could see anything! We could do anything! Isn't that at least a little tiny bit interesting to you?*

I said she didn't convince us. But that's not fair; I'm trying to tell the truth, and I only know my part. What I should have said is—she didn't convince me. Polly would tell me later that she had already been sold. She said it hadn't taken much: Cleo had sent her the very first video, and it felt right and true, like something dislocated inside her had clicked into place. She had been along for the ride as Cleo found each piece of the puzzle and dreamed up the plan that we would, together, make real.

As for Talia, she claims she was still skeptical. But given what happened later in the summer, I find that hard to believe. I think the moment Cleo made us watch the first girl disappear on video, Talia was caught, the hook of that promise lodged firmly in her cheek.

3 LAST SKATER STANDING

"We start letting people in at six. You take their money here—"

"Cash only."

"Yeah, if they don't have cash, you can tell them there's an ATM at the Putt-Putt place across the street. It's five dollars for entry and skates, two dollars for socks. You put the money here, give them their change. Then you give them their skates and the socks if they want. And that's pretty much it."

I swept my hand across the limited vista of the Little Beach Skating Rink as Talia and I concluded our new employee training. Polly, arms crossed, nodded.

"Any questions?" Talia asked hopefully.

Polly shrugged. "Seems pretty straightforward. I mean, the rules are posted right there."

She nodded at the rule board, which was, indeed, centered on the wall at the end of the seating area where kids put on their skates. No smoking. No alcohol. No jumping. No running. End of list.

"Cool," Talia said, turning away with a sigh. It *was* straightforward. We still wanted Polly to ask a question.

All year Cleo had been talking about Polly. Cleo had lots of friends—she was like that; everyone loved her—but she'd always been clear that we were her best. That year she started saying "my best friend here," creating a brand-new category. Polly, I was told, worked on the stage crew for school plays; she was funny, in a weird, quiet way; she was beautiful, sweet, and "great, so great." Every time we got on the phone, we heard about Polly. Reading between the lines, I suspected that though Cleo had many friends, Polly had only one, and the possessiveness I imagined in Polly made me possessive myself.

Cleo had called Talia on a Wednesday in March and, after confirming we were together at Talia's house, told us that Polly would be coming with her to Little Beach this summer. I had acted excited over the phone, then immediately went outside and stress-ran eight miles. By the time I returned, Cleo had called Talia back with what was arguably the more critical news: that Polly would also be working with us at the rink. Miss Abby, the rink owner, needed four girls for the summer, and while Talia and Cleo and I were locked down, Maddie Stenson from last summer was off at App State for college and not coming back. Cleo had seen the opportunity, called Miss Abby, and somehow convinced her to hire Polly sight unseen. And without even the paper application, which felt wrong somehow.

Talia and I spent that entire night glumly doing math homework and saying things to each other like, "Maybe Polly will be great," and "Maybe we'll really like her," and "Maybe we need to mix things up." It is possible that Talia believed these reassurances. I was not so optimistic.

Now, looking at her, I didn't hate her as much as I'd feared; I don't think you could. It would be like hating a tree or an empty building, something that's never done anything to anybody, because it's never done anything at all. But I didn't like her, either.

"So that's it?" Polly said. "Nothing else to know?"

Talia shrugged. "I mean, if you want to practice skating at all—"

"I can skate," Polly said, and for the first time I heard a hard-edged confidence.

"Great," I said, trying to force cheer into my voice and push aside my skepticism. "We've got fifteen minutes to finish getting ready before we let in the hordes. Anyone else want to sweep?"

"Me," sang Cleo.

"Come on, I'll show you how to work the popcorn and sno-cone machines," said Talia, leading Polly into the employees-only area.

I went to the supply closet and pulled out the two big cloth brooms. I passed one to Cleo, and we slipped out of our shoes and started pushing them across the floor, side by side. The evening light spilled through the open windows, though the rink was so big that it still felt dim. I was sweating, but that was nothing new. There was no air-conditioning. I sweated constantly, all summer, every summer.

"So," Cleo said, "have you thought about my plan?"

I sighed. "Cleo, it's not real."

"It is," she said fiercely, almost angrily, and I looked at her in surprise.

"Do you really believe that?" I asked.

Her face softened. "I do."

"Why?"

She looked down at the worn floor, our brooms gliding across it. Sweeping was my favorite. Technically we only needed to do it once between sessions, either with cleanup at night or our prep work before opening, but I did it both times. The brooms were wide and soft and they picked up everything, making clean, even lines. And padding across the rink barefoot, when I was so used to wearing skates, felt strange and nice, like walking on water. Talia didn't mind sweeping one way or the other, but this work was Cleo's favorite, too.

"There's all those posts online," Cleo said. "And the videos."

"You know that could all be fake."

She was quiet for a moment. "Yeah," she said. "I know. But the news articles about the disappearances, and the scientific studies. Those are real."

"Yeah, but, Cleo, we can't even understand those studies. If there were any real findings, it would be a huge story. And those news articles—sometimes . . ." I hesitated. In my peripheral vision, she looked sad. "Girls just disappear. It happens."

"I know."

"Then why do you believe it?"

She shrugged as we walked. "I just believe it," she said. "I can't explain why. I just do."

I didn't say anything. I looked back at Talia as she showed something to Polly behind the counter. While we were working that first night, in text conversations that day, and once or twice on the beach, I had brought it up with her. Each time I had said some version of: "This plan is unhinged and I think our best friend has lost her mind, how about you?"

The first time, she'd rolled her eyes and said, "God, I know, we'll have to pull her back from the brink." It pacified me, and she changed the subject.

But the next time I raised my objections, she had just sighed.

The times after that—she hadn't responded to my texts, or she'd looked away from me, bit her lip, retied her hair back from her face. I knew Talia as well as I knew the feeling of the sand on the soles of my feet, and I had learned the language of her silences. I didn't understand why, but she was in, even if she hadn't said it yet.

And Polly—well, Polly had been in before she had ever crossed the Carolina border. I was the last one Cleo needed to convince. I knew it, and Cleo knew it, too.

"What's the worst that can happen?" Cleo said in a low voice. We had reached the end of the rink, and she leaned against the wall by the emergency exit, folding her arms. Light fell in through the window beside her, making her look like something out of a vintage photo: cutoffs and crop top, dust motes and sweat-sheened skin. I could hear Talia's loud voice coming from the front, Polly's tentative echo. "We spend the first few weeks trying to learn this . . . this skill, let's call it, and then it doesn't work. So what? Then we come up with a project for the rest of the summer."

I undid and redid my ponytail higher on my head. My dad's friend hadn't said the radio need was urgent. The jobs would still be there in a few weeks.

"You promise if nothing happens by the middle of July, we can switch to something else?"

"Sure. We'll have to do the ritual at the new moon, and we're too late for the one this month—"

"The ritual? The new moon? Jesus, Cleo."

"Yeah, well, the next new moon will be in the beginning of July, so if it doesn't work then, it's not gonna work at all. And yes, if it doesn't work, we can do something else." She started pushing the broom back toward the front of the rink. "I take it you have something in mind?"

"Nothing important." It was important to me, but I thought it would sound stupid, especially when I knew none of my friends cared about music quite as much as I did.

I imagined the summer we'd have if I said no. We'd fight. I'd get more and more annoyed with the three of them insisting on something so silly, and they'd get mad at me every time I doubled down. Maybe they would go ahead and try it anyway, without me, and then the three of them would have something together that I lacked.

A little ahead of me, Cleo's profile shone in the dim light of the rink, her jaw set.

"You really think this is gonna work?" I asked her.

"Callie, honest to God, I do."

Kids were starting to gather at the door. I could see their shadows shifting behind the window. The cash register dinged as Talia pushed it in, and the sno-cone machine gurgled to life. Another night at work. But the first night at work with Cleo this summer. The beginning, really.

"Okay," I said.

"You'll do it?" She whipped around.

"Yes, I'll do it. I'm in. Whatever."

She threw her arms around me. I could feel her smile against my shoulder, and it made me smile, too. I was so glad to have her back, to have all of us back together. If this was what it took, so be it. We could play at fantasy again, like little girls. We could pretend to be magic, and the magic of being together would have to be enough. But then again, it always had been.

"Thank you, Callie."

"Thank me when it works," I said.

She pulled away from me, that familiar determination stark on her face. "I will."

When we reached the end of the rink, Talia opened the doors.

Technically, only Cleo and I were working that night, because technically, there were only two shifts available. But last summer, it hadn't been uncommon for all of us to be there, me and Cleo and Talia and, on her shifts, Maddie—two working and the other two skating or helping out, just to have something to do.

That night it was busy; Sunday nights often were. For tourists, it was the end of their first full day after checking into their rentals on Saturday, and they wanted to explore. For locals, it was the last night before the workweek started. We took money and gave out skates and socks and sno-cones and packets of popcorn. We comforted little kids who had fallen. We told children to stop jumping and/or put their clothes back on, and we DJed.

I say we, but the music was the one responsibility I claimed. Cleo and Talia would just put on the radio. I took music seriously. Like a good playlist, setting the right mood at the rink was an art form. It required a blend of old classics, pop hits, and just a little bit of something brand-new.

"What are we listening to?" Talia asked. She was painting her nails and holding them in front of the fan to dry, adding a chemical tang to the sweaty air.

"Do you not like it?" I asked. I was working on Talia's taste, but it was a work in progress.

"I like it just fine. But it's weird."

"It's Kishi Bashi," I said, pleased. *Just fine* was more than I often got from Talia. It was a good thing she had me to expand her horizons.

Polly, unwrapping a new package of socks in the corner, nodded. "This is my favorite song of his."

I spun to face her. "Really?"

"Yeah. I like this part . . ." She looked up to the speakers, as if gazing heavenward, as the strings of "Manchester" crescendoed. She had a look on her face I recognized. It was the way I felt whenever I heard a new song that resonated with me on exactly the right frequency, a lyric that made me change the way I looked at the world. "I think about it a lot. On sunny days. If I'm feeling down."

I made a noise in my throat, which I had meant as agreement—I thought about it that way, too. But she must have taken it in the opposite way, because she looked away and flushed.

"I think I'm going to get out there with Cleo," she said. "See how the rink feels."

"Just don't get knocked down," Talia advised. I thought it was wise to warn her. A husky seven-year-old could take down Polly, and there were plenty of those to go around. At this very moment, Cleo was on the other side of the rink, giving a lecture to two kids who had been running in spite of the very clear NO RUNNING signage.

"I won't," she said. She pulled out her skates from where she'd stashed her things under the counter. I hadn't noticed them when she and Cleo had come in, but now I saw they were worn and scuffed, classic brown leather like the ones we rented, but much higher quality. The same brand my parents had gotten me as a sixteenth birthday present, though mine were bright blue.

"I love those," I said, despite not particularly wanting to find common ground.

She looked at me as she was lacing up and smiled. "Me too," she said.

And then she set out onto the floor.

Talia came to stand beside me to watch.

"Huh," she murmured.

The rink was full of people, but Polly looked like she could have been entirely alone. Eyes drifting, long thin hair streaming behind her, she wove around families and couples like wind blows through alleys. She switched to skating backward, smoothly and easily, and crossed her legs one over the other over and over again, stitching her path into the air.

"Show-off," I whispered to Talia, but it was a lie. I didn't think she looked like a show-off at all. She looked like someone who was moving through a different world, some secret place superimposed over the sweat and the dust of Little Beach.

I was about to turn away, when Cleo slammed into the half-height door separating the employees-only area from the rink.

"Last Skater Standing time," she said breathlessly.

Polly skated up just behind her, looking more alert as she slowed. "What's going on?"

"Already?" Talia glanced at the clock.

"Yeah," Cleo said. "Can I host?"

"Host what?" Polly asked.

"I wouldn't dream of stopping you." I turned down the volume as I said into the mic, "Can everyone please clear the floor?"

Slowly, the crowd of skaters completed their counterclockwise rotations and tumbled into the waiting area. Some collapsed onto benches; others clomped their way to the walls and tried to lean without sliding down. Talia ushered Polly into the employees-only area.

"The Sunday Night Skate always ends with Last Skater Standing," she explained to Polly. "Ever since the rink opened in 1974. Ironclad tradition." Looking at the assembled crowd, you could tell who'd played the game before. New folks, if they're good skaters, get excited anticipating a race or a competition. If all they can do is cling to the rail and pull themselves along, their faces fall with the same anticipation. Locals just wait it out. This crew was mostly new. I saw a lot of interest.

Cleo grabbed a small wooden cube from the shelf beside the door and skated alone to the center of the rink. Her small frame looked tiny in the empty space, but she commanded it completely.

"The game," I said into the mic, "is Last Skater Standing. All y'all are gonna come on in—"

Cleo made a come-on motion; then, when the first person stepped onto the rink, she shook her hands emphatically—not yet, you bozo—to laughter.

"And skate around, slowly, until the music stops."

Cleo skated in a slow circle and stopped.

"When the music stops, you're gonna skate to a window with a number."

She skated to the window on the back-right side of the rink. New folks looked at the black metal numbers, one through six, nailed on the wooden boards above each of the windows.

"Then my good friend Cleo here is gonna roll the die—"

Cleo held up the cube, which was so worn at the edges it was on a journey to becoming a sphere. She turned it over so the audience could see all six sides.

"—and whoever is standing under that window is gonna be *out*."

A slashing motion.

"And then we'll go again."

She twirled her finger in the air.

"All right now."

Cleo beckoned to the audience again, and everyone funneled onto the floor.

"Cleo's so good at this," Polly said, a little awe in her voice.

"It's not rocket science," Talia said. "Callie does half the work."

"Still," Polly said, and she was sort of right. It wasn't exactly difficult, but it was a performance. Last summer, each of us had developed our own spin on the routine. Cleo had this clowny, goofy shtick that kids and corny parents loved. Talia did a flutter-her-lashes model thing. I just tried to be pleasant.

And to make Cleo or Talia do it whenever possible. I didn't mind calling from the mic, but I didn't like being in front of a crowd.

The game proceeded. Family friendly, quick and easy, everyone had a good laugh. When the time came to roll the die, Cleo would pass it to a little kid, who rolled it on the floor with a clatter. Finally, once there were only six people left—one under each window—Cleo had a blond woman roll the die three times. These were the numbers of the three winners, who all received a pass for a free night of skating. The runners-up got a free sno-cone, flavor of their choice. The winners skated to the window to collect their prizes, and I allowed everyone else back onto the floor.

Last summer, Talia, Cleo, and I all separately argued with Miss Abby that the game shouldn't be called Last Skater Standing if, in fact, six skaters are left standing at the end, but Miss Abby was adamant about the name. Not that she was ever around to enforce the rules.

I put on Delta Rae, Polly made sno-cones, and Talia handed out free passes and fielded the accompanying questions (no, they never expire; yes, they include skate rental, but no, not socks). Cleo held court with a few small children in the waiting area. Everyone wants to roll the die.

There were five minutes left in the night when Adam Liu ambled in and looked around. It had been just a handful of days since I'd seen him at our end-of-year track team party, but I swore he had already gotten tanner, maybe a touch taller, his shaggy black hair just a little more carelessly unkempt. And he'd already been tan and tall and looked incredible just pushing back his hair from his eyes. It was unfair. Talia nudged me forward to the front desk. I leaned. Tried to be casual. He saw me and smiled.

"Callie! I didn't know you were working tonight." He noticed Talia behind me and nodded. "What's up, Talia? Have y'all seen my sister? Dad sent me to pick her up. All the tourists, you know . . ."

"Driving like crazy," I finished. "Yeah. She's over there." I nodded to the far end of the waiting area, where Jen Liu was giggling with a bunch of other middle schoolers.

"Cool, thanks," he said. He gave me another smile, small but genuine, and caught my eye. He had gorgeous eyes, dark brown and sweet and soft. Here, with just the counter between us, I could see the lines of his collarbones beneath his thin white T-shirt, the lean curves of his biceps. "Great to see you."

"You too." I hesitated, but he hadn't moved away yet. "You here this summer? I thought you always stayed with your mom for summer break."

"Yeah, well, Jen and I staged a coup." He shrugged. "It's my second-to-last summer at home, right? I don't want to spend it in an apartment in Atlanta."

"Cool." I smiled, too. "I'll see you around, then."

"Yeah. For sure."

He extricated Jen from her friends and left, his arm protective around her shoulders. " 'For sure,' " Talia whispered, bumping me with her hip. " 'For sure,' he said."

"Shut up. We're just friends."

"You said he's been flirting with you all year."

"Talia, *you* said that."

"Oh, right, I forgot who said it first because it was so obviously correct."

Polly looked blank. "Who was that?"

"Just a friend," I said. I grabbed the mic and said into it, "Folks, we're closing in five minutes, it's time to get going."

Cleo pulled herself away from the kids and held the door open for the crowd slowly filtering out into the humid night. Over her shoulder, she said to Polly, "Adam is Callie's secret love."

"Good God," I hissed. There were still a few people from school in the room—all younger than us, and they didn't seem to have heard anything, but still. "Calm down, Cleo."

"He's cute," Polly offered.

"Talia," I said, "will you please do me a favor and kill me?"

It was another ten minutes before we locked the doors behind the last stragglers. The emptiness of the rink and the moonlight through the windows comforted me, as they always did. Talia pulled out the cleaning supplies. I started sorting skates by size. If we took our time now and did our jobs right, we wouldn't have to get to work as early tomorrow. Sometimes we took our time. Sometimes not.

Cleo had just finished showing Polly how to sweep the seating area, when Polly called my name. I turned.

"Yeah?"

"Can you put on Kishi Bashi again?"

She looked like Cinderella, beautiful, holding a broom on the dusty floor. I didn't know what to make of her. "Yeah," I said. "Of course."

"Honestly, I was just teasing you earlier," Talia said. "I like that song, too."

"Me too," Cleo said as she ran a cloth over the countertop.

We sang together as we cleaned, letting the minutes fall away into the soft warm night.

4

DAYTIMES
IN JUNE

We spent them in the ocean. In the early mornings, I woke up to go for my run, feeling my body slowly come awake on the sand and relishing the feeling of being alone on the beach after the long months of crowded track and cross-country practices. That spring, I had finally given up on getting a scholarship at even a Division III college—I was the fastest of the girls on our team, but you have to be near superhuman for scholarship money—and so now I got to run just to enjoy it, the air on my face and the thump of my heart. Afterward, I ate some eggs with my parents, sometimes showered and sometimes didn't. The four of us met at ten or eleven at one of our houses. We lined up our skates at the bottom of the stairs, packed our beach bags and the cooler, and shook the sand from our towels, preparing to get them sandy again.

Cleo and Talia slept too late to let us be the first on the beach, but we always carved out a good solid square among the sandcastles and Shibumis. We anointed each other in sunscreen—after the first week, at least, once we had burned. Talia's hands smoothing down my back, mine working between

Cleo's shoulder blades, Cleo pulling aside the straps of Polly's one-piece, not missing a spot.

And then we pushed out past the breakers to the calm waves beyond. The beach in front of my house was sheltered by the end of a sandbar, so at low tide, we had to walk what felt like forever, up to the sandbar and then past it. There, the shore looked scary far away, so far that sometimes women shouted at us to be careful. At Cleo's, farther down the beach, there was no sandbar. It got deep quickly there, so only Polly and I could stand; Talia and Cleo had to bounce on their tiptoes and tread water.

The first time Polly came out, it was high tide and rough. A savage part of me thought, *Good, let her feel it.* Then she got knocked down and didn't come up, and I started to worry. She was barely there, stained-glass fragile; I might not like her, but I didn't want her to die. But then she burst out of the ocean, yards away from where she'd gone down, pale and joyful in the sun.

"This is fucking great," she said, and Cleo said, "Pool's got nothing on this, right?" and inside I felt a part of me soften toward Polly, just a little at the edges.

We would float, alone together, staring up at the scorched-bright sky. And talk. About school. About boys and girls. About why, how, and when to disappear.

It was June 23—a Saturday, though if you'd asked me what day of the week it was at the time, I wouldn't have been able to tell you. One day blended seamlessly into the next. My parents, who acted as small-business consultants during the off-season, spent the busy season running a bike and kayak rental themselves, so their days off were sporadic during the summer months. My schedule at the rink changed constantly, not least because I was always working shifts I wasn't paid for. Summer, nebulous, continuous, unending. I only knew it was June 23 because it was exactly two weeks before the ritual.

We had our towels positioned so we could all face each other lying on our stomachs, our bodies fanning out like the spokes of a pinwheel. I had packed lunch: peanut butter and jelly sandwiches, apples, and a family-size bag of pretzels. I sifted through my bag to find the food.

"Cleo, lunch, catch." I tossed her a sandwich and an apple.

"Awesome." She caught them deftly, one after the other. "Thanks. I didn't even think about packing lunch this morning."

"What the hell is in your bag, then?" I eyed the enormous tote next to her. I had assumed—okay, hoped—she'd brought a package of cookies or something.

"You'll see." She bit into her sandwich. "Ooh, blackberry, my favorite."

I picked up another sandwich and said, "Talia, catch."

"Just the apple, please," Talia said quickly.

I threw her an apple. "Okay, but I'm making you eat your sandwich later. Polly?"

"I'm good," she said. "I had a big breakfast."

"No you didn't," Cleo said, frowning. "You had a banana."

Polly drew a line in the sand. "Yeah, I guess I'm just not hungry."

I looked at Polly's slender frame, at Cleo with her mouth full, at Talia running her fingers over the red skin of the apple.

I knew that Talia wanted to lose five pounds, or ten, depending on the day. I knew her thrill and discomfort at the chest and hips that had come out of nowhere in the past few years. And I knew that as her best friend in the world, it was part of my job to help her keep eating.

But I didn't know Polly.

Cleo did, and after a pause, she shrugged and pulled a notebook out of her bag. Polly took a sip of her iced coffee.

Cleo opened the notebook to a page packed with her handwriting, looped and curled so that from upside down it looked like hundreds of circles. "I've done some research," she said. This explained what she'd been scouring on her phone during slow times at work, and why she had been glued to her laptop every morning we'd arrived at her house.

"More than the videos you showed us?" Talia asked.

"More than the videos. Well, those videos, yeah, but there are more videos, too, and more blogs about those videos. Honestly, a lot of girls less impressive than us have done this. The grammar on one of the write-ups was awful. Almost unreadable."

"Oh, well, if the girl doesn't know how to use commas properly, you probably can't take her seriously when she talks about how she turns invisible like a superhero," I said.

Cleo ignored me. "Step one is meditation," she said. "Every night for a month, so we're already behind, but I think we'll be okay if we start tonight. You have to practice getting into a kind of trance state. Focusing on being invisible."

"How am I supposed to trance when Angelica and Olivia are yelling at each other?" Talia tipped down her sunglasses, her dark eyebrows arched. Talia's little sisters were twelve and fourteen and argued with each other almost as much as they did with her. I still thought of them as babies sometimes, but they were grown up now, with the vocabulary to match.

"Before you go to sleep, maybe," Cleo suggested.

"Or we could come out here," I said. "On the beach."

I had heard the words *trance state* and envisioned the four of us in a circle on the sand, the night sky a curved bowl above us, pinpricked with stars. But immediately I regretted voicing the thought. The dark came on late this time of year, and we were at work most nights starting at six or earlier. I had no interest in asking my parents to extend my curfew so I could meditate on an impossibility.

"It's quiet in the rink after we close up," Polly said. She was right, but I almost snapped at her anyway, annoyed that we were discussing this so seriously at all.

Talia settled her chin in her hand. "All I'm saying is sometimes in my house, silence is scarce."

"Right, well, okay, let's brainstorm solutions later, because that's just the first part. We have to get really good at that, and then on July seventh—" She traced her writing with a fingertip. "That's the new moon—we have to fast for twenty-four hours beforehand, so starting around eleven p.m. on the sixth—"

"We have to fast?!"

Cleo ignored me again. "And come out here to the ocean on the night of the seventh. And in theory, if we do our meditation while we're floating in the ocean, on the night of the new moon, in a fasted state . . ." She snapped her fingers. Her gold nail polish glittered in the sun. "Boom. Invisible."

"So we just get to do it the once?" asked Polly, sounding a little dubious.

Cleo shook her head and flipped a page in her notebook. "The way it's supposed to work is that after the ritual, it's activated. You maintain it as long as you can keep your concentration, and then you should be able to do it again later. But it's always gonna be easier to start off in the dark—that's why the new moon—and in the ocean. Something about the salt water being some kind of conductor."

"Didn't the first YouTube girl live in Oklahoma?"

"Yeah, she made herself a salt bath and turned off all the lights in the bathroom. But I figured we have the world's largest salt bath right here, so."

"How do you come out of it?" I asked, then mentally kicked myself. There was no point in asking about how to stop something that was never going to happen.

"I am so glad you asked, Callie," Cleo said cheerfully, flashing me a grin. I stuck my tongue out at her. "Meditating the same way, just thinking about the opposite. Being visible, being seen. I watched some videos of girls coming back from it— they're pretty freaky, honestly, I'll send them to you—and they all use slightly different words, but it's the same vibe. Any other questions?"

"Yes," Talia said at the same time I said, "Absolutely not."

We talked about it for ages. What Cleo knew from her research and what Cleo made up, I will never know. But it turned out that Talia and Polly had been doing research of their own, so there were some arguments: how long you had to meditate, what you were supposed to wear, whether it mattered if the moon was directly overhead or if it could be a minute or two before or after midnight. I ate Polly's sandwich while the others talked and talked.

I had not done my own research. I had other things to worry about, like my mile time and Adam Liu. Talia had exaggerated his interest, obviously. But it did feel like he was paying more attention to me than he used to. The thought gave me a glimmer of excitement each time it crossed my mind.

We had drifted in and out of each other's spheres through-out high school, sometimes ending up in the same classes or on the same group trips to Wilmington, always on the track and cross-country teams together. I had made varsity for both as a sophomore two years ago, him as a junior. The varsity boys and girls teams had a lot more interaction with each other than the JV teams.

I'd had little crushes here and there, girls and boys I liked or just liked looking at. But I had never had a boyfriend or a girlfriend, never so much as gone to a dance with anyone. Not a lot of people knew I was bi—and sure, in part that was because, even though there were plenty of queer kids out at school, I was acutely aware that I lived in a part of the state that always voted red, and I didn't want to draw attention to myself. Part of it, though, was that I'd never liked anyone of any gender enough to really pursue them. I had Talia and Cleo, and I had running, and I had the wide, wide ocean, and that had always been enough.

But one night in January, I had been stretching on the cold grass after practice, and Adam had done one last lap—and I remember seeing him passing under the fluorescent lights of the track, the cling of his shirt to his chest, the silhouette of his face against the dark. I had seen him hundreds of times and I had never seen him before. In that moment I felt a knife of desire slide beneath my ribs, making me breathless. It had happened that fast.

After that, it seemed like I always found him in a group, ending up talking to him more than the rest of the team. And he found me, too. During practice, he teased me and cheered for me—and yeah, we all teased each other and cheered for each other, but maybe he was a little funnier and a little louder for me than for the other girls. I wasn't sure if what we were doing was flirting. It felt like flirting, but how would I know?

Now, on the beach, a long shadow fell over us, and I looked up. I couldn't tell who it was at first, just a shape against the mid-day sun. But Talia squealed, "Michael!" and hopped up.

The peanut butter was suddenly too sticky on my tongue.

They embraced and kissed. I looked away; I felt uncomfortable watching them, all that bare skin pressed together. Over the past year, Michael—who had always had the kind of symmetrical face that made me distrust a guy—had discovered the weight room and gotten stronger and stronger, until you could see every muscle in his body as clearly as if he were sketched in a biology textbook. He wasn't as tall as I was, but the width of his shoulders and the thickness of his chest made him an overwhelming physical presence. He made me feel shorter and slighter than I was, which always threw me off-kilter. Talia told me once that she felt the same, but she framed it as a good thing, feeling small.

Cleo arched her eyebrows at me: *So this is Michael?*

Finally, just when I was starting to worry about Talia getting enough oxygen, he and she separated. He knelt on her towel, getting it sandy, as she stepped out of the circle.

"You must be Cleo," he said, sticking out a hand. "I've heard a lot about you."

She shook it. "Likewise," she said drily.

He turned to Polly. "I'm Michael," he said.

She shook his hand, too, awkwardly, because it was an awkward thing to do, making someone shake your hand on a beach. "Polly," she said. "Nice to meet you."

His gaze lingered on her a little too long before he stood up again.

Michael and Talia had been together since last October, but this was the first time he had met Cleo. It might've been my fault that Cleo's impressions weren't 100 percent positive. Michael was charming. He had a sense of humor, nothing interesting or unique, but he could make you laugh. He wasn't school-smart, but he wasn't stupid. He played soccer—Talia and I would watch him from the sidelines, the muscles of his thighs, the lean lines of his chest when he lifted his jersey to wipe sweat from his face. Talia always looked at him with her lips parted, like she was waiting to take a bite.

He was gorgeous, if you liked that kind of thing, and maybe that's part of why he didn't treat Talia very well. Everything would be great between them for a while, and then suddenly, they'd fight for a day or a weekend or a week. He ignored her when he didn't want to deal with the difficult parts of her—her family, her insecurities—and when she was happy, he took up too much of her time. He wasn't mean, usually, but he could be dismissive. Flirtatious with other girls. He got offended easily.

In fairness, Talia shared a lot of these qualities, not that I ever would've said that aloud.

Michael kissed Talia again and said, "A bunch of us are grilling burgers up the beach. Wanna join?"

"Yeah!" She kissed him back, smiling big. They had just gotten over their most recent fight a few days ago. He had said he'd call after he got home from work—he was a lifeguard at the community pool—and he didn't. When she got annoyed at him, he blew up. Pretty standard.

"Great," he said. He started to leave, before remembering the rest of us were there. "Do y'all wanna come, too? Everyone's welcome. We probably have enough food."

Polly looked at Cleo. Cleo looked at me.

"No thanks," I said. "We just ate."

"Well, swing by later if you want. We're maybe a quarter mile toward the pier." He and Talia went up the beach, hand in hand. Talia glanced over her shoulder to give me a guilty look and mouthed *Sorry*, to which I rolled my eyes and smiled. It was more flippant than I felt.

"Why didn't you want to go with them?" Polly asked.

"It doesn't matter." I pushed up from my towel and brushed the sand off my stomach. I felt hot and restless. "Come on, let's go swim."

"Aren't you not supposed to swim right after you eat?" Polly asked.

"Old wives' tale," Cleo said as she got up, brushing sand off her bright pink one-piece. She pulled Polly with her. I didn't wait for them. I ran in, splashing.

The water was warm, but it still felt so good, as familiar as my own hands. I dove under the first big wave and swam out with my eyes closed for as long as I could hold my breath. I loved the feeling of the waves passing above me while I was underwater. It was like watching someone strong throw a punch. A great unstoppable force, and my body an unharmed witness.

I surfaced past the breakers and waited for Polly and Cleo. I had to squint against the light of the sun on the water.

"I wonder," Cleo said breathlessly when she finally reached me, "if this'll be easier when we're invisible. You're supposed to be less corporeal. The water might go through us."

I barely resisted grimacing. "I don't know if I'm that excited to be *less corporeal*. I like my corporeal body, thanks."

"Yeah, I get it."

That response surprised me. "Then—" I didn't want to argue, but I couldn't not say it. "Why are we doing this?"

Cleo hesitated for a moment. "It's not exactly invisibility per se that I'm excited about," she said. She ran her hands through the water, making trails with her fingers, catching and flicking away a thread of seaweed. Polly, beside her, bounced gently up and down. "It's that it's a real-life superpower. You know?"

"I guess. It's not the superpower I would choose."

"So what superpower would you choose, if you got a choice?" Cleo asked. "You don't, but if you did."

"Breathe underwater," I said without hesitation. I could already hold my breath for a long time. Talia and I used to have competitions, and I would always beat her. "Those runner's lungs," my dad would say fondly, a runner himself. But it wasn't the same as being able to stay under forever. I used to dream about tracing the seafloor down deep, into the open ocean, being able to open my eyes and see the world clear as day. Like a mermaid, but without the fishy bottom half.

"Would you have gills?" Cleo giggled.

"Yeah." I made a face and tucked in my hands like flaps on the side of my neck. "Would you be a fish with me, Cleo?"

"No, I'd fly." She kicked her feet up to float on her back, gazing at the sky. "I know it's a cliché, I don't care. It would be so fucking cool. You could see everything. I dream about it sometimes. The air is so soft up there."

Above us, a small plane was buzzing into sight, trailing an advertisement for two-for-one lobster specials at the Shack. An arrow of pelicans crossed its path hundreds of feet below. The sky was dress-shirt blue, unbroken blue, sweet-summer-perfect blue.

"Good answer," I said. "Polly?"

She shrugged and didn't say anything.

Cleo righted herself and looked between us. Seawater dripped from her long eyelashes. She opened her mouth, but then Polly answered, "I'm happy with invisibility."

"Well, right," I said, trying not to sound unkind, "but if you got to choose, what would you choose?"

"That's what I'm saying," she said. "I'm really happy with invisibility. I wouldn't choose anything else."

"Why?"

"I would love to not have a body," she said.

Her expression was unreadable, the sun hitting the water and reflecting back on her face.

I said it before and I'll say it again—I never believed any of it was possible. Rituals, new moons, all of it was bullshit, a joke we were playing on ourselves. But there in the ocean, in the middle of a conversation I had meant as small talk, I felt myself getting angry. If this was real, why weren't we aiming higher? Who said we were only capable of shrinking ourselves into nothing? Who would choose to be invisible?

I kept my voice light. "Well, all I'm saying is if I get my pick, I choose breathing underwater."

Cleo said, "You don't get your pick."

Polly slipped under the surface and came up with her hair slicked back. The sun flared against her skin, turning her briefly into nothing but water and light.

5 MEDITATION PRACTICE

I could have done the closing routine at the rink with my eyes shut. I knew it by heart, like the lyrics of my favorite songs, the rhythm of it with two people and with four. It took between twenty-two and fifty-five minutes, depending on how busy the night had been, how many of us were there, and how thoroughly we wanted to clean. And I liked my job, but my favorite part was being done. Stepping out of that big, humid room into the breeze of the night, the air cool on my skin for the first time since I had woken up in the morning. Skating home, no one but us on the road.

Except now, there was another step.

"Can't we do this by ourselves when we get home?" I asked, as I had asked every night for the last week. "Cleaning up that sno-cone syrup took forever. We're not gonna make curfew if we don't go home now."

"You can leave if you want," Cleo answered tartly, "but the rest of us are doing it here."

"But curfew is—"

"At eleven," Cleo finished, "and no one's going to be mad

if we're a few minutes late because Cherry Blast got blasted all over the floor. It's not like it's never happened before. They know we're not out, like, doing drugs or . . . I don't know, carousing with strangers."

"All I'm saying is that maybe we don't have to do this every night."

"This is the best place," Talia said, unbothered. "It's quiet and we're together. And it's only ten minutes."

"She's right," Cleo said.

Polly looked at me and arched her eyebrows, somewhere between sympathy and too bad. I exhaled and put away the broom. The others were already moving out to the middle of the rink.

"Callie, get the light?" Talia called over her shoulder.

I flipped on the disco ball. Moths' wings of light flickered and turned on the floor. I followed my friends; they had formed a circle, leaving a me-size gap. Talia and Cleo had their legs crossed like they were in preschool or doing yoga. Polly was in a ball, her knees tucked up to her chest. I sat and stretched my legs out in front of me.

Cleo looked around. The light passed across her face and disappeared, over and over again. "Ready?"

All of us nodded. Around me, like a chain of dominoes, the three girls closed their eyes.

Time to give it another shot, I thought.

For the seventh or eighth time in as many days, I closed my eyes and tried to match my breathing with the rhythm of my heart. In. Out. In. *Relax your shoulders,* the girl had said in the meditation video Cleo sent us. *Relax every part of your body, one by one.* I tried.

I opened my eyes a millimeter, feeling as if I were breaking a cardinal rule by doing so. Cleo looked exactly like the girl in the video, her pose such a specific match that I was sure she'd practiced with a mirror. Polly looked so tranquil she was almost asleep. Talia's breathing was steady and even, but her eyes were screwed shut tight in concentration, her shoulders up around her ears. So maybe you didn't have to relax.

I closed my eyes again and thought, *I am invisible.*

I kept thinking it, repeating it to myself, even as I thought about the grain of the wood beneath my fingers, the snack I was looking forward to at home, the skates we hadn't gotten to and would need to re-lace tomorrow. Below the meditation, I thought, *this is such a waste of time.* If we had chosen the goal I'd wanted for the summer, we might be driving Talia's mom's car back from the radio station, the music turned up loud and the night spread out before us on the road. Not sitting here in the dark and the dust, praying for the impossible.

At least, I reminded myself, we were together. Being together was enough.

Minutes passed. I don't know how many. Somewhere in the circle, there was a shuffle and a sigh. I waited, my back starting to ache, and kept waiting. And a part of me did drift and soften as I focused on my breath. In, out, in.

Finally, I felt a gentle touch on the back of my hand and opened my eyes. Cleo, beside me, smiled, and I touched the back of Talia's hand as Cleo had touched me. Talia startled. Polly, across from her, opened her eyes and stretched.

No one said anything.

Even to me, the silence felt a little bit sacred.

As we got up from the rink, I broke it anyway.

52

"How late is it?" I asked Cleo.

She checked her phone. "Just before eleven. I guess we went a little long."

"Shit," Talia said sleepily.

"Cleo, I told you!"

"Sorry!" She didn't look sorry. "You'll be home in twenty minutes anyway. Just call your parents and tell them cleaning up took longer than usual."

Dad answered on the second ring. I told him exactly that, and told the twinge in my stomach that it wasn't a lie. Sno-cone syrup malfunctions were reasonably rare.

"Are you sure you don't want me to come pick you up?" Dad asked. "It'll be almost eleven-thirty when you get home. And the traffic . . ."

It was a Saturday, meaning that there were more than the usual number of people on the road. "It's almost all gone now," I said. "You can't even check into a rental this late."

"I know, but if you guys get even the slightest bit uncomfortable—"

"We'll call. Promise."

"Wear your helmets."

"We always do."

"Okay. Love you, Callie."

"Love you too, Dad."

I hung up the phone. "Talia?"

"No need." She rolled her eyes. "Either they're already asleep or they'll be mad that I broke curfew, period, and they won't care if I called."

We locked up and made our way down the stairs, awkward on our skates, to the road. The night air was cool and sweet.

I hadn't been lying about the traffic, at least. It was gone, everyone's cars nestled tightly in their long rented driveways, all the pool toys and changes of clothes unpacked, people going to sleep exhausted in unfamiliar beds.

We took our time, even though we were late. Going slow like that, it was fifteen minutes to Cleo's place, another five to Talia's, another five to mine. We skated four astride down the middle of the road. In and out of pools of yellow light.

"Let's play Questions," Cleo said.

"You start," said Talia.

"Okay. If you could add one, and only one, new flavor of sno-cone to our sno-cone offerings, what flavor would you choose?"

"Watermelon," I said.

"I wouldn't add a flavor, but I'd fix the orange flavor so it tasted good," Talia said. "Right now it's weirdly acidic."

"I find that to be part of its charm," Cleo noted.

"I like plain," Polly said dreamily, looking off in the direction of the ocean and skating with long, graceful strokes. Absolutely fucking useless. Who ate a sno-cone plain? That's not even a sno-cone. That's just ice.

"My answer is lemonade," Cleo said. "Callie, your turn."

"Why me next?"

"You answered first."

"Fine. On July seventh, what are you going to do with your newfound power?"

Cleo skated ahead and turned, skated backward, gave me a look. "Forgive me, but that sounded like you're making fun of our endeavors."

"I just want to understand what we're gonna be doing with

the second half of our summer, is all. I mean, is it going to be all sneaking into locker rooms, or . . ."

"By locker rooms do you mean Adam's house?" Talia asked innocently. I shoved her on the shoulder, very lightly—we were not, in fact, wearing our helmets. After the heat of the rink, the wind on our scalps felt too good.

"Okay, fuck you. I asked my question. The rules say everyone else has to answer first."

"What am I *not* going to do?" Cleo asked. She was still skating backward, her legs crossing behind her, relying on luck to keep her away from puddles and potholes.

"Name one thing." I wasn't sure what I was trying to get at, but I wanted to hear their answers. If we were going to dive so wholeheartedly into this fantasy, I wanted to understand the future they saw.

"I'm going to sneak into the movie theater," Talia said. "Whenever we go to Wilmington. I'm gonna bring in food from the mall and watch movies for free."

"Ambitious," I said, but I shut up when I saw the look on her face, her jaw set and eyes staring hard into the dark ahead. Not the whole truth. I thought of her house, always loud with the arguments of two younger sisters and two frazzled parents. I thought of her and Michael. How often they fought.

"I'm gonna make my own version of that video," Cleo said. "But better. More detail. Maybe a whole series. Also, I think I'm gonna have better on-screen charisma. People are going to absolutely love it."

"We'll be famous," Talia said, laughing.

"I'm going to eavesdrop on my parents," Polly said. "Not this summer, obviously. But when I get back home. There's something going on with them."

"Something like what?" Talia asked. Cleo turned around again and skated next to Polly, grabbed her hand.

"I think they're going to get divorced," Polly said. Her voice was almost too soft to hear. The wind took her words and swept them away, high up in the air, disassembled them and tossed them down around us like droplets of water.

"Shit," I said after a moment. "I'm sorry, Polly."

"Yeah," said Talia quietly. "Me too."

"It's fine," she said, and I didn't know her well enough yet to tell how much of a lie it was. "Honestly, I don't think I'll feel a need to do much. Just being able to get away from all of this"—she pressed her hands to her stomach, concave beneath her baggy dress—"will be so nice."

Polly sped up, and she and Cleo skated together a few yards ahead of me and Talia, two and two again instead of four across. No one said anything until we got to Cleo's house. I gave Polly a real hug goodnight this time. I could feel every bone in her back.

Five minutes later and a mile farther down, Talia squeezed my hand and slid into her driveway. I kept going alone.

In Questions, you're supposed to answer your own question last. The theory is that you're not there just to talk about yourself, but you also shouldn't ask your friends something you're unwilling to answer. You play not because you're looking for dirt, but because you want an equal exchange of truths.

I didn't mind not getting to answer my question, except that I didn't know what my answer was. What would I do? Certainly not creep into Adam's bedroom, although the idea of being in

Adam's bedroom—quite visible and at his explicit invitation—was something I had thought about a number of times. I had never really wanted to eavesdrop on my parents, and I had no wish for fame. I would happily sneak into movies with Talia, because I didn't feel guilty about robbing Hollywood of my five-dollar matinee ticket price. But that wasn't an answer. Not for her, and not for me.

I imagined lying on my bed and seeing the pattern of my quilt beneath me. Being in the ocean, looking down at an empty space in the water where my torso should have been. It was a pretty cool idea. It didn't feel like anything to aspire to.

At home, I took off my skates at the bottom of the stairs outside. My parents had left the porch light on for me, like always. I entered the house in my socks and tucked my skates into their spot beside the door, and down the hall in the kitchen, my dad poked his head around the doorway.

"You made it!" he said, mostly enthusiastic, maybe a little annoyed.

"Sorry," I said. I set down my bag and joined him at the table, where Mom was eating leftover pasta salad out of the bowl we'd made it in the day before. "The syrup was everywhere. It looked like we'd killed somebody. How long have you guys been home?"

"Since ten," Dad said.

"Busy day," Mom said. She slid the bowl to me.

"Busier than a normal Saturday?"

"Felt like it. One of those big houses down the island wanted twenty bikes delivered. Twenty! And then we had someone come in yelling about how their canoe was all wrong."

"They didn't believe us when we explained the difference between a canoe and a kayak," Dad said drily. "How was work apart from the syrup, Callie?"

I took an enormous bite of pasta salad before answering. I swear meditation made me hungrier. "Good," I said. "Busy there, too. Technically I wasn't working, so Cleo DJed, but she put on some of the songs on the last playlist I made her, so that was nice."

"I still think you shouldn't go to work if you're not getting paid," Mom said, but I just shrugged. I knew it wasn't a great precedent to set for my boss. But what else was I going to do? Especially on a Saturday night, when my parents were still busy delivering to the new crop of renters, I wasn't just going to sit at home. I was going to hang out with my friends. Even if they were at work.

"How are your goals for the summer going?" she asked when it became clear I wasn't going to respond.

"Good," I said again. I focused on the pasta as if it might help me lie more convincingly.

Obviously I didn't want to discuss this stupid invisibility plot with my parents. But they knew our history and I'd had to come up with something, so I had told them that we were doing individual goals this summer instead of a group goal.

"I liked the old system of a goal for the whole crew," Dad said, nostalgia softening his voice. "But the individual goals are good, too. How many of those fifty books for the summer has Cleo gotten through?"

"Twelve. She's behind. But the next few are graphic novels, so she thinks she's gonna catch up pretty fast." Like the rink cleaning, this was only a half lie. Cleo really was trying to read fifty books.

"And how's Talia doing on her SAT practice tests?"

I rolled my eyes. "What practice tests? She says she's going to work on studying, but she doesn't really. And thanks for asking about my goal, my mile time is going great."

"Oh yeah?" Mom perked up. "What are you down to?"

"Five thirty-six on the road yesterday. This morning it was higher, but it was hotter today. And I ran on the beach."

"That's awesome," Dad said. "Really amazing. You're gonna make it under five thirty before the summer is over, I'm calling it now."

"That's the goal," I said. This, too, was true.

My parents didn't know Polly well enough to ask about her goal, which was fortunate, because I had made it up out of whole cloth. We were claiming she wanted to learn the ukulele. Cleo's grandparents had a ukulele that sat on top of the dresser in the guest room, and honestly, it was just the first thing I thought of when I pictured Polly in the room. When this had come up with Polly several days later—Cleo's grandparents had asked, so we'd needed to coordinate our stories—Polly had said, "As good an answer as any."

I had wanted to ask her what her actual goals were, what she'd come into the summer wanting. But I didn't.

I took a last bite of pasta salad and pushed the bowl back to my mom. "I'm going to bed. I'm pretty tired."

She yawned, an enormous yawn that overcame her whole body. "Probably a good idea for all of us."

"You girls go to bed," Dad said as he grabbed the bowl. "I'll clean up down here. Callie, sleep well."

He was holding the bowl in one hand but tried a two-handed hug anyway. I hugged back tight. It sometimes felt weird, being as tall as my dad. New.

I hugged Mom, too, because even if Dad told her to go upstairs, I knew she would linger in the kitchen with him. I climbed the stairs by myself. As I brushed my teeth, I sat on the top stair, like I used to when I was little and couldn't sleep, and listened to the familiar sounds of them—the murmuring between them, quiet giggles, the clink of silverware as they slid it back into the drawer.

6 THE DAWN OF JULY

I was awake for the dawn of July. Sitting on the bottom step of the stairs, tying the laces on my sneakers, I felt the morning air clinging to the damp, dark chill of night. The breeze raised goose bumps on my stomach. I jogged across the empty street and onto the beach and turned right, to the east. I would run into the sun, so I could watch it rise.

I started off slow and broke into a sprint after a quarter mile. I felt my legs burning, heart skipping, lungs flagging, and kept pushing and pushing until I couldn't anymore. Then I settled back into my normal jog, gulping air and seeing stars.

I liked July. It was the only month of the year that had no school on either end. It had no landmarks: the tide of renters came in and went out on Saturdays, and the town held a cookout for the Fourth of July, but otherwise nothing much happened. In July, no one had birthdays or crises. It was pure, undiluted summer, molten and sweet like ice cream at the edges.

This July was different. It had a hole in the middle: the new moon. The night we were all looking forward to, meditating for, when nothing was going to happen.

I ran past Talia's house, Cleo's house, the old general store, the seafood stand where sometimes Talia and I had gotten free lemonade when we were little kids. I was almost at the skating rink when the half-hour timer on my phone went off. It wasn't the farthest I had ever gotten in half an hour, but it was close. I turned around.

While I was running, the sun had grown full and bright. Early walkers were out in pairs by the water's edge. A few intrepid families were setting out tents and coolers for the day, and I passed three or four elderly folks sitting in beach chairs and drinking their coffee. So even though it was still very early, when I saw the girl by the ocean letting the water wash over her legs, it wasn't that weird. I wouldn't have stopped. Except as I got closer, she took the elastic out of her hair and shook it out over her back, and I saw that it was Polly.

I almost kept going anyway. She was sitting in the sand, looking out at the water. It would've been easy to pretend I'd never crossed her path.

But it was so strange, seeing her there alone this early, the memory of sunrise still lingering in the pale sky. She looked tiny and distracted. The tide rushed up her skinny thighs to kiss the bottom of her shorts, the hem of her oversize sweatshirt, and she didn't even move back.

I slowed and got my breathing under control before I said, "Polly."

She startled and turned toward me. "Callie!" Her eyes were big and bright blue. "What are you doing here?"

I gestured at my body, sweaty and shaky. "Running," I said.

"Oh." She shook her head a little, as if clearing cobwebs. "Of course."

"What about you?"

"Same."

I raised my eyebrows. "Really? I didn't know you ran."

"Yeah. In the mornings, every other day."

"I'm surprised I haven't seen you. I'm out here every morning."

"Oh, I usually run on the road. Just a few miles." She looked up at me and smiled. "Today was the first time I tried the beach. It was a lot harder."

"It is harder," I admitted. "But I prefer it."

"I get that. Being by the ocean is nice. But my feet are killing me. I barely made it a mile that way before I turned around. I was gonna go inside"—she nodded back toward Cleo's house, behind us—"but it's such a gorgeous morning. I thought I'd sit here for a bit. I still can't get over how big the ocean is." She paused. "That probably sounds stupid."

"It doesn't sound stupid." I sat down next to her. The sand was damp, but my shorts were already sweaty. "I've lived here my whole life and sometimes it's still incredible to me. Especially during a storm, when it gets so high. It feels like something I shouldn't even be allowed to witness."

"Have you ever been through a hurricane?"

"Yeah. Every year."

"Every year?" Polly's eyebrows arched high. "That's so scary."

I laughed. "It's not, it's fine. I mean, sometimes it's scary, but it's normal, too. It's the one time it's nice to have a house that isn't beachfront. And besides, the whole island, if you look at a map—" I traced an imaginary coastline with my finger in the air. "We're kind of tucked in underneath Wilmington, here, so we've been lucky. Not perfectly lucky. When Florence came through a few years ago, that wasn't great."

"Did you have to evacuate?"

"For that one, yeah. We stayed with Talia's aunt in Raleigh. We were all worried, and there was a lot of flooding here, but my and Talia's houses were fine. The worst part was having to spend so much time with Talia's sisters and cousins."

I was smiling at the memory: all those kids, the tears and giggles and yelling, the complex games we had made up and then abandoned.

Polly was staring at me in horror. "Evacuation doesn't sound lucky."

"Maybe it's just because I grew up here. Everywhere has their own kinds of natural disasters, right? Although I guess DC doesn't have much of anything."

"I wouldn't know."

"What?"

"I only moved there last summer."

I looked at her more fully. "I didn't know that."

"Yeah. Before that I lived in Boulder. And before that Cambridge, and before that Oklahoma City, and before that . . ." She waved her hand vaguely, as if the memories of all those places were clouding the air in front of her. "Cleo didn't tell you?"

I shook my head. "She said you were new. I guess I assumed you just switched schools or something."

The truth was, I had never even wondered.

"Yeah. Well." There was a bitterness in her voice, and I thought for a second she was mad at Cleo for not telling us her story, which wouldn't have been fair. But she was still staring into that invisible cloud in front of her, or through it, out to the unknowable ocean. "I did switch schools, that's true. But to answer your question, DC doesn't seem to have a lot of natural disasters, no. The hurricanes usually don't stretch up that far north and the snow this winter wasn't nearly as bad as it was in Colorado. Supposedly the heat is bad in the summer, but . . ." She gave a tiny shrug, a tiny smile. "I'm here. So I wouldn't know."

"The heat is bad here."

"Yes. But there's the ocean."

"Yeah." I waited a beat before asking, "Why did you move around so much?"

"My dad's work. He's a consultant. He gets a placement in a city for a few years, and then they move him somewhere else. So we move somewhere else."

"Oh."

"He always says the whole idea of me and my mom moving with him is so he can spend time at home with us instead of going to work during the week and commuting home on the weekends. But he's mostly not home anyway."

I wasn't sure what to say to that, so instead I asked, "What kind of consultant?"

She smiled. "I don't really know."

It was the most I had ever heard Polly talk, and I didn't want to push it. We fell into silence for a few minutes. I scooped wet sand into my palm and let it fall and puddle into itself again.

Polly spoke up after a bit: "What was it like growing up here?"

"Good." I thought about it. "I don't know, I've never grown up anywhere else, but I feel like here is as good a place as any. I guess it's sort of strange because so many people come here every summer for vacation, but for me, for us, it's not special all the time, it's just . . ." I smoothed out the sand under my fingertips again. "Just home. There are good parts and bad parts like anywhere. But I do like being by the ocean."

"I think I would have liked growing up here," Polly said quietly. "I'd like living here."

"A lot of people say that."

"I'm sure. But I mean it."

I believed her.

I was about to get up when she said, "Hey, I wanted to say thank you."

"For what?" I tried to think about anything I had done over the past few days to deserve thanks.

"For being willing to do this. The meditation. The ritual." Her eyes met mine, and they were blue as the ocean, just as deep. "I know you don't want to," she said, "so thank you. For doing it anyway."

"I don't not want to," I said slowly.

She gave me a wry smile. "You don't have to lie."

"I'm not lying," I said, and I found that it was at least a little true. "I admit I'm not convinced it'll work, okay? But maybe it doesn't matter. Like—for me, the most important thing is that Cleo and Talia are happy. And you," I added quickly, but she hadn't missed the slip. She didn't look offended, just inclined her head for me to keep going. "If they're happy, and we're together, and we're all laughing about this in ten years, then okay, it's worth it. That's what I want."

"You really think," she said after a second, "that we'll all be friends in ten years?"

"Yes," I said. "Of course. The idea that we wouldn't be—" I shook my head. "It's absurd."

She hadn't stopped looking at me. I didn't want to look back. I could hear the fear in my own voice. The fear of losing them, to new places and new friends and the slow-pulling tides of time.

"Why do you want to do this, anyway?" I asked her, then cleared my throat.

"I told you," she said. Her voice was soft and clear. "I don't want my body."

I finally looked back at her, torso invisible beneath the folds of her sweatshirt, though it was at least eighty-five out and climbing. I thought of the way she sat at lunchtime on the beach, holding a black coffee, tracing patterns in the sand and not eating anything at all.

"I need to go," I said. I felt, suddenly, like I needed to stretch my legs, feel my blood moving everywhere and the breathlessness of a hard sprint. I got up and dusted the wet sand off the back of my shorts as best I could. "But hey," I added, "we should run together sometime."

"I'm sure I can't keep up," she said, laughing. "I'm not on the track team or anything. I just run for the exercise and to get outside."

"That's okay, I don't mind slowing down."

"Then that'd be great. Thank you."

"You should have breakfast," I said. "After you run. I know Cleo's grandparents always evangelize that weird wheat cereal they like, but it doesn't have to be that. You could make scrambled eggs or something. It's important. My coach always says so."

"Yeah," she said, but it was barely a sigh, nothing to it but air and salt.

I wanted to stay on the beach with her. I wanted to take her home with me, sit with her at the kitchen table, eat eggs and bacon and thick slices of buttered toast together until I saw pink rise in her cheeks. Instead I said, "See you in a few hours," and started off home, running fast, watching the colors in the waves.

7

THE
BASEMENT

My family as a whole doesn't have a ton of interest in town events. On a warm Saturday night, if they aren't working, my parents would rather stay home with me or hang out with Talia's family than go to the pavilion for a concert or attend a fundraiser for the turtle rescue. And I, personally, almost never want to spend time with strangers. But the Fourth of July at Little Beach is an exception. Everyone, tourists and locals alike, converges on a half-mile stretch of beach right in the center of the island. There's a stand that sells turkey legs, another for mini donuts, and a big fireworks show at the end of the night.

Talia, Cleo, Polly, and I met at my house and skated down together. We wore our helmets this time, because Talia's and my parents were biking with us, and they thought we still wore our helmets all the time. Cleo's grandparents drove, trailing us in their old green station wagon.

"So what should I expect?" Polly asked, skating between me and my mom.

"Uh, I don't know," I said. "A party?"

"There's food," Mom supplied helpfully.

"A party," Polly said, as if she were a Martian hearing the word for the first time. I waited for the stab of annoyance that typically came when she was spacey like this, but what bubbled up instead was a laugh. She glanced at me and started laughing, too.

We found a spot at the edge of the festivities and tossed our things on a blanket while the adults set up their chairs and coolers. Talia and I led Cleo and Polly through the maze of towels and tents to find people from school. Michael was somewhere, and so was Adam.

"This is not what I pictured," Polly said, hopping over a sandcastle.

"What did you picture?"

"You said a party."

I looked around. "This is a party."

I had been to plenty of beach parties, and it seemed like one to me. People were grilling burgers and passing around beers. Everyone had their own speakers, all blaring overlapping songs, giving the air a tinny, pop-flavored filter. Little kids ran back and forth from the ocean to the safety of the dry sand, and families sat in clumps, sunburned and gossiping. Honestly, it was a lot like a normal summer day, except the density of people was about twice as high, and there was something else indefinable and good on the breeze—the feeling of strangers coming together.

"Yeah, but I pictured, I don't know, more like—"

"Miami," Cleo interrupted. "You know, like on TV? Tons of superhot people in string bikinis and Speedos playing beach volleyball and drinking champagne? And somehow also there are sports cars?"

"That is not what I thought," said Polly, indignant, but Talia and I had already stopped in our tracks.

"Cleo, do you mean to tell me," Talia said, "that you brought this poor girl down to Little Beach, North Carolina, with the promise of Miami television parties?"

"We are literally called Little Beach," I said, starting to giggle. "It's in our name."

"Polly over here expecting our Fourth of July party to be some kind of flashy event from, God, I don't know, Myrtle—"

"It's not like we're Wrightsville, we're only a simple town—"

"Myrtle Beach is in South Carolina and there's more of a nightlife there," Cleo explained to Polly, rolling her eyes with a smile as Talia and I kept riffing, now gasping from laughter. "And Wrightsville is near Wilmington, which is a college town."

"God, Polly, I can't imagine how disappointed you've been in us all this time—"

"—all this time thinking she was entering a world of glamour—"

"—a world of, of, I don't know, clubs with bouncers—"

"—and DJs—"

"Okay, you two, come on, I want to say hi to these people I see once a year who think I'm amazing." Cleo pulled Polly ahead and charged toward our classmates, while Talia and I did our level best to get our breathing under control.

"Miami," Talia muttered under her breath, and we burst into laughter again.

The folks from school were gathered a little ways down the beach, a huge crowd of kids, some in the ocean and some on the sand around a charcoal grill. Michael split off as soon as he saw us approaching, then jogged over to Talia with a grin that broke his face in half.

"Babe, you look incredible," he said, grabbing her around the waist before kissing her, which shut both Talia and me right up. She did look amazing—her dress was floaty and yellow, bright against her tan, and scooped low in the front. "Hey, y'all," he said to us, barely glancing up.

"Hey," Cleo and Polly chorused. I didn't say anything. Michael pulled Talia away without further preamble, murmuring something into her ear, leading her toward a group of soccer guys who were drinking soda I was sure they'd spiked. Talia raised a hand and shrugged as she left, as if to say, *Oh well.* I pinpointed that group of guys in my memory—away from the grill, close to the water—so I could keep an eye on her, just in case.

"Swim?" Polly asked, raising her eyebrows at me and Cleo.

"Yes."

The heat was brutal, sweat already covering us in a sheen like lotion, and it was easy to leave our dresses in a pile and tumble into the waves. Past the breakers, fifteen or twenty people floated, talking and laughing and throwing a ball around. When they saw Cleo, a few people waved hello, and others who hadn't yet seen her this summer yelled in excitement.

"I'm back," she called, like a queen greeting her subjects. Our school friends loved Cleo. Talia and I fielded questions about her all year. "How have things been? Kaylee, how's your little sister? Parker, are you still with Alexis?"

"How does she remember all of their names?" Polly, beside me, looked mystified.

"Cleo loves people. And she loves, you know, being loved."

"Yeah." She looked at me, smiled ruefully. "I couldn't do it."

"God, me neither."

"Polly, come here and meet Kaylee!" Cleo called, and with a bewildered glance back at me, Polly bounced her way over to the group. I ducked under the waves to get my hair wet, squeezing my eyes shut against the salt water. My hair was a frizzy disaster, and I had clocked Adam with some guys at the other edge of the group.

I floated next to Cleo, basking in the fringes of the attention directed at her. By listening, I found out that Parker was indeed still with Alexis, that Kaylee's little sister had recovered well from her gymnastics injury last year, and that a variety of other things had happened that I never would've thought to ask my classmates. As my gaze moved from the sky to the shore—Talia was still on the beach, Michael's arm around her waist like a vise—I wondered if I should feel guilty. I could have gotten to know these people better. And I could still, now. It wasn't too late. It would only be one more year, after all, before we graduated and scattered into the rest of our lives. I should take advantage of the time I had with them.

But then again, it was only one more year. If I hadn't grown close with them yet, I probably wasn't going to. Better to stay where I liked best, on the edges. I tipped my head back into the water and listened there, the laughter and shouts softened by the sea.

"Catch!" yelled a familiar voice as I came up for air, and I turned just in time for the ball to smack me in the forehead.

I felt like it was the universe telling me: the edges aren't good enough.

"Oh, fuck," said the voice, and Adam appeared in front

of me, grinning bashfully. "That's not how that was supposed to go."

I rubbed my forehead, picked up the ball, and tossed it back to his friend, who was laughing at Adam several yards away. "You know just because I can run doesn't mean I have hand-eye coordination, right? That's why I don't play a real team sport. No need to handle balls."

Adam raised his eyebrows, and I sank into the water, groaning. "Jesus. Not what I meant."

"Uh-huh. So what've y'all been up to this summer?" Adam asked. He reached past me to pluck a piece of seaweed away, and his hand brushed against my shoulder.

"Working at the rink," I said against the tumble in my stomach. "Beaching. Reading. You know. I haven't seen you in a few weeks."

"Yeah, I've been working at Cappuccino by the Sound, it's open most of the day. Been running?"

"Always. You?"

"Of course." He grinned. "Got my mile time down to five forty-five. I'm comin' for you, O'Connell."

I kicked up into a float. "Keep trying. I'm almost at five thirty."

He groaned and splashed me a little. "I'll never catch up. Hey, I saw the new girl running on the road the other morning, what's up with her?"

"Polly." A low, dismal panic cut into my weightlessness. Polly was very pretty. Of course Adam had noticed her. "Cleo's friend. She's nice. She's really weird, but she's nice."

Adam tugged very gently on a strand of my ponytail. I turned over in the water to look at him. He was smiling. "No one's as weird as you," he said, and even though I knew I was not that weird, and anyway, weird wasn't necessarily good—the way the words came out, they sounded like the sweetest compliment. I touched my hair where his hand had been.

As if on cue, Cleo dragged Polly over and introduced her to Adam, who gave Polly a goofy, waterlogged handshake. "Callie's been telling me about her summer," he said. "Sounds thrilling."

Cleo's head inclined toward mine, her mouth tightening, and if I could've seen her eyes behind her sunglasses, I swear they would've been like knives. I shook my head with the smallest movement possible and made a mental note to ask her later if she thought I'd lost my mind. Obviously, I wasn't going to tell Adam. We had promised each other we wouldn't tell anyone.

Not like I wanted to tell anyone. This fantasy project was at best childish and at worst deranged.

But just in case Cleo didn't get my drift, I said, "The thrilling life of the rink and the beach."

"Literally anything would be more interesting," Cleo said, relaxing into the water. "Good thing I don't come here for interesting."

"Cleo! I'm offended!" Adam said, miming a dagger in his heart. "Is Little Beach not metropolitan enough for you?"

"It's exactly the right amount of metropolitan."

The ball that had hit me a few minutes before landed again, perilously close, and someone yelled Adam's name. He threw the ball back—the lines of his back, the curve of his wet shoulder in the sun—and said, "Ladies, apparently I'm overdue returning to the group of assholes I call my friends. Polly, good to meet you. Cleo, good to see you."

Polly nodded. Cleo said, "I'm sure we'll see you soon."

"Of course." He turned to me. "Listen, I was going to ask if you wanted to go running together sometime. My grandparents are visiting this weekend, but maybe after that . . ."

"You think you can keep up?" I immediately cursed myself. Why could I not be like Talia, sweet, easy for boys to talk to? But Adam grinned big.

"I can give it a shot," he said.

"Then yes," I said, relieved. "I'll make us a running playlist."

"Cool. Looking forward to it." His name rang out over the waves again, and he rolled his eyes and swam toward the sound.

"Well, look at that," Cleo said, kicking off my thigh to float a few feet away.

"Look at what?" I said, and did a quick somersault under-water. I stayed there for an extra second or two, letting myself smile, my eyes squeezed shut tight. Running together. I wondered what Adam wore when he ran on the beach in the morning.

I propelled myself back to the surface. "See, he was nice," Polly was saying to Cleo, accusation in her tone.

I looked between them. "What?"

"Mason was also nice," Cleo protested.

"I guess if by nice you mean boring. He had nothing inter-esting to say. And he stared at my boobs."

"Yeah, that sucked. Though in fairness," Cleo pointed out, "you have great boobs."

"I honestly do not."

"What are you guys talking about?"

"I just wanted to introduce Polly to—"

"Cleo's trying to set me up," Polly interrupted; it was prob-ably the first time I'd ever heard her interrupt anyone, and it pleased me. "With some guy whose face I can't remember even though I met him five minutes ago. Cleo, I'm going to find the girl with the squeakiest voice in that group and tell her you think she's cute."

Cleo rolled her eyes and splashed Polly half-heartedly, though there was something in the set of her jaw that looked—angry, maybe? Not angry. Worried. "I was not trying to set you up. I don't even really like him, and I didn't think you would, either. I was just trying to introduce you to some of my many fans. Who, by the way, do not know I'm queer, and I'd appreciate it if you didn't tell the entire beach. I have zero interest in any of these girls, and coming out down here would be more trouble than it's worth."

"Amen to that," I muttered. Cleo and I were both out to our families—and to each other's families and Talia's—but in her visits to Little Beach, she had never told anyone else she wasn't straight. I hadn't, either. Coming out to Polly, which I'd done during a video chat with Cleo in the spring, had been an accident: I made an offhand comment, having fully forgotten she was sitting there beside Cleo on-screen.

"I'm sorry," said Polly, looking genuinely abashed. "I would never out you. Or you, Callie."

Cleo splashed her. "I know, you doofus."

"Can one of you please tell me who we were originally talking about?" I asked.

"Mason Moretti," Cleo said. "A perfectly nice guy. Not someone you would want to date, but nice. Right?"

"Oh, sure. Mason is fine." I had known him since middle school but couldn't put my finger on any of his particular characteristics. I seemed to remember him being on the yearbook staff. He wore a lot of hair gel.

"Yes, exactly, fine," Polly said. "And all I was saying was that Adam was actually nice, if by nice you mean funny and charming." I didn't mean to change my expression, but something must have crossed my face, because her eyes went wide and she said, "But, Callie, that's not— I'm not— I don't want to date anybody. I don't want a summer boyfriend. At all. I just want to hang out with you guys and, you know—" She looked around to make sure no one was listening. "Gain a new superpower."

"Adam is great," I said carefully. "And if you want—"

"I don't," Polly said. Her voice was clear and strong. "I don't want to date anyone. As I've been trying to tell Cleo."

Cleo shook her head. For a second she had a strange look on her face, but then she tipped onto her back to float. "I try to help you make friends and am persecuted for my efforts. Someday you'll thank me."

"I have you," Polly said. "I don't need more friends." Cleo smiled up at the sky, and her whole body softened a little, like she was becoming part of the surface of the water.

"Are you sure?" I asked Polly. "About Adam, I mean."

"I am." Polly's eyes were gentle. "But I meant it. He's nice. Really nice. You should date him, if you want."

"So say we all," said Cleo to the sky, and having nothing left to add, I fell back into the water myself.

The day lasted forever. Of course, we always spent a lot of time on the beach, but not usually like this, from morning all the way till night. I ate cheeseburgers and corn chips with my parents and Popsicles with Cleo and threw a ball around with Adam and his friends. Adam tackled me in the ocean once, ostensibly trying to get the ball before I caught it, and I felt his solid chest come into contact with mine and propel me back into the water and thought—*this has to be intentional, right?* I came up gasping and laughing, clutching the ball, and Adam said, "Got me, O'Connell," with a grin. I felt like the heat of the sun was shining all the way through my skin to my heart and my lungs and the marrow of my bones.

At one point later in the afternoon, Polly and Cleo and I crossed paths with Miss Abby, who was predictably drunk off her ass. She threw her arms around us and told us how proud she was that we were continuing her legacy at the skating rink, whatever that meant. We had to peel her off us and assure her that the Sunday Night Skate was still running exactly as it always had. When it got dark, there were fireworks, and then people started to go home.

The only thing missing was Talia. She had been glued to Michael's side all day. When Michael had come out into the ocean, she had come, too, but she hadn't gone on walks or eaten dinner with us or done any of the things we normally would. It was strange. I was used to wandering around in a group of three, but in Talia's usual place there was Polly, her blond hair plastered to her neck, laughing over a cup of iced coffee.

When the fireworks started, I'd returned to my parents to lean against my mom's legs, an old tradition. Talia usually sat with her family for the fireworks, too, but she wasn't there. She still wasn't around when Cleo's grandparents loaded Cleo and Polly into their station wagon. Cleo promised through the open window to see me on the beach the next morning. I walked back from the parking lot through the cool, soft sand, letting the happiness of the day sink into my skin. This was the first time in ages that we hadn't practiced meditation at the rink, the first day that hadn't been entirely occupied with talk of the ritual, the plan, the superpower that I knew would never really manifest. It had been normal. Like summers used to be.

Across the beach, a few clumps of people lingered. A couple walked hand in hand near the water. Families standing beside a grill packed up their things, tossing plates into a trash bag and folding up chairs. My parents were sitting around a bonfire with Talia's, our mothers tipsy and laughing, our fathers taking turns poking the fire ineffectually with sticks. Talia's youngest sister, Angelica, was stretched out on a beach blanket asleep. Her middle sister, Olivia, was giggling with her best friend, Hazel, over a plate of chips and guacamole.

Down the beach, the area where Michael and Talia had been was empty. I texted Talia *where are you?* but it didn't go through. Her phone was dead, probably. She was always forgetting to charge it.

I tapped Talia's mom on the shoulder. "Mrs. Maris?"

She turned, smiled, leaned back in her chair. "Hey, honey, what is it?"

"Have you seen Talia?"

"She was with Michael, right?"

"Yeah, but I don't know where they went. They were right down the beach before the fireworks."

"Oh, she said they were going to Parker's house." Mrs. Maris pointed vaguely in that direction. "I told her we were leaving at nine-thirty. Hey, Catherine, what time is it?"

My mom checked her watch. "Nine."

"So she should be back soon."

I frowned, and Mom looked at me gently. "I wouldn't worry. Parker's house isn't far, and they were with a big group. We saw them head off. Parker's parents left a while ago, too. Why don't you text Talia?"

"I did, I think her phone's dead." I looked down the beach. "I might just go catch up to them."

Dad furrowed his brow. "I don't want you going by yourself, Callie."

"You guys just said it wasn't far," I pointed out. "It's no big deal. I'll be back by nine-thirty."

"You promise nine-thirty?" Dad said. "You can't claim that you took too long cleaning the rink this time."

"I never lied about cleaning the rink!" I protested, feeling a snake of guilt coil in my stomach. "Yes, I promise nine-thirty."

"Fine by me, then. Catherine?"

"Okay, but nine-thirty," Mom said. "And call us if you run into any trouble."

"I'll be back by nine-thirty, everything's fine, I love you."

"Love you too," called my parents in unison as I set off.

Parker's house really wasn't far, but still, as soon as I was out of sight of my parents, I started jogging. My legs ached from walking around all day, and stretching them felt good. But there was something urgent driving me, too, something in the same family as panic. Maybe it was the sound of the explosions over the sea still echoing in my ears; maybe it was so many hours in the sun. Maybe it was nothing.

"You are being stupid," I muttered to myself.

It was just—I didn't like Parker or his house. It was one of the big new McMansions on the island, containing a ground-floor apartment with a second entrance, and it wouldn't matter if his parents were home; people could be doing anything there. I knew this because Parker's house was where Michael and Talia went when they wanted to hook up and the weather didn't permit them to go out to the beach. There was a futon, Talia said.

By the time I got there, it was completely dark, and I was panting a little. I steadied my breathing as I found the right private walkway and followed its crisscross path over the dunes. The light was on in the basement, curtains drawn. I knocked on the door.

It opened partially: Alexis, Parker's girlfriend, peeked out. Her face was wary at first, but when she saw it was me, she laughed and opened the door fully. "Callie's here," she called over her shoulder to the room, where Parker and a few other guys were playing pool. They nodded at me, called hello. A girl lounging on a couch raised something in a koozie in acknowledgment.

"Hi," I said.

"Hey, Callie, what's goin' on?"

Alexis gave me a tight hug. I had known Alexis for ages, in the way you know people at school you never hang out with, but she had never hugged me before. The smell of alcohol hung around her hair like a cloud.

"Not a lot," I said, attempting to extricate myself. "I'm just looking for Talia, I heard she was here."

"Oh, yeah," Alexis said, waving her hand at a doorway on the other side of the room. Indistinct yelling came from behind it. "She and Michael are, they're here, somewhere." She moved in close again and whispered, as if it were a great secret, "You should take her home. Michael's being mean."

I swallowed hard, breathing in the harsh, sweet smell of flavored vodka, and fought the reflex to gag or run. I had tried the odd sip of beer or wine at family dinners, but I was rarely at parties where kids my age were drinking. Apart from a handful of furtive experiments in the quiet of our homes, Talia and I had always agreed that the risks of alcohol (furious parents, arrests and fines, permanent record) weren't worth the benefits (still not totally clear, as we both thought that most of it tasted terrible). I didn't want anyone to offer me anything, look at me, pay me any attention at all. Being in this basement full of boys and a few drunk girls switched on a fight-or-flight instinct.

I walked through the room and opened the door.

Inside was an unfinished space with a big TV, a couch, an armchair, and three guys playing a video game I didn't recognize. Michael was one of them. Their yelling was the yelling I'd heard, and none of them looked up from their game when I entered. Relief hit me in a quiet ping, like a raindrop on water, until I saw Talia curled up in the armchair. Her yellow dress looked sickly in the blue light of the screen, and she had been crying. When she saw me, her face twisted—part relief, part shame.

I didn't go any farther. Just jerked my head back, *Can we go?*, and Talia nodded and got up, sliding into her flip-flops and picking up her tote bag.

"I'm going home, Michael," she said.

"Okay, see y— Ah, motherfucker, Paul, you fuckin' asshole!" He shoved the guy next to him, who was laughing at whatever had just happened on-screen, and didn't even look at Talia. The guy fell over from the force of the push, still laughing.

Talia stared at Michael for a second before setting her jaw. I held the door open for her and let her lead me through the adjoining room. As we stepped outside, I heard Alexis call tipsily from behind us, "Bye, Talia! Bye, Callie! I love you so much!"

The silence, the heat, the humidity, the dark. The smell of the salt on the air. They were welcome after the harsh, cold fluorescents of that basement. We walked in silence down the long path, and when we got to the beach, I took Talia's hand. She squeezed mine, and I felt another little rush of relief, that she hadn't flinched away. I can't explain why, but I thought if the worst had happened, she would have flinched away.

"After the fireworks." She spoke very quietly; I had to tilt my head toward her and concentrate to hear over the white noise of the waves. "I wanted to go back to you guys. Say good night to Cleo and everything. But Michael wanted to go to Parker's. We were arguing about it and he said—" She swallowed. "He said I was being a bitch, and I never put him first, and a real girlfriend would spend more time with him, and if I didn't go back with him I would embarrass him."

We walked in silence for a moment. I wanted to say something, but it felt like she was just taking a break before she kept talking. And eventually, she did speak up again.

"He sounded so angry," she said. "And people heard, which made it worse. He wasn't yelling, but we were just standing a little ways away from the barbecue, so I know at least Alexis and her friend heard. I mean, I don't know if I'm getting it across, how angry he sounded."

"You're getting across plenty," I said. I felt cold. I wanted to tuck Talia into a soft, warm bed and then run back to Parker's house as fast as I could, a five-minute mile, four-minute, three, and knee Michael in the balls. Watch him double over and vomit like I felt I might any minute.

She shook her head, like she couldn't believe it. "It was so weird. I keep thinking about what I could have done to make him mad. But he was so nice, all day. It was such a nice day. And then this happened and I said I'd go back with them, and once we got there he just started playing that game and he didn't even pay attention to me. It was like after all that, he didn't even want me there."

"Oh, Talia." I felt shaky, and beside me, she sighed.

"Thanks for coming and getting me," she said. "I didn't know what to do. I thought he might get mad again if I left. And my stupid phone had died so I couldn't even text you."

I focused on the light of the bonfires in the distance. I didn't know the right thing to say or do, so I said the thing I wanted to say. "You need to break up with him."

She withdrew her hand, and it was like her whole body got a little smaller. "I can't."

"You absolutely could."

"But I love him."

She sounded so pitiful, so desperate, and I wanted to turn a mirror on her and say: Look. Look at my best friend. Look how beautiful she is when she laughs; look at how good she is at bringing that laughter to other people; look at her smile. Look at her concentrating, how smart and thoughtful she is; look at her when she sings. Look at all the love and care and loyalty she brings to everyone in her life and then tell me how it makes any sense that a boy like Michael should deserve her.

Talia stumbled on a shell beside me and almost fell, and a more urgent thought pushed out my anger: "Talia, are you drunk?"

"Are you kidding?" She looked as horrified as I had felt a moment earlier.

"Sorry." I shook my head. "It's just, everyone was drinking back there. I wouldn't have judged you." This wasn't entirely true, but it didn't top my list of concerns.

She sighed. "Michael did offer. Several times. Someone had a flask on the beach. Maybe he was mad because I didn't join in, maybe that was it. I don't know." She nudged me. "But you know I don't like liquor. Or beer."

"Now, if they'd had sangria," I teased, and Talia laughed. Talia's dad's sangria was world—well, island—famous. Last year, the year we'd turned sixteen, we had each been permitted one small glass. It tasted like sweet, spicy fruit juice with a sort of gross aftertaste, and the one glass had made me feel sleepy and silly, a sensation that I only half understood why someone would want to chase. Talia, though, had loved it, begged for a second cup. In the months after that, in secret, we'd experimentally tried sips of other alcohol our parents had stashed at the backs of their cabinets and fridges. But it had all tasted terrible. "Sangria or nothing," Talia had said to me after trying a whiskey that tasted like grass clippings left too long in the sun.

"Please. I drank my own water and lemonade all day," she said now, still smiling. "I wouldn't trust anyone back there to pour me a drink."

"Not even your boyfriend?" I asked, and the smile faded.

We were within sight of our parents. In the light of the streetlamps and the few remaining bonfires, I could see their silhouettes: dumping ice out of coolers, looking for us in the darkness. It was 9:32. My phone was going to buzz any minute, my dad asking me where we were.

Talia stopped. She folded her arms in front of her chest.

"It would've been nice today," she whispered.

I didn't ask what she meant. I knew she was talking about the ritual, just three days away.

My legs were tired, and I had a headache. "Come on," I said. "Let's go home."

8 GRADUATION MORNING

Three days are nothing. Three days go fast. Three more days of the beach and work, sun-warmed sandwiches and meditation practice, each day an echo of the day before—except for the singular fact of July 7, almost here.

I had been rolling my eyes at my friends, but that wasn't entirely honest. Maybe I believed more than I said I did. Because a small, hopeful part of me did think this night could change us. It could turn Talia untouchable, make her see Michael for the jerk he was. It could give Cleo the victory she wanted, pulling off the most extraordinary summer project there ever was. It could impress into Polly whatever missing piece she had been searching for.

It could make me— What? Faster, maybe. Stronger. Better. Or maybe it would just tie us tighter together, and that was all that mattered. I had been calling myself a skeptic, but I was meditating every night with the rest of them. Whether I'd intended to or not, I had bought into the power of ritual.

Before falling asleep those three nights, I put in my earbuds and listened to a playlist on repeat, all sad songs that blended into a single low melody. Julien Baker whispered softly in my ear; Indigo De Souza wailed, and I listened. I meditated, and I looked at the disappearing moon in the sky, and I listened. And I waited for the night we had been waiting for.

When I woke up on July 7, I felt like I did the mornings of races. Excited, aimless nervousness ran up and down my arms and legs. I texted Talia !!!!!!!!!, but unsurprisingly, she didn't respond; it was far too early for her. Instead, I thought of Polly running and pulled up the group text I had with her and Cleo and Talia. I sat there for a minute, the first soft light of the day drifting in through my window, and I could not imagine a version of the conversation that made me feel less nervous. I set down my phone and put on my sports bra and shorts. When I stepped outside, I thought how strange it was that the air tasted exactly the same as always.

About a mile into my run, I remembered that I was supposed to fast today, so I wouldn't be able to eat breakfast. I turned around. I couldn't run for an hour and not eat anything. But two miles was better than nothing; days off made me jittery. I didn't want to be jittery today.

Overall, I was trying to act normal. Set aside the magic and the science, ignore the ways that Cleo said, self-seriously, "This could change our lives forever," and still I was left with the fact that today, we were doing something unprecedented. We were breaking the rules.

All four of us would be sneaking out at midnight to the beach across the street from Talia's house. I had negotiated a sleepover there, and her parents usually went to bed at nine. Still, though. As I ran back home, I kept envisioning one of our parents or grandparents waking up and finding a girl gone. They would panic. They would call the others. And when we came back, all of them would be terrified and furious.

When I got home, still breathing heavily, Dad looked up from his plate of eggs and said, "How was the run?"

"Good," I said. "Fine."

"Why so short?"

"Trying to work on speed. Do some sprints."

"Nice. Want some breakfast?"

"Nah, thanks, I'm going to Talia's," I said, and then I dashed upstairs. No real lies. I *was* fine. I *had* sprinted most of the last half mile, trying to make my calves flex and burn. I *was* going to Talia's.

Though I had lied about breakfast. I wanted some eggs.

I skated to Talia's house on skittish legs. At the door, as I took off my skates, I could already hear yelling coming from inside. Angelica's twelve-year-old whine met Olivia's screech and Mrs. Maris's quiet, exasperated rebuttals.

If I had known Talia for anything less than my entire life, I might have waited, or at least knocked. But I had held both of her little sisters in my own baby arms on the days they came home from the hospital. I took a deep breath and opened the door.

"—hid my fucking book. I need that today! I'm way behind on my summer reading!" At the end of the hall, Talia's sisters and mom were gathered in the kitchen, Mrs. Maris washing dishes and Olivia and Angelica squared off like fighters. Olivia had her arms crossed as tight as a tangled necklace. She saw me enter and raised her chin a fraction in acknowledgment.

"Olivia, language," Mrs. Maris said automatically, her back to me.

Angelica didn't even notice me. She was starting to cry. "I wouldn't have taken anything if she hadn't taken my towel!"

"I was getting out of the shower! I didn't want to drip all over the floor!"

"Well, where the hell was your towel? You made *me* drip all over the floor!"

Talia came down the stairs in a bikini top and shorts, yelling, "Where the fuck is my pink tank top?" She spotted me. "Oh, Callie, thank God you're here, you can tell my terrible sisters that they can't just take my fucking clothes whenever they want."

I raised my hands. "I'm not part of this."

"Oh, Callie, hello—" Mrs. Maris pulled a breakfast casserole from the oven and placed it on the table. "Nice to see you, have some casserole. Girls, come on, don't fight when we have company."

"Callie isn't company," Angelica said without looking at me. "And I didn't take your pink top, Talia. I guess Olivia is taking all our stuff today, huh?"

"I didn't take anything," Olivia said. "Except a towel that could've been mine."

"It wasn't yours!"

"Have you checked the laundry, Talia?" Mrs. Maris asked wearily.

"I'll check now," Talia grumbled, and returned up the stairs.

I hung back. I had witnessed plenty of Maris family fights, and I knew from experience that the best course of action was to pretend you weren't even there. One time a few years ago, I had decided that since I was practically family anyway, I should get involved and stand up for Talia. That had ended with Talia's mother, both sisters, and, somehow, Talia herself yelling at me. Better to wait in the hallway and hope that everyone went back to forgetting I had ever arrived.

"Callie, get in here and have some casserole," Mrs. Maris called. Angelica and Olivia sat down, still sniping at each other, though so quietly I couldn't quite hear what they were saying.

"I'm okay, thank you," I said, coming into the kitchen. I looked with longing at the breakfast casserole. Mrs. Maris made it with the week's bread ends soaked in eggs and cream and sharp cheddar, with peppers and sometimes bacon between the layers. She made it only on Christmas and summer breaks, when she didn't have to get up early to teach second grade. It was in my top five breakfasts of all time. But we were fasting. "I had a big breakfast at home," I lied.

"Oh, all right. Angelica, Olivia, Talia—" Talia walked back into the room, pulling on her pink tank top. "Have some food."

"I'm not hungry," said Talia.

"Me neither," said Olivia.

"More for me," said Angelica, who had always been skinny and didn't show any signs of gaining weight as she got taller. She cut a huge slice of casserole as Mrs. Maris folded her arms and looked at her other two daughters.

"Girls. Come on. Eat some breakfast."

"I'm not hungry," Olivia whined. "I don't want any."

"Me neither, and we have to go," Talia said. She ducked around her mother to walk through the screen door and get her towel, which was hanging on the porch to dry.

Mrs. Maris looked at me and threw up her hands. "I spend all morning making casserole and no one's going to eat it? What is wrong with everyone today?"

"I don't want to get fat," Olivia said tartly as Talia came in with her towel and started sorting through a pile on the coffee table, looking for her phone.

"You're not fat!" Mrs. Maris exclaimed. "And you're not going to get fat from casserole!"

"You might, we don't know for sure," Angelica said. Olivia, now, burst into tears.

For a second there it all felt ordinary. Not good, exactly— Talia's sisters could be so mean to each other—but unexceptional. Too many mornings to count I had spent like this, the girls arguing, the light through the window, and Talia bouncing around getting ready for the day we had laid out in front of us, as bright and familiar as a beach blanket.

Mrs. Maris said, "Angelica, come on," and circled the table to put her arms around a sobbing Olivia. She looked up at me and said, "Speaking of work, I'm assuming the two of you will be late again, right?"

And Talia, picking up her sunglasses from the couch behind her mother, said, "Yes, we're closing, and you know how Saturdays are." Her mother said, "Yes, well, we need to be in bed early, so just let yourself in," and Talia said, "No problem," and held a finger up to her lips, so only I could see. Behind her finger she smiled. And I thought I might pass out.

9

THE NEW MOON

We had one blessing: The rink was busy that night. The week after the Fourth of July was always a little wild, but this night was especially feverish, high-pitched with hysterics and tears, and we were short-staffed. Normally, all four of us would be working. But it was Cleo's grandparents' fifty-fourth wedding anniversary that night, so while they were out to a nice dinner, Cleo and Polly were deep-cleaning the house as a gift. When I stopped to think about it, I couldn't decide whether the anniversary was a good sign or a bad sign for us. Fifty-four years was stability, solidity, permanence. We were aiming for the opposite. Would it help us, to mark that occasion as a counterweight? Or would it keep us tethered?

It was a foolish thought. Their anniversary didn't have anything to do with us. But that's where my brain was that night. Every time I stopped to take a breath, it was busy tying me in knots, making connections out of nothing.

We had spent the day on the beach as usual, restless and twitchy. Cleo kept talking through the plan, saying the same words over and over again. Polly hung on Cleo's every syllable, and Talia just stared at the ocean. I tried to read and failed. As Cleo launched into her twentieth recap of the evening to come, I got up and went into the water alone. I was starving. I had a headache.

I floated and watched them on the beach, my three best friends killing themselves with anxiety over nothing. I felt apart from them. We were afraid of different things. They were worried that it wouldn't work. I knew it wouldn't and was worried about what would happen next.

There in the ocean, I let myself think ahead to the approaching night. I envisioned us walking quietly back to our houses, soaked and shivering, our skin as solid as it had ever been. I wanted to think they would bounce back fast—that I'd bring my radio station plan to the beach tomorrow and they'd be excited about it. Engaged again in something achievable, something real. But this nervousness was acid, eating at my bones. I was scared that my friends believed too hard.

We left the beach early so Cleo and Polly could spend more time with Cleo's grandparents before dinner. Talia and I went to my house and watched TV. I almost started painting my nails to have something to do with my hands, then, against my will, thought better of it—*What if it interfered with the ritual?*—and set the polish back on the shelf. Half an hour earlier than we would've normally left for the rink, Talia looked at me and said, "Let's go, right?"

It turned out to be a good idea. After we set up, I unlocked the front door to discover a line of families ten deep. Relief nearly made me collapse. I couldn't have faced the whole shift with no one else around, just my stomach rumbling and those preperformance jitters hanging in the air between us.

As the first skaters filtered in, Talia said, "Hey, can I run the playlist tonight?"

"Why?" I asked, genuinely curious. "You never care about the music."

"I just want something fun."

"MUNA is fun, Talia," I said, but she had asked and she never asked, so I said yes. Her choices were all sharp, spangled pop and hip-hop, the summer's biggest songs and remixes thereof. I disdained anything super-popular, even the songs I secretly liked. But tonight, it felt right—Glass Animals murmuring throughout the hall, Taylor Swift's heartbreak reaching far into every dusty corner.

Talia turned it up loud. That felt right, too.

Then the night fell into a familiar chaos. "I'm going to make Miss Abby pay us double for this shift," Talia grumbled as she skated past me to berate a boy who was running. Said boy fell a moment later, broke open a cut on his elbow, and burst into tears. Two minutes after that, a blond woman screamed at me for giving the wrong size skates to one of her four children. During a slow song, a tourist couple in their twenties started making out so aggressively—hips and everything—that they had to be separated. Talia and I did rock paper scissors for who had to take on that task. Talia lost.

The hours zipped by, loud and messy, circling tighter and tighter around us until finally I heard my own voice ring out over the loudspeaker: "Final skate!" It was 10:15. Talia put on "Mr. Brightside." It was a song that had always made me feel as if someone had struck a match against the inside of my rib cage. Tonight especially, it filled me up until I thought if I opened my mouth to speak I might breathe fire.

And then it was over, though with the night so busy, we didn't shut the doors for good until 10:45. We left most of our usual cleaning and prep for tomorrow, when Cleo and Polly could help us, and gathered our things fast.

We skated side by side in the quiet. Our wheels clicked and whirred on the pavement. The humid night air was velvet and water on my skin.

Inside Talia's house, we unlaced our skates and set them by the door, like always, and went upstairs. Talia's parents' bedroom and Angelica's bedroom were silent; Olivia was at a friend's house. The clock on Talia's bedside table read 11:14.

"Do you think they'll get here in time?" Talia asked. Her brown skin looked pale in the glow of her bedroom lamp.

"Yes," I said. "Cleo will make sure of it."

"I'm worried they won't make it."

"They will."

"I'm texting them." Talia pulled out her phone and typed out a message. It buzzed a few seconds later, and I peeked over her shoulder. *are you leaving yet?* she'd asked. Cleo responded, *can't yet, but soon. grandma just got into bed. I think we'll be able to get out of here in ten minutes.*

Talia bit her lip. *that's cutting it close,* she typed.

it'll be fine, Cleo said. *gotta go. see you soon.*

I stepped back. Talia stared at her phone, then up at me. She looked like a child, hopeful and afraid. I had an inexplicable urge to bundle her into bed with a cup of tea.

Instead I said, "Should we change?"

She nodded, exhaled.

The white dresses had been Cleo's idea. She had talked about Roman priestesses, baptisms, ritual. I had agreed for practical reasons. The island had a rule that you had to turn off your house lights at night so the turtle hatchlings didn't get confused and walk farther inland instead of out to sea. It meant that at night, under the new moon, it was completely dark out there. I didn't want anyone to drown. We would be able to see each other better wearing white.

Talia was wearing a dress she had bought for a dance with Michael ages ago. It was short, with a halter neck, and it showed off just about everything she had to show. She twisted, looking at me over her shoulder. "Can you tie my straps?"

I did, feeling the cheap, silky material slip between my fingers, imagining what it was going to feel like when it was wet. It was surreal, and I wanted to stop, tell her to put on some pajamas and go to sleep like we had a thousand other nights.

"Thanks." She turned around and adjusted the bodice. "Tell me what you're wearing."

I pulled my dress out of my bag, made a face, and said, "This."

Talia broke into a smile for the first time in hours. "Seriously?"

"I wasn't going to spend money on a dress I'm just going to ruin."

"This is the most important night of your life and you're wearing your fourth-grade Halloween costume?"

"It's the only white dress I own!"

"Come on, put it on, let me see."

I changed, turning away for the comedic value of the reveal. I knew what I looked like in this dress, and it wasn't good. When I turned back to her, she burst into laughter.

"Shut up!" I hissed, though I could feel myself about to start laughing, too. "Angelica will wake up."

She clapped a hand over her mouth but shook with giggles. After a few seconds, she whispered, "Sorry, but you look ridiculous."

She was not wrong. I had been an angel for Halloween when I was nine years old. Before my growth spurt. Seven years and a full foot and a half later, the bottom of the dress came to midthigh. Under different circumstances, this might've been sexy, but the seam separating the skirt from the bodice hit me at midboob, negating any of my torso's already limited appeal. Thankfully, the dress was sleeveless, but I'd had to expand the neck- and armholes with kitchen scissors. I had tried to cut smooth lines, but they hadn't turned out great.

The summary effect was one of a slutty Flintstone at her rehearsal dinner. I could hardly blame Talia for laughing.

"You are not going outside in that," she said once she got her breathing under control. She wiped tears from her eyes. "Jesus, that's funny."

"It's not *that* funny," I said. I was glad that she was happy.

"You're lucky I have another white dress." She disappeared into her closet and emerged with a frilly, scoop-neck number embroidered with flowers. I arched my eyebrows.

"Never seen that one before."

She rolled her eyes and tossed it at me. "My grandma got it for me. For Easter."

"When are you going to tell your grandparents that you don't go to church?"

"They'll find out when they're dead. Put it on."

It didn't look as bad on me as I had thought it would. I smoothed my hands over it as I looked at myself in the mirror. The skirt, knee-length on Talia, was a little short on me. And I definitely wouldn't have chosen it for myself—nothing about it, from the layered ruffles to the embroidery, was my style. But it basically fit, and it was comfortable.

"So much better," Talia declared. A smile played at the edges of her lips. "You should keep this after. Wear it for Adam."

I made a face. "You can't pawn it off on me."

"Can't blame a girl for trying." She glanced at the clock. "Shit. We gotta go. Cleo should be almost here."

It was 11:48. I felt, as if from beneath the floorboards, the thump of my heart in my chest.

10 RITUAL

It was stupid, I thought as we walked across the street, how easy it was to sneak out. How had we never tried it before? Why were we just now discovering it? We arranged pillows under the blankets in Talia's room, like you see in the movies, and then we just tiptoed down the stairs and walked outside. Closed the door quietly. There was nothing more to it than that. Her parents' trust had left our path open and easy. I felt, then, the first shivering premonition of the night to come: that we could do anything.

We crossed the narrow walkway to the beach, the wood cool and splintered under my bare feet. It was very dark. Talia drifted ahead of me in her white dress like a dandelion seed. I was struggling to take deep breaths and simultaneously marveling at the ordinariness of this night, not so different from nights with my parents when we had come out to see a turtle hatching. With one breath, the air felt charged with something electric and new. With the next, it felt as it always had: hot, humid, homely. The ocean at the end of the walkway spread dark and infinite in front of us.

For a few minutes, we stood there in silence alone. I tucked my phone into my bag—I had brought it in case something went wrong, though who knows what—and concealed it in the sand at the edge of the dunes. Beside me, Talia braided and unbraided her hair.

Then Polly and Cleo appeared as a blur in the dark, gradually brightening and forming into the shapes I knew. Polly wore a shift that made her look like a hospital patient; Cleo, a maxi dress dipping low at the chest. Their eyes shone in the night.

"What time is it?" Talia asked as soon as they were close enough to hear us. They dropped their skates in a heap beside us.

"Hello to you too," Cleo said, glancing at her phone. "It's eleven-fifty-six." All of us exchanged hugs. I felt the tension in their shoulders and wondered what they were feeling in me.

"Well," I said.

Talia took a deep breath.

Cleo tucked her phone into her skate and straightened up.

"Shall we?" Polly said.

Cleo led us into the waves.

The water was black underneath and around us. It still held the warmth of the sun. My dress floated where it wasn't plastered to my skin, and I asked myself why we had chosen cotton and polyester when we could've just worn our swimsuits. Or skinny-dipped, for that matter; nakedness seemed appropriate.

But I couldn't very well bring it up now. We kept moving out until the water was calm and halfway up my chest. I could barely see the others. We stood there together, four formless shapes bobbing gently up and down.

"Is it time?" Talia asked.

"It's time," Cleo said. There was a beat when I could hear her considering, though I couldn't tell exactly where she was. "Let's hold hands while we meditate. So we don't drift away from each other."

I groped in the water and found Talia's hand on my right and Cleo's on my left. In sync, like we had talked about, we kicked up our legs and floated. Their fingers were tight around my own, but they kept me on the surface. They didn't pull me down.

"I'm nervous," Polly whispered.

"Don't be," I said quietly.

"It'll be okay," Cleo said. "Just do like we planned."

Black above us, black below. The stars were faint and far away. There were stingrays and sharks, riptides and winds. We could have been carried anywhere. We could have drowned. But I wasn't afraid at all. I was just sad—sad that we had come here to this wild, climactic point and that nothing would come of it.

Still, though, I had to try.

I closed my eyes like I had taught myself to and thought: I *want to be invisible.*

I breathed in and out like we'd practiced and thought it over and over, isolated everything in me down to those five specific words.

I'd had so much trouble with it this past month, struggled to focus and contain my skepticism, but as I kept thinking it, I started to find it easy. More than that: I started to find it exciting.

We were so small to the ocean and the sky, as small as plankton glowing in the water. We were practically invisible already. Call it science, call it magic, but as I silently chanted to myself over and over, it felt more than possible to slip those last few degrees into transparency. It felt, in fact, inevitable.

I breathed in. Breathed out. *I want. I want. I want. I want to be. I want to be invisible.*

I am invisible.

Beside me, Talia gasped.

And then I felt it.

When I was a little girl and too hot to sleep, my mother would come into my room and push all the covers onto the floor, untuck the top sheet from the bottom of the bed, and shake out the sheet in the air. She would hold her arms high so it fell on me slowly. It drifted down and settled on my body, melting into me like ice cream, cool and soft.

When the invisibility came over me, that's what I felt. That coolness, that softness, that sweet, welcome embrace, over my whole body, back and front and head to toe. It attached to me like a second skin. I swear to God I felt it in my blood.

To my right, Polly made a noise like a bird, and Cleo laughed in triumph.

I did not open my eyes. My heartbeat raced as if I had just run ten miles. I felt my breathing speed up. I didn't believe it. It couldn't be. Any minute now, I was going to wake up.

Then my friends' clasped hands on either side of me loosened, and all my shapeless fears coalesced into something that felt real: The tide was pulling them away. In the back of my mind, the small calm part, I recognized that the ocean was steady that night; there was barely any motion at all. My friends had let go of their own accord. But the rest of me was terrified. My eyes snapped open.

There was no one.

I gulped in air. The sand under my feet felt unsteady. "Talia!" I yelled, too loud, panicked. "Talia!"

"I'm right here, silly," came her voice, elated and playful, to my right. I spun around. Nothing.

"It worked." Polly, in awe, somewhere in front of me.

"I told you." Cleo. "I fucking told you."

"Y'all, this isn't funny," I said. I couldn't stop the shake in my voice. If I had been standing on land, I might have lost my balance. The water held me up.

"Callie, calm down," Talia said. "It worked. Just like we thought."

"It really worked." Polly, whispering.

"I'm not joking," I said.

"Neither are we," Cleo said. "Look down."

I looked down.

I didn't have a body. The ocean went through me, rocking gently in the breeze.

I opened my mouth, but no sound came out. I touched where my stomach would be. My hand—there was no hand—went right through. The air and water were warmer there, body temperature, but there was nothing visible or tangible.

It worked.

It really worked.

"Oh my God," I murmured.

"Believe me now, Callie?" Cleo asked, giddy. There was a huge splash beside me, and she burst into laughter.

And then there was splashing all around me, and laughter all around me, and I was terrified but splashing and laughing, too, the water kicking up around us like a living thing in the night. "Come on, let's see what we look like in the air," someone cried, and the splashing made its way toward the shore. I ran with my friends and felt the sand under my feet and the pressure of the water slowing my motion, but there was that cool sweet feeling, too, that incorporeal release, and it made it easier, the water flowed right through me. When I made my way out, I felt the sand against my feet but also inside my feet, the wind around me and inside of me.

We were all laughing violently. I don't think I could have stopped. I looked where the laughter was coming from, and now, in the air, I could almost see the slightest golden glimmering—like sunlight reflected and refracted through hundreds of mirrors until only the memory of the light remained. But that was all. Just a flicker you could have mistaken for a firefly, or an optical illusion, or a memory. I spun in a circle again and again, dizzying myself, and that golden whisper was everywhere around me.

"Come on," Talia called, softly, a little ways down the beach, and I ran toward her. Running, I could tell I was faster. As if I were untethered from the earth.

We ran and walked east beside the water, aimlessly, our laughter holding us together like the links in a chain. When it finally died out, Cleo said, "Let's sit." I saw a small puff in the sand, and I sat down next to it, feeling as I did an odd sensation in my thigh. Hot like the heat from a campfire—indirect but blazing. Cleo giggled. "You're on my hand," she said.

"Oh my God," I said, probably for the twentieth time in the last ten minutes. I scooted back and the heat disappeared. Had I not been invisible, I would have flushed. I had liked that heat. "I'm sorry."

"No worries," Cleo said easily.

"I thought," Talia said, out of breath, "that we would just be invisible. I didn't know everything would go through us."

"This fucking rules," Polly said. The fierceness in her voice was as new as everything else. "This is so much better than I thought it would be."

"Another summer of success," Cleo said, the sound rich with satisfaction.

I dropped back so I was lying down. The stars looked bigger than normal, as though they had grown to encourage us, or I had become, with this change, more sensitive to light. I groped to my right and left and found that same heat in the shape of a hand. Cleo on my right, now, Talia on my left. I heard both of them inhale sharply. Holding their hands like this, occupying the same space and simultaneously not occupying it at all—it felt strange and breathtaking and too, too good, and no one pulled away. Polly gasped on the other side of Cleo, and Cleo made a soft, pained noise from her throat, and I knew that they had reached out to each other, too.

I don't know how long we lay there, catching our breath. Long enough that the tide started to slip in. The wind cooled the wet fabric plastered against me, and I shivered. The heat and pleasure of our linked hands began to feel almost ordinary. Never once before had I thought about kissing Cleo, but after one wave reached up high enough to brush through our feet, I wanted nothing more than to roll over and into her, to feel that honeyed flare of connection through my whole damn body.

"I thought it would take concentration," Polly said quietly, the first words any of us had spoken in what felt like an hour. "Like, we'd have to really focus to stay this way. But . . ."

"It's easy," Talia said.

"So easy," Cleo echoed.

Too easy, I thought and didn't say. It required no effort to stay invisible. Less effort, even, than being visible. The sand didn't scratch me; bugs didn't get in my hair. I didn't worry about my dress riding up too high on my legs or whether someone could see the acne at my hairline. All the movements and mindfulness necessary to live in a body, all of it was gone, left in the ocean with the salt and the fish.

We lay there for ages and finally, feeling more reluctance than I wanted to, I said, "We should go back."

"Do we have to?" Polly, from the ground a few feet away, longing and distant.

"Yes," Cleo answered. Her voice rose as she stood. "In fact, we should probably change back now. So we know we can."

A new fear rose inside me. I looked out at the ocean. While we had lain on the sand, the waves had gotten restless. I didn't want to go out there again.

As if reading my mind, Talia said, "Cleo, it's supposed to be that we can just change back and forth like we want now, right? Now that we've . . ."

"Activated it," Cleo finished. "Yes."

"But . . . ," Polly started, then stopped. The pause hung in the air between us, or I assumed it did. The others could have wandered away from me and I never would have known.

"We just need to meditate the same way we did before, but the opposite." Cleo sounded less certain of herself. "We talked about this. It should be simple. The hard part is done." A vicious part of me wanted to say, Why did we not practice this meditation? Isn't this just as vital as the rest of it? But I didn't. After all, I had never thought it would be a problem.

"Just exactly the opposite?" Talia asked. "Like, 'I want to be visible'?"

"Yeah. I think so. Let's give it a shot," Cleo said. After a beat, she added, "No one talk," as if we would.

Though we hadn't talked about going back into the water, I waded in up to my knees and closed my eyes. I wanted to undo this much more than I had wanted to do it in the first place, and I thought the water might help. I thought, *I am visible, I am visible, I am visible*, and at some point it turned into *you can see me, you can see me*, and then just *see me, see me, see me, see*, and it happened fast. The sheen on my skin receded. There had been, I only now realized, a very slight buzzing in my ears; it went away. My hands had been hanging by my sides feeling nothing but air, and as I came back to myself, the wet fabric of my dress brushed against my fingertips. Beneath that, the warmth of my thighs. I opened my eyes and looked down. There was my body, whole and familiar. I touched myself all over like I was looking for keys in a hidden pocket, just to make sure—but everything was back to normal. I let out a shaky breath and turned around.

The others were still on the beach, and they hadn't finished yet. Without meaning to, I clapped a hand over my mouth. I tasted seawater on my palm, brine and sand. It helped me not cry out at the strangeness of what I saw.

All three of them were transparent. Cleo was the furthest along; she looked almost complete, but textured gritty from the sand stretching out behind her. Talia was next closest, maybe half-opaque, her hair disappeared at the ends. I could see each individual rib, translucent and flexible, beneath the wet gleam of her dress.

Polly was still almost completely invisible. She looked like a ghost of herself—all of them did, but she most of all looked like a dream or a fairy tale, something cursed into the in-between. She stood absolutely still. Her lips were pressed tightly together, and her eyes moved under their lids. It looked like this return was hard for her, like it was an effort to become visible, and for long seconds I was seized by the fear that she would never be whole again.

But I took a deep breath and pulled my hand away from my face. They were all solidifying. It was taking a while, but it was happening. Every second, they were a little more real. I saw the moment when each of them finished. Cleo sighed and patted her torso like I had, then turned to her right, to Polly; I saw her jaw drop a little, her eyes fixed on Polly, that slow transformation. Talia shifted on her feet as if feeling the sand between her toes. She ran her hands through her hair. Polly was the hardest to spot, but finally, her shoulders slumped. She opened her eyes.

I waded back through the shallows to join them on the beach. Without speaking, they came nearer to me, until we stood in a close square and draped our arms around each other in a group hug. The solidity of them underneath my hands and the simple, unconscious nature of the movement calmed my galloping heartbeat. We were all still here.

After a minute or two, Polly pulled away. She looked dazed. "We should go home," she said.

Talia sighed, as if waking up from a dream. "Yes, let's," she said.

All in a line, we started walking back. I relished the weight of my feet in the sand. We were quiet. The ocean was loud.

In the back of my mind, I realized that I had stopped worrying about our parents finding out. They seemed very far away. Of course they were sleeping, secure in their dreams that we were where we said we'd be. Of course we would get back before they woke up. It didn't matter tremendously whether that was at two a.m. or three or four. The whole night was ours, to do with as we pleased.

No one spoke. I don't know why. Maybe Cleo's mind was racing with the possibilities. Maybe Polly was starting to get afraid that we'd become test subjects in a mad scientist's lab, like what happened to people in comic books. Maybe Talia was wishing we hadn't started walking back.

I will never know, and that's another thing I regret. I wish now that when we'd got back to the narrow wooden walkway that led to the street and home and bed, we had sat and talked about everything until the sun started to whisper on the horizon. How it had felt, what we wanted to do, what the rest of the summer would hold. I like to think that could have helped.

Instead, no one said anything until we got back to the road. As Cleo and Polly laced on their skates, Cleo said, "Noon, tomorrow, on the beach in front of my place?"

Everyone nodded. She stood up and glided a few feet toward me and Talia. Cleo wrapped her arms around us and whispered, fiercely, "I love you," and all of us whispered it back, and then she and Polly turned and left, blurring again into the darkness.

Getting back into Talia's house was as easy as opening the door. No lights were on; no one was awake. It was 3:52. We went quietly up the stairs and changed into pajamas, got into bed without brushing our teeth or showering. I felt the grains of sand gathering between the sheets and the salt and grime hardening on my skin and Talia there with me, awake.

But all of that was familiar. How many times as children

had we protested a bath? Tomorrow we would wash the sheets and vacuum the rug, which was necessary every week anyway, being on the beach as much as we were. And how many times had Talia taken longer to fall asleep than I had? She'd always had insomnia. She once told me that when she closed her eyes, all her thoughts got louder, like a staticky radio with the volume turned up.

The normalcy soothed me. I fell into sleep hard and fast, and Talia lay beside me, eyes open.

11 THE DAY AFTER

The sunrise through the window woke me up early, and I thought it had been a dream. I wish I were more original—a dream, really?—but the memory was filmy and loose. And like a dream, it was impossible, so it was easy to think, *How odd; I wonder what happens next?* I put a pillow over my head and slipped back into unconsciousness.

When I woke up the second time, it was because of the heat, that same sun through that same thin glass. I was sweating and hungry. The clock on the bedside table said 11:00. For a moment I still thought I had imagined it. Then I moved my foot and felt the grit of the sand against my skin, pulled myself out from under the pillow, and turned to face Talia. The fog dissipated, fast.

She was awake. It looked as if she had barely slept. She was turned toward me, her hands tucked under her cheek. I didn't know if it was the light of the sun or something inside her that was making her eyes blaze like that.

"We really did it," she whispered. She sounded wild. As if her voice, so quiet, could turn into a scream if it were pushed just a degree or two to the left.

I swallowed. My mouth tasted horrible and my skin was sticky. "Yeah," I whispered back. "We did."

Her face softened, as if my confirmation had reassured her it was real. I couldn't remember the last time I had seen her look so happy.

"We should shower before we go out to the beach," she said. "You smell terrible."

I laughed and shoved her out of bed. I was glad, really glad, she had been the first to suggest something as mundane as a shower. If I had been the one to bring it up, I would've felt like I was dragging her out of that mystical memory. But maybe the two could coexist side by side, the visible daylight and the invisible night. Besides, we really did smell.

She went into the bathroom first. The house was quiet. I grabbed my phone from the bedside table and saw a message from Cleo from a few hours ago: *did y'all get home okay????*

yes—just woke up though sorry! I typed back. *you???*

no worries, talia texted me ages ago, she replied. *coming home last night was almost a disaster, my grandma woke up as I was brushing my teeth. but I managed to convince her I had just woken up from a bad dream.*

whew. All the fear from last night rushed back into me, delayed and unnecessary but present all the same. But no one had discovered us. We were fine.

correct, Cleo said. *do you want to meet up now? polly and I are ready to go.*

no, I wanna shower.

I'm so impressed you slept, she said. *I couldn't. I gave up and took a shower at like six a.m.*

I can't not sleep, I told her. *I love sleep.* But I thought of Talia beside me, awake when I had closed my eyes and awake when I woke up, and I felt a flicker of a different kind of fear. Something I couldn't put my finger on. Maybe I wasn't taking this seriously enough. Or maybe the opposite; maybe they were too serious.

But: *polly's the same way, apparently, she conked out as soon as she got into bed,* Cleo said, and I relaxed a little. I didn't think I could ever be close with Polly in the way I was with Cleo and Talia, but she had the undeniably positive effect of balancing us out. She was quieter than Cleo, more practical than Talia, more nervous than me. If she had slept, it had been okay for me to sleep, too.

Down the hall, the shower switched off. *gotta go,* I typed to Cleo. *see you in 45.*

I've got lunch, Cleo responded, and I set my phone down.

It took twenty-six minutes for me to shower and for us to get dressed and lace up our skates. Talia led as we set off down the street. Her yellow sarong trailed behind her like a bird's tail, like wings. She skated in the middle of the lane and only moved when cars came up behind us and honked. .

"Talia," I yelled after a truck got too close on my heels, "maybe we should stick to the side of the road." Like we usually did.

She inclined her head back toward me, but she sped up and kept skating in the middle. A group of guys in a pickup truck yelled something unintelligible to us before their laughter disappeared into the distance like the sound of a siren. I followed Talia, fast, adrenaline crackling in my muscles.

Cleo and Polly were already on the beach when we stepped off the public access holding our skates. They sat with their backs to the ocean. Cleo waved when she saw us. She had brought her grandmother's biggest beach blanket and spread it out close to the water, daring the tide to rise.

"My beautiful compatriots," she said as we got closer. She

stood up and dusted the sand off her butt before hugging me first, then Talia.

Polly was behind her like an echo, one hug, two. I held the hugs longer than usual. I wanted to feel their solidity. All around us were everyday colors and sounds—music blasting, a Frisbee whistling through the air, a giggling baby—but it was too easy to erase all that in my head. To come back to twelve hours ago. The dark and the quiet and the absolute emptiness.

Polly said, "Ow." I had squeezed her too tight.

"Sorry."

"I brought sandwiches," Cleo said, gesturing to the spread on the blanket below.

"You sure did." *Sandwiches* was an understatement. There were three kinds, plus pasta salad and fruit and cookies, the chocolate chips melting in the sun.

"I might've gotten carried away," she said cheerfully, folding herself onto the blanket. "I figure it's for a good cause. We don't know how this whole thing affects our bodies. Maybe it takes up a lot of energy, maybe we have to eat more. Here, everyone, choose your sandwich."

She took two for herself. Talia picked up the thinnest vegetable sandwich in the bunch. Polly passed an orange between her hands, back and forth and back and forth, as if she was about to pitch it like a baseball.

I grabbed a ham-and-cheese and hoped it would work magic. My body felt all wrong. My perception of time was off-kilter; I had never taken a trip far enough to have jet lag, but I imagined it might feel like this. Apart from the obvious, exhausting things we had done last night, we had been up very late, and I had woken up very late this morning, much later than my usual. And this was the first morning in ages I hadn't gone for a run. I ate my sandwich in five huge bites and picked up another. Thank God Cleo had brought extra.

"I call the group to order," Cleo said, clapping once. "To talk about next steps."

"Next steps? Are we on prom committee?"

"Next steps are we do it again," Talia said, ignoring me.

"When?" Cleo asked. A grin played at the edges of her mouth.

"As soon as possible."

"How?" I asked.

"You know how," Talia said. A little impatient, as if she wanted to run into the ocean and disappear right then and there. "You've done it now."

"I mean, do we need the water again?" Polly spoke up.

"I don't think we do," Cleo said. "I mean, obviously I don't know for sure. But I think that was just for the first time. Like an activation. I think it's in us now. This power. I mean—" She looked around at us, took a bite, swallowed. She was the only one not wearing sunglasses, and the sun drifted into her eyes and made her squint. "I feel it inside me now," she finished. "Don't you?"

"Yes," Talia said.

"Yes," Polly said.

"I guess," I said. I didn't know what it was supposed to feel like. I felt sort of how I did if I ate too much sugar and then took a nap, wired and sick and shiny. But I remembered how I had felt last night, and yeah, this faraway feeling was some kind of echo of that.

Cleo said, "Right," like she had proved something.

Talia said, "So when?"

"I was thinking tonight at the rink. After everyone leaves."

"Invisible cleanup?" Polly laughed.

"Yeah. Exactly. What better place?"

"It'll be a long night," I said. "Since we also have to get there early to clean up from last night." And I'd been at the rink the last three nights. But Cleo waved her hand dismissively.

"Technically Polly and I are working tonight, we'll clean up from last night. You and Talia can get there whenever." I looked at Polly for her reaction to this. I would've been annoyed if Talia had signed me up for that—we had left a mess, and it was going to take at least an hour to prep for opening—but Polly just nodded. Cleo must have thought I was skeptical, because she added, "What else are you planning for tonight? With all your other friends?"

"Ha ha," I said. "Nothing."

"We'll be there," Talia said. She was still vibrating at the same intensity.

"Everyone eat your sandwiches," I said. "We need our strength."

Polly peeled her orange, slowly, laying the bits of peel on the sand in the shape of a star.

———

I left the beach early. It was even hotter than usual. I was used to being hot, but every summer there were a few unbearable days, and this was one of them: well over a hundred degrees, muggy and brutal. You had to be in the water, but even the water was hot. We floated in silence.

I had expected my friends to talk over the main question: what we were going to do with this new power. To me, that was the center of everything. Okay, we had committed a miracle;

now what? But they didn't discuss it at all. They barely talked. Maybe they felt the same thing I did, the extreme eeriness of being in the exact inverse position that we had been in twelve hours ago. Then, midnight, invisible; now, high noon, the sun reflecting off our sunscreen-shined skin. It was unsettling. At two, we all went home.

My parents were at work. I ate half a pint of strawberry ice cream, sitting in my bikini at the kitchen table, then showered again and took a nap.

I woke up at five. My eyes had sleep gunk in them and I had a slight stomachache from the three sandwiches and the ice cream, but I felt better. More like a human. I got dressed in my comfiest clothes: running shorts and a soft black T-shirt I had gotten at a concert at the Cat's Cradle in Carrboro. And then the door opened downstairs, and my dad called, "Callie? You here?"

"Yeah," I yelled back. "About to go to the rink."

My stomach flipped over and I took a deep breath. I had never kept a serious secret from my parents before. I liked them, after all. We liked each other. And I had never had a secret to keep.

I walked downstairs to the kitchen, where Dad was taking vegetables out of the refrigerator. He looked up as I came in.

"Work again?" he asked. "I thought you had off tonight. I'm making dinner."

I shrugged. "I do. But the rink is busy. I told Cleo and Polly I would help."

"You shouldn't—"

"Work for free. You've said it before."

He grinned and came out from behind the kitchen counter to give me a hug. "Took the words right out of my mouth," he said. I held on a little longer than usual.

"But it's not really work," I said as he pulled away. "It's just running the playlist and hanging out with my friends."

"Well, as long as you get to run the playlist," he said. He'd liked the most recent playlist I'd made for him. He said it reminded him of listening to Ani DiFranco and Bruce Springsteen when he and my mom were first dating. He started slicing the vegetables. "I was hoping you could have dinner with me and your mom tonight, though. We haven't spent much time together recently."

"That's true," I said.

I wished I had not eaten all that ice cream. I wished I could leave.

"Hey, your mom and I decided to take a day off this coming Friday, let Martha handle all the bike repairs for the day." Martha was the most reliable of their three employees, but still, I raised my eyebrows. My parents rarely took time off during the busy season. "We were thinking we could hang out with you," he continued. "Maybe grab some lunch. Do some Putt-Putt."

I wrinkled my nose, but a lump grew in my throat. I wanted to throw my arms around him again, tell him everything.

Instead I said, "Ew. Putt-Putt?"

Dad smiled. "It used to be your favorite."

"Yeah, when I was six." I tried to match his smile. "And besides, Little Mimi's Putt-Putt has been the sworn nemesis of anyone who works at the rink for thirty years. You know that."

"Well, there's that new course down in Sunrise Beach. I know it'd be a little bit of a drive, but I hear they have good soft serve. Hey, Callie, are you okay?"

He looked worried, and it took me a second to realize that I was crying.

"God, yeah, sorry," I said. I wiped my arm across my eyes. "It's the onion. Pungent."

"I guess so," he said.

"Maybe I'm extra sensitive."

"Yeah." He looked at me, close. "You sure you're okay? You've seemed awfully tired the past few days."

"I'm sure." I nodded at the clock. I tried hard to make the lump in my throat recede. "I'm gonna be late if I don't get going. Can I . . ."

"Yeah, yeah, go on, but if they make you do more than the playlist, you tell Miss Abby she has to pay you for your time. Oh, and hold on just one minute." I leaned against the doorway and watched him whip out bread and peanut butter from the pantry, making a sandwich in a few quick, practiced motions. He wrapped it in a paper towel and handed it to me. "If you can't stay for dinner, I want to make sure you at least *eat* dinner."

"Thanks, Dad." I gave him another hug, taking a deep breath, letting it go. "Have a good night."

"You too. Friday will be nice, yeah?"

"Yeah, definitely."

"I love you."

"I love you, too, Dad."

I tucked the sandwich into my bag and dashed out the front door, swiping my hand across my eyes again. Thank God for onions. "Pull yourself together," I muttered as I walked down the rickety wooden stairs toward the sidewalk. Still, the tears blurred my vision as I skated on the side of the road toward the rink, my own forward momentum pushing them down my cheeks.

12 CLEANING UP

I hadn't meant to get to work early. Honestly, I wasn't sure if I wanted to be at work at all. But I also hadn't wanted to stay home with my dad, trying not to cry. So I skated fast and got there a few minutes before six, when kids were starting to queue up outside. I went through the parking lot to the back entrance and knocked until the door cracked open. Polly's face showed, skittish in the opening before she saw it was me.

"I thought you weren't going to help clean up," she said as she led me toward the front of the building. We were both in our socks on the rink floor, which always felt weird to me—illicit in a childish way, like breaking into school on a Saturday.

"Y'all aren't done prepping?"

"Well, we're mostly done. There's some front-office stuff still."

Cleo's head poked out from the window to the office. "Oh, thank God," she said. "The hordes are gathering and I still need to sweep. Can you restock the chips?"

"Hello to you too," I said. "Talia not here yet?"

"Nope. Haven't heard from her. I wasn't figuring you'd come until later."

"Same, but I woke up from my nap early."

"You napped?" Cleo arched her eyebrows as she dragged the broom along the wooden floor in the waiting area.

"You didn't?" I tore open a new bulk pack of individual chip bags. "I was exhausted."

"Too excited," Cleo said, shaking her head. "Too many thoughts to sleep."

"I dozed off," Polly added helpfully.

"My sister in snoozing," I said, nudging her with my shoulder. It was only half on purpose, because the area behind the counter was so small, but she grinned.

The front door slipped open, letting in a sliver of daylight, and a child's face poked through.

"Can we come in?" a small voice said.

"No," Cleo said.

"It's six o' clock," said the small voice.

"Our clock says five-fifty-eight," Cleo snapped. "Synchronize your damn watch for next time."

"Fine," the kid sighed, and the door fell closed again.

"It's true what they say," Cleo said. "If you love what you do, you never work a day in your life."

The evening passed as a hundred other Sunday evenings had. Talia showed up at seven, and Miss Abby didn't show up at all. None of our customers broke any bones or vomited. We traded off shifts skating around playing chaperone and working at the register, and in between, Talia texted Michael and Cleo messed around on her phone and Polly—well, Polly just skated by herself. I was feeling restless so I played Sleigh Bells, the kind of loud, messy music that let me get lost in the noise of it, which didn't go over great with the crowd, but whatever.

An hour before closing, Jen Liu came in with a group of her friends, and a nervous light skimmed through my body. Adam didn't follow, though. I had all but given up on seeing him, when at last he appeared in the doorway, just as Cleo was clearing the floor for Last Skater Standing.

"Look who it is," he said, smiling broadly. "I haven't forgotten about that run you promised me."

I laughed. "Me neither," I said, "but I've been busy."

"The rink is demanding, huh?"

"So demanding," I said, and I thought of last night, the water all around me and inside me, the heat of my friends' hands inside my own, how I had felt like the world was melting into us, how the four of us were everything and nothing together. I shivered.

"You okay?" Adam asked, and I realized I'd been quiet too long.

"I'm great," I said. I met his eyes. He didn't look away, and I felt a different kind of heat. A different kind of demanding.

"Y'all, sorry to interrupt, but she's doing it," Talia hissed beside me. I startled and turned toward the rink, where Polly was making her way toward the center. "She's hosting Last Skater Standing for the first time," Talia informed Adam, just as Polly tripped and nearly fell. It was the first time I'd ever seen her look ungainly on her skates.

"She's nervous," I said to Talia, and Talia shrugged, taking a spoon of a plain sno-cone. To my bafflement and frustration, Polly had converted her to the gospel of plain.

Polly got the hang of it pretty fast. Cleo called the numbers, as encouraging and funny as always. It helped that there were a bunch of cute kids playing, too, so Polly could hand the die to a different round face every time. And the people were nice. No one argued. No one catcalled her; that happened a lot, but not that night. Talia, Adam, and I cheered at every opportunity.

As soon as the Skate ended, Adam said, "I'm gonna head out now, try to get Jen home before Dad goes to bed." He put his hand on my shoulder, lightly, for just a moment, and smiled. "See you soon?"

"Definitely," I said. I wanted to keep his hand on my shoulder, warm and dry, to jump across the counter separating us.

But I also wanted him to leave. I wanted everyone in the rink to leave so the four of us could be alone.

"Cool," he said, and he and Jen disappeared out into the night. Talia made ridiculous faces at me as she distributed free passes and sno-cones to the winners of the Skate. Cleo teased me about him as I took the music back over, and I played Seinabo Sey for the last song, and it was closing time.

"Have a good night," Talia called as the last person left the rink. The door shut behind them and we were left in silence. None of us said anything as she came out from behind the counter and locked the door. When she turned around, she was smiling, and I knew it wasn't about Adam.

"Do we want to clean first, or—" I started, but Cleo shook her head.

"Invisible cleaning," Cleo said. "Per Talia's request. Meaning let's get invisible first. Wow, that's fucking cool to say." She switched off all the lights and switched on the disco ball. "Everyone put on your skates, please."

"This is extremely silly," I said, but no one replied, so I asked what I'd wanted to know all along. "Do we want music or no?"

"Huh." Talia wrinkled her brow. "What do you think?"

"It'll help me," I said. "I don't know about y'all."

"I say let's give it a shot," Polly said. "I liked that song you played before closing a few nights ago, what was it?"

"It was by Sharon Van Etten," I said, pleased that she had enjoyed it. I had not gotten rave reviews from the skaters on that one. I put it on, and the low guitar and high voice drifted out over the dark rink. The disco ball rotated slowly, casting starlight onto the floor. I glided out onto it, following Polly, following Talia, following Cleo. We stood in a circle underneath the circling mirrors.

The others closed their eyes, but I kept mine open, just for a moment. Just long enough to admire them in the flickering light. Talia's heart-shaped face, Cleo's long eyelashes, the sharp, clean line of Polly's nose. The thought shot through my head: *How could you want to disappear when you were this beautiful?* Then I closed my own eyes and thought: *I want to be invisible.*

This time it came faster, the shift from *I want to be* to *I am.* It happened almost as if someone's hand were pulling me along, as if I had suddenly remembered the answer to a question on a test. The cool-blanket feeling, again.

I heard giggles, laughter. Skates whirred across the ancient boards, softer than usual, as if muted by distance. I opened my eyes and my friends were gone. I was gone.

"Yes!" came Talia's exuberant shout somewhere in front of me.

"God," Cleo said. Her voice was rich with joy. "This is the best."

I pushed off and glided across the floor. Like last night, I felt faster than usual, lighter. I could almost feel the waves of sound and light going through me, as if they were tangible. The music bled into the next song on the playlist.

Maybe the others hadn't decided what they wanted to do

with this new power because the power was the point. This feeling was the point. I had never felt the constraints of my physical body so keenly as now, when I was finally free of them. I felt like I could fly. I jumped experimentally in front of the NO JUMPING sign and came down with a clunk. Lighter and softer than normal, but a clunk, still. No flying, then. Okay.

"I tried, too," Polly said softly, closer behind me than I had realized. I startled. "We're not weightless, unfortunately."

"Good to know," I said, my heart racing. Over to the left, Talia and Cleo were laughing, zooming back and forth, heedless of Polly and me.

"I wonder . . ." I heard the sound of wheels, and a bottle of cleaning solution in the middle of the floor levitated. In context, it seemed like the most normal thing in the world—it was like when you're dreaming and you're at school, and then you walk through a door and you're at your friend's aunt's house, something that shouldn't fit, but in the dream it does.

And then, in front of my eyes, the bottle started fading. Not disappearing entirely. Just becoming a little bit less of itself. It was as if the bottle was getting farther away, or losing its saturation, or maybe as if my own vision was getting fuzzier.

"Interesting," said Polly breathlessly. Her voice was in the same place as the bottle, which—like a video in reverse—came back into focus and fell to the ground.

"Whoa," came Talia's voice. The zooming of her and Cleo's skates had stopped, and they were close by.

"Did you do that on purpose?" I asked.

Silence. Eventually Polly laughed and said, "Yeah. Sorry, I did it on purpose, but it was hard. Like, it took a ton of effort. I don't know if I could do it again."

"Maybe this explains why our clothes disappear," Cleo said. She had her scientist voice on. "Maybe the more we're touching something, the easier it is to take it with us. Or maybe it has something to do with weight and, like, how substantial the thing is. I mean, our clothes disappeared, right? And our phones in our pockets?"

"I don't understand any of this," Talia said, but she didn't sound mad. She sounded delighted. I was sort of with her. It felt dangerous to think too hard about how this power worked. "Can we just clean and be invisible and be excited about how incredible this is?"

"Tomorrow I want to talk about it," Cleo said.

"But tonight can we just enjoy it?" Talia asked softly.

"Yes," Cleo said. "Of course. Tonight we can just enjoy it."

So the brooms swept the floor. The trash picked itself up and threw itself away. The sno-cone machine rinsed its own sugar-stained components, and the cash register counted the money, which stored itself in the safe beneath the counter. The soda stain on the bench disappeared of its own accord. The backpack someone had left in the corner drifted through the air to the lost and found and nestled in among the lonely headbands and socks. And when the rink was as clean as it was going to get, the disco ball switched itself off, the music quieted, and the four of us came back to ourselves in the dark.

13 REAL LIFE

It turns out that if you drop a bomb in the middle of your life and only three other people know it's exploded, your day-to-day doesn't change that much. For the next week, I woke up and ran every morning, like always, and ate breakfast with my parents, like always, and went to the beach and to work with my friends, like always.

Really, only a handful of things were out of the ordinary.

The first was that we disappeared ourselves at work before cleaning and going home. It was getting easier to disappear. Sometimes it felt as if it took no effort at all, as if the difficult thing was staying visible. Sometimes, in fact, I thought it was harder to turn back than to turn in the first place, but maybe I was just imagining that.

"We know our clothes disappear, too, but it's harder if we're wearing heavier clothing," Cleo said in a low voice on the beach one day. She had said this at least three times before, but it didn't seem to matter. We talked constantly about how it worked.

"I think it's easier if I haven't eaten much beforehand," Talia said, and Polly nodded.

"I think it doesn't make a difference," I said stubbornly, though after eating an entire delivery pizza at work on Thursday, I *had* noticed it was slightly more difficult. I just didn't want to give my friends yet another excuse to not eat.

"And we know we can make other things disappear if we're touching them," Cleo continued.

"But it's hard," Polly said. Cleo nodded.

"It's very, very hard," Cleo said. "And there are limits." She had tried to disappear one of the heavy wooden benches in the waiting area at the rink a couple of nights before. She said she'd put in as much effort as she possibly could, and it hadn't even shimmered in the air. "Like trying to lift a car," she'd said, panting. Apart from our clothes and small items in our pockets, the largest thing any of us had made disappear was the broom at work, and Polly was the only one who'd been able to make it entirely transparent.

"And that's it," Talia said. "That's what we know."

Cleo nodded. "That's what we know."

The second odd thing was that on Friday, instead of hanging out on the beach, I went to the new Putt-Putt place in Sunrise Beach with my parents and did a low-country boil with them on our porch. I lost to my mom and beat my dad at Putt-Putt. I got to eat the extra corn at dinner. We talked about my senior year classes, and how their business was doing, and my grandparents, who lived in Florida and had just moved into a new house.

It was all fine—nice, even, to be with people who didn't know about the disappearing—but it was also sort of weird. I had barely seen my parents all summer. It was easy to forget sometimes that I even had parents, that I hadn't been born fully formed like Athena and linked only to those three other girls.

The last strange thing happened on Sunday, when Talia and I were swimsuit shopping.

The shopping wasn't strange at all. After a fight with Michael, one of the ways I helped Talia feel better was taking her to the smoothie-shop-slash-swimsuit-emporium in town. The stated goal was for me to buy her a low-fat strawberry-banana smoothie, but inevitably she would also buy a swimsuit from the sale rack. She owned an enormous number of swimsuits. I had drunk a lot of smoothies.

"Maybe I should've said I was sorry," Talia said for the fourth time.

"*He* should've said he was sorry," I said for the fifth time.

We swayed slowly through the aisles. Talia's hand drifted over the racks of bikini tops, the cheap material sliding under her fingers. I took a gulp of my mango smoothie.

"I just think it's reasonable to not want to mess around if I'm on my period," she said.

"Yes. Of course it is."

"I just don't see any reason for him to be such an asshole about it. We can have sex again in, like, two days."

"He should never get to be an asshole about it. It's your body."

"Yeah." She sighed. "But I still feel bad. I mean, I could've done something for him, I guess."

"You have nothing to feel bad about," I repeated.

She sighed again as we turned the corner to the next aisle. I fiddled with my straw. Talia had gotten increasingly casual about discussing sex with me. When she and Michael had first started doing it, she had been secretive about it, coy, and that had been just fine with me. But now, she was comfortable giving details. Sometimes a lot of details. I didn't know what to say to her. I had never even kissed anyone. The only thing I knew was that Michael shouldn't pressure her to do anything she didn't want to do—that was an easy rule.

"Oh, this one is good, right?" Talia held up a yellow bikini top patterned with illustrations of blueberries.

"You don't need another swimsuit."

"But don't I?"

"It's pretty cute," I admitted. "Yellow is good on you."

She flipped over the tag. "It's on sale. I'm trying it on." She grabbed the matching bottom and started toward the fitting rooms.

"Seriously, you shouldn't apologize to him," I said as I followed her. "I don't like when he's a jerk to you, Talia. You deserve better."

She stepped inside the fitting room and turned to me, biting her lip.

"I know," she said quietly. Then she swept the curtain closed. I leaned against the wall outside and took a sip of my smoothie, let my eyes wander over the store. On the opposite wall hung a swimsuit I coveted, a red one-piece that had never been on sale and was cut way too high on the sides for me to get away with anyway. A few women laughed together as they browsed novelty Little Beach T-shirts. An older couple asked if the smoothies were made with real fruit. Adam lazily spun a rack of towels.

Wait. Adam?

The curtain beside me swept open, Talia stepped out, and Adam looked up and saw us.

Shit.

"How do I look?" Talia asked me, turning to glance over

her shoulder at herself in the mirror. She looked incredible, of course. She was always beautiful, but the swimsuit really was great on her. "What do you think, too skimpy or no?"

"No," I said. "It's perfect." Adam was making his way over to us, and I couldn't pretend I hadn't seen him. I raised a hand and Talia, noticing, turned around and grinned.

"Adam!" she said cheerfully. "Hello!"

"Hey, Talia. Hey, Callie." He sounded as friendly as always, though he looked slightly uncertain about where his eyes should land. I couldn't blame him. We saw each other half-naked on the beach all the time, but context was everything. Here, with Adam and me fully clothed and Talia in a garment that showed more of her than her bra and underwear, it was impossible to have a totally normal conversation.

Perhaps sensing this, Talia took one final look at herself and stepped back into the fitting room, pulling the curtain shut behind her. "Out in a minute," she said.

"Hey," I said to Adam.

"Not trying on anything yourself?" His eyes swept over me in the briefest of glances.

"Not today." I tried very hard not to blush. "All set in the swimsuit department. I've got my smoothie, though." I held up the half-empty cup. Very cool, Callie. "What are you shopping for?"

"Oh, our dog chewed a hole in Jen's favorite towel, and she insists that she got it here and they still have it. But I've looked through every towel rack and they definitely don't, so I guess just whatever towel's cheapest."

"Why are you shopping for Jen's towel and not Jen?"

"Well, I might've been in a heated game of tug-of-war with the dog and thrown the towel over him. Just to give myself an advantage. But it didn't go how I'd hoped."

"You didn't win the game?"

"I did," he conceded, "but in a larger sense, one could argue that I lost. In that I am here, buying a towel for my sister out of my own paycheck."

Talia emerged. "I'm buying this," she said before heading for the register.

"Well." I nodded at her. "Looks like she's got what she needs. I'll see you on the beach later, maybe?"

"Yeah, maybe." He shifted, a little awkward, and a shot of worry cut through me—I had said the wrong thing, somehow. But as I made to step past him, he cleared his throat. I stopped. "Actually," he said, and my worry deepened. "I was hoping I could maybe see you, um, not on the beach."

"What?"

It had not sunk in.

He laughed. "I didn't say that very clearly. I was hoping that I could take you to dinner, Callie. Tomorrow, actually. If you would like. If you don't have work, that is."

"Oh!" Heat spread across my chest, and I prayed it was a sunburn. I bit my lip so I wouldn't smile too big. "Um, yes. I would like that very much. I don't have work."

I did have work, but I could worry about that later.

He grinned, big and broad, and I couldn't believe it was because of me. "Great," he said. "Yeah, okay, great. I'll pick you up at six-thirty? We could go to the Shack?"

"Yeah, that sounds great."

"Cool. Um—I have your phone number, I think, from track. You have mine, right?"

"Yeah, definitely." I tried to sound very relaxed about the idea of private conversations with him. All the people in our grade on the track team had a group text, but I never would have reached out to him alone.

"Okay," he said, shy again. "Cool."

Talia appeared, holding her shopping bag. Her eyes darted back and forth between us, mischievous. "Callie, do you want to get going? Or I can go back by myself."

"I don't want to keep you," Adam said. "And I've gotta get this stupid towel. See you tomorrow, Callie."

"See you." I raised a hand and he laughed a little, not in a mean way, and turned down the next aisle. I walked as quickly as I could out of the store and into the sun, my smile bursting off my face, as Talia hissed next to me, "What was that? Callie, what was that?"

14 FIRST

The next day, I sat outside on the steps of my house, listening to Jacob Banks and waiting for Adam, like Talia and I had waited for Cleo a month prior. It was the middle of July, and the heat had deepened into something remorseless and unrelenting. Sweat beaded on my collarbones, and I adjusted the strap of my dress. It was green with white flowers; I had borrowed it from Cleo.

"Obviously you're cute all-around, but your legs are your best feature," she'd said yesterday, as I tried on three of her dresses and four of Talia's. The two of them sat on the bed in Talia's room, where we had gone immediately after our shopping trip yesterday. Talia had called Cleo and asked her and Polly to come over. An emergency, she'd said.

"This is too short." I plucked at the hem. "He's gonna think . . ."

"What? That you want him to look?" Talia stood up behind me and pulled my hair out of its ponytail holder, arranging it over my shoulders. "You do want him to look."

It felt embarrassing to admit. Embarrassing to want to be wanted.

"Wear the dress," Polly advised. She was sprawled on the floor in a sweatshirt and shorts, making her hand appear and disappear. I thought it was eerie, but no one else seemed bothered.

"You'd look great in this dress," I told Polly. "I do not."

"I would look terrible in that dress."

"Polly," Cleo said sternly, "you would look beautiful in that dress, as you look beautiful all of the time, and as Callie looks right now. Callie, wear the dress," she repeated, "and we will cover the rink, and you will have a great fucking time."

Now, I stretched out my legs and looked at my phone. Adam was supposed to be here in four minutes. I prayed for a strong breeze and pulled my hair over my shoulder, off my neck. I could've waited inside, but I was hoping to slip him past my parents. There was no chance that we'd get away without some kind of interaction, but I did not want to do the thing where he stood awkwardly in the foyer.

He pulled up in his car, a shabby blue sedan, two minutes after six. I stood and waved. He got out halfway, calling, "Sorry I'm late!"

"No problem," I called back, heading down the stairs. I had made it all the way to the gravel and thought my parents might've dropped the ball, when the door behind me opened, and Mom stepped out.

"Hi, Adam," she said from the top of the stairs, squinting into the sun.

Adam straightened. "Hi, Mrs. O'Connell! It's good to see you!" Dad appeared next to her. "Hi, Mr. O'Connell," Adam called with the same—impressive—amount of enthusiasm.

"How's your father doing?" asked Dad after a pause that was

just a beat too long. "We see him so often during the school year, it's strange to go months without talking."

"Oh, you know. He's good. Same old, same old." Adam smiled as I reached his side.

"And Jen? Good, too?"

"Yep, she's great."

"Good to hear." Dad nodded and Mom lingered just outside the doorway. Their expressions were unreadable.

It's not that they didn't like Adam. They had known him since we were both on the middle school track team, and they thought he was great. When the other boys had gone through phases where they pretended to be too cool to talk to adults, Adam had been consistently polite, especially to parents, even after his own parents got divorced. When I had told them he'd asked me to dinner, Mom and Dad had been, if anything, too excited.

But this was my first date ever. I felt that my parents might be experiencing an unpredictable cocktail of emotions, and it was best to make a quick escape.

"Where are you working this summer, Adam?" Dad asked. He leaned against the railing. I had seen him lean against that railing and have conversations with the neighbors that lasted upward of an hour.

Adam started to answer, but I cut in: "We'll be back by ten, Dad." I opened the passenger-side door of Adam's car. "Okay?"

"Yeah, yeah." Dad laughed, and Mom smiled and shook her head. "Have a good night, you two."

"Be safe," Mom called. I chose to interpret this as an absurd statement about driving safely on the local roads, with their 25 mph speed limit, rather than an implication that she expected us to have sex. I got into the car as Adam cheerfully responded, "Will do!"

He closed the door behind me, then got in the other side. In the cool silence of the car, he smiled. It was a different smile than I was used to from him, a little more nervous. It was cute.

"You look beautiful," he said, and I wasn't sure what to do with my hands. A boy had never called me beautiful before.

"You look really nice, too," I said, because he did. He had on a light, long-sleeved button-down and good shorts, which was a pretty standard date-night uniform for guys in Little Beach, but he wore it well. The pale blue of the shirt shone against his tan.

"Well," he said, starting the car. "Shall we?"

"We shall."

The full name of the Shack was the Seaside Seafood Shack and Grill, but I had never heard anyone say all of it aloud. The building was not, in fact, a shack, but a perfectly nice single story on a dock on the sound, with wood-paneled walls and lots of windows. The food was fine, the views were great, and the place was always packed. As a result, they were a significant source of summer employment for Little Beach High School students.

Adam opened the door for me and I stepped through. We wound our way up to the host stand past the crowd of sunburned families in the entryway. The stand was occupied by Steph Stewart, a field hockey player I knew vaguely as part of the wide, nebulous circle of Adam's friends. She nodded at us, and for a second I panicked at the idea of being the subject of gossip.

But this wasn't something I had to hide.

"Hey, Steph," Adam said. "Still got that two-top for me?"

"Yep. All the way back on the right. Hey, Callie."

I raised a hand, and behind me, a woman in the line we

had skipped cleared her throat menacingly. "Better get going," Steph said under her breath before plastering on a smile. Adam grabbed my hand in the crowd, and my breath caught in my throat as he pulled me gently off to the right.

We had just sat down at the table in the corner when a waitress—no one we knew, thank goodness—dropped off the red plastic basket of free hush puppies. I grabbed one immediately.

"Great choice for dinner," I said to him. I bit into one. God, hush puppies ruled.

He grinned. "Not like I had a ton of options," he said. "There are six restaurants on this island. I didn't think your parents would let me take you all the way to Wilmington."

"Did I ever tell you that when we took Polly to the Fourth of July party, she had been picturing a *real* beach party?"

"It is a real beach party. It's a party, and it's on the beach."

"No, but I mean, like, a Miami Beach party."

He laughed loud enough for a couple a few tables over to take notice.

"I know," I said. "We still haven't stopped making fun of her."

"So is that what y'all are always giggling about?"

"There's plenty to giggle about. We live in an absurd world."

"Uh-huh. Really, though, what do you talk about all day? Every time I see you, you're with Talia and Cleo and Polly, or at least just Talia, and you're always talking. I don't think I even have the ability to talk that much. I'd run out of words."

His eyes were warm and sweet, and I looked away. We talked about plenty, but the most frequent topic of conversation was the only thing I couldn't tell him. The idea of him knowing—of anyone else knowing—was unthinkable, abhorrent, like the thought of intentionally breaking a bone. But I didn't know what to say.

"It's not an insult," he said, a little quieter. "I'm just curious."

I looked in his eyes again, smiled, and settled for the truth. "Books and music, a lot," I said. "And secrets."

He arched his eyebrows. "Secrets?"

"Secrets," I said, and bit into another hush puppy.

"Well," he said, piling a few onto his plate, "okay. I won't ask. Instead I will say that I am really glad you said yes tonight, and I am really happy to spend some time with you without everyone else."

"Me too," I said. "Me too."

And just like that, my secrets were forgotten.

We lingered over dinner, but we couldn't ignore the waitress's glares forever, so at nine, we went to get ice cream. We sat in the rocking chairs on the front porch of the ice cream parlor, rocking and laughing and licking our cones. It was dark by that time. The store was busy, other couples talking and holding hands, and I felt like a part of something. I had felt like a part of something all summer, but that something was "a coven of invisible girls" and not "the rest of the world," so I leaned into this new feeling. I treasured the way Adam's eyes lingered on me, and I met his gaze, letting myself not look away.

I had looked at him this same way almost every day at practice last year, but I had thought it wasn't allowed. Now it was.

He dropped me off at home at nine-fifty, insisting on walking me up the stairs to my door. My parents had left the porch light on, despite the turtles. He hugged me beneath it and didn't let go.

"Thank you," I said into his shirt. "For dinner. And ice cream. I had a really nice time."

"Me too," he said. I could feel his voice in his chest, deep, and I felt the startle that was coming more and more often lately—he was almost a grown man. All of us were almost adults.

"Could I call you sometime?" he asked, still holding me. "After you get off work. Or we can just text. But I kind of like talking for real."

I smiled against him. I liked talking, too. "Of course. As long as you don't mind if it's late."

"I don't mind. I have insomnia."

"Okay." I pulled back and looked up at him. "If you're sure."

"I'm sure," he murmured, and he tipped his head down and kissed me.

It was my first kiss. It took me by surprise. I had hoped for it, maybe even expected it as we stood there under the porch light, but I hadn't known *what* to expect, not exactly. He was gentle, his mouth was hot and soft and felt strange against mine. Before this moment, I had worried about what to do with my tongue, but we didn't even get that far; he didn't try. It could have been almost chaste except that it struck a spark deep in my belly, a ferocious curiosity that shocked me almost as much as the fact of the kiss itself.

He was still for a moment and then stood up straight.

"Good night," I said. "Thank you. Again."

He laughed quietly. "My pleasure. Good night, Callie."

He kissed me on the forehead, and turned and walked down the stairs.

I stepped inside and flattened myself against the back of the door, covered my mouth with my hand. Adam Liu. Kissing me.

It had just happened—I had been there, right there inside of my body—and I still couldn't believe it.

"Callie?" Dad called from the living room. "Is that you?"

"Yeah," I managed. "Be there in a sec."

I took off my shoes and set down my purse slowly, trying to stay in the moment a little longer. When I finally came into the living room and sat down in my usual chair, my parents both looked up from their books with expectant faces.

"Did you have a good time?" Mom asked.

"Yeah." I wanted to be cool about it, but I couldn't help smiling. "A really good time."

"What'd you guys do?"

"Just dinner at the Shack, like I told you. And then we got ice cream."

They were quiet for a moment, and when I didn't say anything else, Mom shook her head and smiled, shot my dad a look. He smiled wryly in return.

"Well," he said, "that sounds good. Thank you for being back home on time."

"Of course I'm home on time," I said. Internally I winced at my own indignance. I didn't have any right to be self-righteous, not with sneaking out a few weeks ago and coming home late from the rink every night.

Mom and Dad ignored me. "Now that you are home safe, we are going to bed," Mom said. She came over and kissed me, just a few inches above where Adam's lips had been, on my forehead. Dad followed in her wake.

"Thanks for waiting up for me," I said as they went up the stairs. "I love you."

"Love you too," they said, one an echo of the other. I curled up in my usual chair in the living room as I listened to the sounds of them going to bed above me. The running of the water on and off, the flushing of the toilet, their indistinguishable voices murmuring to each other. Finally the creak of the bed frame as they got in bed.

I should've taken this rare opportunity to get to bed early, but I was wide awake. I could barely imagine closing my eyes, let alone falling asleep. I took a long, hot shower and brushed my hair; I picked up and, five minutes later, put down the book I was reading. It was nearly eleven when I sat down at the kitchen table and opened my laptop. I thought I might start a playlist for Adam.

But my phone buzzed with Talia's name. *HI, you still up?* she asked.

yes, just got back from my date with Adam, why are you??? I said.

oh my god, she replied. *how was the DATE?*

I hadn't planned on texting her, but now that we were talking, all I wanted was to hear her voice. To tell her about tonight. She was going to be so excited. *can I call you?*

yes of c, she said, and I called.

"Hi," she said, her voice quiet. "Hold on a sec, let me go outside." I heard shuffling on the other end of the line as I, too, moved, going upstairs into my bedroom and closing the door, climbing into bed. A door opened and closed on Talia's end before she said, "Okay, hi, can you hear me?"

"Yeah." The wind was soft white noise in the background.

"Okay, good. So how was it?"

"It was . . . really good." I curled up into a ball, trying to contain the giddiness still ricocheting under my skin. "It was so nice. He's so great. We just talked all night."

Talia laughed, not unkindly. "And?"

"And what?"

"And did you make out?"

"We did not make out," I said, feeling myself flush in the dark. "But, um. He did kiss me."

"Yes!" Talia whisper-shouted. "Oh my God, was it amazing? First kiss!"

"It was amazing," I admitted. "Just really . . . just really nice."

I felt so stupid saying *nice*, like a little kid who didn't know any other adjectives, but as much as I had wanted to talk to her just a few minutes before, I could feel myself pulling back from the desire to tell Talia everything now. I wanted instead to keep the memory locked inside myself where it would stay perfect, shining, untouched.

"That's great," she said. "God! Seriously, Callie, that's amazing. Adam is the best. I mean, not as good as you, but as good as you're going to find in this town, probably."

She sounded sincere. But there was something strained in her voice. Most nights, she got home from the rink and fell immediately into bed, but tonight she was still awake. And she had texted me, not the other way around.

"How was work?" I asked, taking a stab in the dark. Nothing weird ever happened at work, but maybe there had been an exception.

"It was fine," she said. "I mean, not the best. A whole family reunion came in. All wearing these bright green T-shirts. They were awful. Like, didn't have any cash, argued about the music, all the little kids kept getting into fights . . ."

"The classics." Family reunion groups typically made for either great nights or really bad ones—either they were all polite and friendly, or all jerks.

She coughed. "And Michael came by."

"Oh yeah?"

"Yeah, he wanted me to ditch work. We were maybe going to hang out, and I forgot to tell him that I was taking your shift tonight."

"Oh," I said. I bit my lip. "I'm sorry."

"It's fine, we hadn't committed to anything," she said. "At least that's what I thought. But maybe I was wrong. He just kept telling me I needed to keep better track of my schedule. And he— I mean, you know how he gets. It was in front of everyone and he wasn't yelling but he wasn't keeping it quiet, either, you know?"

I lay in the dark, staring at the ceiling. The ocean breathed its quiet rhythm outside.

"That sounds really shitty, Talia," I said. I heard a small sniffle on the other end of the line. "He shouldn't be trying to embarrass you like that."

"He's not," she whispered. "He's right. I should keep better track of my schedule."

I rolled over violently. "He's not right. He should treat you better."

"He's doing his best," she said. Her voice was a little louder and stronger now. "And I'm doing my best. Relationships are hard, right?"

"They don't have to be," I said. "I mean, not like I know, but I don't think they have to be like this."

"He's trying his best," she said, soft again. "It was just hard, tonight."

"I'm sorry," I said. The line was quiet, and I didn't know if I was apologizing for myself or for Michael or for what I hadn't done—what I wasn't doing now, in not pressing more deeply on the bruises he had wrought.

"Listen," she said, "I'm really, really glad you had such a good date. You deserve it."

"You deserve it, too, Talia."

Another sniffle. "Yeah."

I stayed on the line for a minute or two, just waiting. But she didn't say anything else, just yawned, finally, and said, "All right, I'm pretty tired. I'll see you tomorrow, okay? Cleo's house? Eleven?"

"Yeah. Love you, Talia."

"Love you too. Good night."

15 THE POLTERGEISTS

I didn't see Adam for a few days after our date. It wasn't on purpose. He was at work most of the day, most days, and that week held a series of afternoon thunderstorms that drove us off the beach by the time his shift ended. His sister, Jen, didn't go skating with her friends, so he never came to the rink to pick her up. We texted every day, but just surface-level stuff, chatting about running and our friends and the weather. But he hadn't called me, and I hadn't called him. Every night I told myself I should, but every night I didn't. It was too late after work, I reasoned. I didn't want to wake him up.

I thought about him, though. I thought about him as I ran in the morning, as I fell asleep at night. And I was thinking about him on Friday, as we were invisibly setting up for opening the rink, and someone skated right through me. It took me by surprise: that intangible warmth, the disappearance of it just as fast as it had come. I yelped.

"Sorry." Cleo laughed, and the barely there whir of her skates disappeared behind me.

"You scared me," I yelled.

"It's not like I could see you to avoid you," she teased, and she was closer to me again.

"Callie, you have to relax," Talia said, close to me as well.

"I am relaxed," I said through gritted, transparent teeth.

"Are you okay?" Polly asked.

I sighed and lay down on the wooden floor. "I am lying down," I said. "If you guys want to join me."

"I could nap," Cleo said, and Talia and Polly hummed their assent. I felt the warmth of a hand shift tentatively into the space of my palm, either Polly or Talia, and I didn't move.

"What's wrong?" Polly asked.

"She wants to call Adam and she hasn't," Talia answered for me.

"You should call him," Cleo said, and I sighed again.

"I will," I said. "But it's not that. At least, not all that. It's just— This is so weird, right? I mean, this, what we're doing now. I can't get past it."

Everyone was quiet for a minute. The disco ball circled slowly above us, eerie in the silence. The wind howled outside with the promise of more storms to come.

"But it feels good, too," Polly said gently. "Right? Can you let yourself feel it?"

After a while, I said, "Yeah."

It did feel good. That was the problem.

Being invisible felt like silk. It felt like the cool sea on a warm day. Like the way a pebble feels when it's been worn smooth, slippery under your fingers. Sometimes being invisible felt so good that I could barely imagine leaving that state, and when I did come back into my body, I wanted to scream at it, slice it into pieces—this clumsy, fragile thing that had laced up my soul.

And then I lived in it for a while, and I liked it again. I looked at the gray of my eyes in the mirror and touched the tender skin on the backs of my knees, felt the muscles in my calves stretching and aching as I ran, and I remembered myself.

Only to leave myself again. To follow the siren's call and fling myself with my friends into the chasm.

Sometimes coming back from it felt harder than going in.

Sometimes I thought it would be better if I never did it again.

I always did it again.

"It's almost six. Time to open," Talia said. I heard Cleo sigh beside me, reluctant. I closed my eyes and pulled myself back, back, back until I felt the skin of my calves on the worn wooden floor.

Polly unlocked the door, Talia switched on the OPEN sign, Cleo checked the register, and I turned on the music.

And no one came.

It wasn't that unusual for Fridays to be quiet. You'd think it'd be busy, and in the off-season it is, because everyone from town comes for the start of the weekend. But in the summer, all the families are packing up their beach toys and their laundry, eating their leftovers, making up after the latest iterations of their traditional fights. No one has the time to go out to skate.

Still, though—"It's never this quiet," I said to Talia at seven o'clock. "This is weird, right?"

"Weird," she agreed. "Especially since Little Mimi's is hopping." She nodded across the street, where the mini-golf emporium was swarmed with people in pink T-shirts. "Those are the same folks who came here last night."

"Why don't we have more locals, though?"

Cleo looked up from her phone. "Isn't there a concert down by the pier?"

"Oh, right." I remembered seeing the flyers. Some country artist from Wilmington had gone on a singing-themed reality TV competition recently. He'd gotten sent home third, but most of coastal North Carolina was hailing him as a hometown hero, meaning that anyone who would've normally come out on a Friday was probably otherwise occupied. I switched my own playlist to something a little weirder. No need to bother with pop if it was going to be just us.

"I almost feel bad for Little Mimi's. I really did not like that family." Talia was at the window, peering across the street. Cleo and Polly and I joined her. There were at least fifty people, adults and kids, all blond and all wearing the same T-shirt. One kid was having a meltdown in line for clubs. A couple was arguing heatedly by a fake palm tree.

The corners of Polly's mouth turned up. "We could really mess with them if we were invisible, huh?" she said.

Talia gasped. Cleo shrieked.

I said, "Absolutely not."

"That is inspired," Cleo said with reverence.

"What are we going to do with the rink?" I felt like I was the only one of the four of us who hadn't lost my mind. "We are open. For business. To customers."

"I'll make a sign," Polly said. She had already grabbed a sheet of paper and was writing CLOSED FOR REPAIRS in big letters. Her handwriting wasn't soft and rounded like I had expected it to be. It was angular, awkward, lines spiking out of letters every which way.

"You can't just make a sign," I protested. "What if Miss Abby comes by?"

"We totally can, and she definitely won't," Cleo said. "Oh my God, I'm so excited. Polly, you're a beautiful genius."

"What do you even want to—"

"We can be golf poltergeists!" Talia said, laughing. "Maybe it'll actually be good for them. The first and only haunted mini-golf establishment in the Carolinas."

"This is a terrible idea," I said. I crossed my arms over my chest. "It's dangerous. Someone could see us. Or we could get hurt. Or we could lose track of each other. Or—"

"Or we could play a totally harmless prank," Cleo said. Her voice had gentled a little, and she wrapped an arm around my waist playfully.

"You need something to distract you from not calling Adam," Talia said. She was already unlacing her skates and putting on her sandals. "And besides, what was the point of doing all this if we can't have some fun with it?"

"Right," Cleo said. "Nothing bad is going to happen, Callie."

Polly was taping up the sign in the window. The light came through it and hit her furrowed brow as she lined it up straight. Talia looked up at me from the floor, her eyes bright and wide. Cleo, beside me, squeezed me close.

"We should change first and then go out the back," I said after a moment. "So people don't see us leave."

Polly flipped the dead bolt on the front door as Cleo clapped her hands and Talia said, "Thank God, finally."

It happened quickly after that. We slipped invisibly out the back door, and I followed the sounds of my friends' laughter to the parking spots in the front of the rink. "What is the *plan?*" I hissed into the air. It was broad daylight, kids playing in the park a block down, people walking on both sides of the road less than twenty feet away from us, and I felt the same way you do in a dream of being naked at school.

"There's a clock on the wall at Little Mimi's," Cleo said impatiently. "We meet back here at eight-thirty."

"Eight-thirty?!"

"Fine, eight."

"And until then we just have fun," said Talia. "Come on."

"I'm going," said Polly, her voice already a little ahead of us.

I took a deep breath and started walking toward the road.

And then a truck came barreling past, way too fast, a blur of light and chrome, and I heard a shriek from the middle of the road.

Other people heard it, too—heads turned, faces puzzled at the sound that had come from nowhere. My stomach dropped, and I clapped a hand over my mouth to keep from yelling out Polly's name. I had no idea where Talia and Cleo were. I ran out into the street, now empty, whispering "Polly" as I went, as loudly as I dared. I didn't hear anything.

I tried to keep alert for the feeling of my legs passing through another girl's body as I ran, but I didn't feel anything, either.

I got to the other side of the road, hyperventilating. This, exactly something like this, was what I had been afraid of. We didn't know what would happen if we were knocked unconscious, or worse. I looked down the street. If I could make it back to the rink, with my phone, I could call 911 and I could say—I didn't know what I could say—

I heard a soft giggle in the empty air to my right.

I ran toward it and slipped straight into another girl.

"Who is it?" I whispered.

"Oh my God, that truck just barely missed me," said Polly, her voice quiet but vibrating with adrenaline, and I could've punched her, I could've kissed her, I was so fucking happy to hear her voice.

"You scared the shit out of me," gasped Cleo. Her voice came from barely inches in front of me, and I could hear her breath, shallow and loud in the air.

"It's fine, everything's fine," hissed Talia, a little to my left. "We're here, it's fine, I'm going to go shake some trees. Literally."

I stood in place, breathing hard. "Callie, you coming?" Cleo whispered.

"Yeah," I said. "Yeah. I'll be right there."

I swallowed hard. I wished I had some water.

Then I slipped through the gate into Little Mimi's.

My heart was still racing, and I looked around for a place where I could be out of the way. My eyes landed on the big old oak tree by hole seven. There was a sign at its base that said NO CLIMBING, which was necessary, because it was absolutely ideal for climbing. As a little kid, I had tried to climb it every single time we'd gone to Little Mimi's and been thwarted each time.

Now, I made my way toward it, avoiding the mini-golfers, and pulled myself up by the lowest branch. The leaves shook a little, and a teenager looked up at the tree in puzzlement, but then focused back on her swing. She had looked right through me.

I climbed maybe fifteen or twenty feet, the broad, flat branches making the job easy. Being in the leaves was as wonderful as I'd always thought it would be—cool and comfortable, with a view of the whole mini-golf course and a sliver of the ocean beyond. For the first time since Polly had suggested we come here, I let myself smile. Then I let myself laugh.

That same girl below me looked up, shook her head, looked down again.

I felt light-headed. Invincible.

I leaned back against the trunk and watched.

It looked like Little Mimi's always looked on a busy night, tourists and little colored balls everywhere. For a second I wondered why I had thought it would be any fun at all to observe my friends, when by the very nature of our power they were impossible to see.

But then, just as a woman hit her ball toward the windmill, the windmill started spinning much faster than wind could've set it off. Unevenly, too, slowing and then starting again as if struck by a hand. It was moving so fast that when her ball slipped through the spokes, she couldn't reach through to pick it up. She turned around, half-heartedly called for an employee, then snapped at her daughter, who was dripping ice cream on her shirt.

I couldn't help but grin.

Little chaotic moments started erupting all over the park. Near the front, a man who I'd seen yelling at the cashier was rooting around in the first hole, frowning, unable to find his ball even though he'd gotten a hole in one. Noises that sounded like a bat or an owl—or, suspiciously, like Cleo's all-purpose creepy animal noise—were coming from inside the mock volcano. The water feature splashed of its own accord, spitting droplets of dyed-turquoise water on everyone near it.

I shook the branches of the tree experimentally. The air was still, no breeze, and the same girl looked up again with obvious confusion.

I felt a little bad. But as I watched a gnome levitate and then fall back to earth on the other side of the park, a toddler pointing at it and laughing, I slipped down from the tree branches.

I didn't have a plan. I just walked around the perimeter of the park, two, three times, reveling in the feeling of being there without being there. I had never thought of myself as especially self-conscious, but in a crowded public space with no one's eyes on me, I could feel a weight slip away. No need to check for lingering male eyes. No adjustments of my hair or the hem of my shirt when a girl looked at me like she was sizing me up. I waved my arms in the air two feet from a man ignoring his daughters and tapping on his phone. Nothing.

Very slowly, the plastic toucan at the edge of the water feature slid off its perch and into the electric-blue waterfall below.

I started to laugh, clamping a hand over my mouth when a boy near me turned around to find the source of the sound.

Then I looked past him, across the street, and I was glad my hand was still there to muffle my yelp. A line was starting to form at the skating rink—not a long line, but at least four or five people deep, with another car pulling in.

My heartbeat sped up as I tried to think. I stared at the big blinking digital clock mounted on the wall above the water fountain. It had only been half an hour; we weren't supposed to meet back at the rink until eight. Maybe the others would see the line forming. But maybe not. Or maybe—I thought of Polly and the spiky, bold handwriting on her sign—they would see and wouldn't care.

I couldn't text them. I couldn't yell out their names.

I could think of only one other way to tell them it was time to go, and it seemed like a terrible idea.

I went for it anyway. Speed-walking across the park, dodging golf clubs and groups of kids, to the water fountain and the clock. I sized up the fountain, then decided—fuck it. I hoisted myself on top of it. It groaned, but it held, and part of me wondered whether it would've collapsed if I'd been visible, while the rest of me was grateful for my height.

I felt around on the side of the clock until I found a button and pressed. The hour changed. Not great. I kept pressing until the hour came back to seven, and then I found another button just above it, pressed, and let out a sigh of relief as the minutes started ticking up.

Behind me, I heard a guy say, "What the fuck is wrong with that clock?"

In the distance, the owl-hooting from inside the volcano stopped.

I let the time get to 7:59 and stopped, dismounting as delicately as I could. And just in time: A little girl ran up and pressed the bar for water just a couple of seconds after my feet touched the ground. She looked around with a frown as I held absolutely still. But then she dipped her head to take a drink, and I backed away slowly until I could make my way around the other side of the building. Through a gap in the fence, across a blessedly empty street, around the back of the skating rink, and then— waiting for a moment when no one was looking through the front window—through the door we had left cracked open.

I stayed there, motionless, watching the people waiting outside through the windows across the rink. A couple gave up and went back down the stairs. I felt a soft pang of guilt, even though Miss Abby would almost certainly never find out, even though my job was not dependent on the number of customers we served on any given night. I told myself I'd count to one hundred, and then I'd go into the broom closet, change back, and open the rink, no matter who was there.

I was at a hundred and fifteen when, in the air near the door, Cleo said, "Callie? Are you here?"

"Oh my God, finally." I exhaled. "Okay, we've got to open up, are the others with you?"

"Polly is—"

"Hi." Polly drew out the word with a delighted drawl.

"And I'm not sure about Talia. Um."

"I can change back and call her," I offered, though I wasn't sure if Talia had her phone with her or not.

"I'm here now," Talia said, out of breath, a moment later.

Looking at the dark, empty rink, I felt like I could collapse with relief. "Okay," I said, "let's change in the broom closet, then we open, and we say— What?"

"The roof had a leak?" offered Talia. "I guess it's been sunny all day, though."

"We wanted to play with our new superpower?" suggested Polly.

"Spilled bleach, fumes were dangerous," said Cleo, with the certainty that was appropriate, since hers was the only suggestion that even approached making sense.

"Let's go with the last one," I said. I jogged across the rink and opened the door to the broom closet and storage room, thankfully large enough for all four of us and just barely visible from the window. I changed back as quickly as I could, beating the others—Cleo, standing too close to Polly, had to pull her hand away as they both started to become visible again.

When we were all there again, Talia said she would open the doors, Polly said she'd start the register, and they both jogged out. I was about to follow, when Cleo said, "Wait."

I turned back. She lifted the jug of bleach and poured a little onto a rag. Stepping outside the closet, she waved the rag in the air around the side of the rink.

"There," she said. "See? Easy."

She was standing so far away that in the dark room I could barely see her. I flipped on the disco ball. The door opened. We were back.

It was a normal night after that. Someone told us the concert had ended early, sound system issues, which explained the sudden rush. I ran the music and resolutely played not one speck of country, soothing myself with the songs I liked best, getting my heart rate back down to normal.

When it was time to skate home, we disappeared again. The road was near-empty and the air had cooled, and I took deep breaths. For the first time since we'd put the sign on the door, moving fast and easy through the night with my best friends around me, I started to feel safe.

I got home by curfew, barely. I turned myself visible while I unlaced my skates on the porch. It was difficult, like trying to open the lid on a tightly closed jar. But I did it, and I tried not to worry about it. It had been a long day; it was late; that was all. I stepped inside in my socks. My parents had left a note on the counter saying they'd gone to bed early and that there was leftover gazpacho in the fridge. I wasn't hungry.

I showered and got into my pajamas. I knew I should've gone to bed. I was rattled and exhilarated and a little afraid of what we had done, and a headache had settled in behind my eyes. I didn't want to sleep, though—to have the nightmares that came more and more frequently now, where I wanted to scream but I couldn't breathe, reached out for my mom and my arm went right through her. I wanted to feel good again.

I sat down on my bed and picked up the phone, tapped to Adam's contact.

I put it down. It was late. Past eleven now.

But he said he had insomnia.

I picked it up again and pressed call. He answered on the second ring. There was silence, and then Adam's voice, low and quiet: "Hello?"

"Hey," I said. Almost whispered, even though I knew my parents were asleep.

"Hey," he said, and I heard the smile in his voice. "You called."

"I called." My head fell back onto the pillows. I said, "It's good to hear your voice."

He paused, and I thought maybe that was a stupid thing to say. It was the kind of thing I thought of people saying in books. Maybe that was too much for real life, even if it was true. But then he said, "You too."

"Where are you?" I asked after a while.

"In bed," he said softly.

A shiver trembled through me, thinking of him under the covers. "Did I wake you?"

"A little."

"Sorry." I winced. "I thought it was too late to call, but then you had said it was okay—"

"It is okay, I don't mind. Where are you?"

"Bed."

"Hold on a second." There was rustling on the other end of the line, a bump and a shuffle, and then his voice again: "Okay. That's better. I turned over."

"Comfier now?"

"Yeah."

"Good."

"So what did you do today? How was work?"

I thought of the shriek from the air in the middle of the road, the confusion of the family at Little Mimi's, and shoved it out of my mind. "Not a lot," I said. "I got to run the playlist tonight, which is my favorite. There was a little kid who was so into this Jetty Bones song I put on. It made me happy."

The phone grew hot against my ear as we talked. Adam told me about his workday. The frazzled parents who came in having realized that their rental house coffee machines were broken, the regulars and their orders. Mostly, he said, he sat around and read. He was often the only person on his shift.

"That must be lonely," I said.

"I guess. But I've read some good books this summer. And I didn't exactly expect work to be fun, right? I mean, it's work."

"My work is fun." I thought about when we'd had to clean up vomit or break up fights, or the one time last year that the sno-cone machine had broken in a truly spectacular fashion, and amended that. "Well, most of the time."

"You're lucky," he said. "What you guys have, it's special."

"More than you know."

I regretted it immediately, but he didn't seem to think I had said anything strange. Instead, he said, "You should come by sometime. To the store. I have an employee discount. I could get you . . . What kind of coffee do you like?"

"Iced, with cream, no sugar. I'd like that," I said. "I can get you into the rink for free, too, if you want."

He laughed. "That's kind of Jen's thing. I don't do great on skates."

"Oh, now you have to come."

"No way. I've seen you out there. You're amazing. I'll just embarrass myself."

I curled into a ball, scooting closer to the window. "I'm not amazing."

"You are." His voice softened. "Callie, you are."

A smile spread across my face, and I said the first thing that came to mind, which was: "Why are you being so nice to me?"

He laughed. "What kind of a question is that? Have I been an asshole to you up to this point?"

"I just mean . . ." My eyes started to ache from being open. I felt shy all of a sudden, and I looked down, where I could just barely see my fingers in the darkness, rubbing the fabric of my sleep shirt between them. I let them disappear, reappear, playing with the sensation of it. "You know what I mean. Yeah, okay, you've always been *nice*, but you've never asked me out. We've known each other forever. Why now?"

164

"Well, um." I heard another shuffle and an exhale. I liked that I could make him nervous. "I never really knew you that well, before last year. I mean, obviously I knew you, all of us have known each other since we were little, but I had never really thought of you that way. No offense." This provoked a small pang in my chest, though that wasn't quite fair; it wasn't like I'd been pining after him for a decade, either.

"But then once we got onto varsity together—"

"You mean when you got onto varsity with me," I corrected, and he laughed.

"Yes. You're right. When I got onto varsity with you, we ended up spending all that time together between school and practice. And then," he continued, "in May, you failed that chemistry test and you had to do extra tutorial sessions with Mr. Sims and you couldn't hang out with us for a few weeks."

I groaned. "You remember that?"

"Yeah, of course. Because every afternoon, I was really bummed, and then I was like, what's different about this? And the thing that was different was that you weren't there."

I closed my eyes. He had been sad. Because I wasn't there.

"Anyway," he said, then cleared his throat, "you asked why now, and that's why. I just realized it, I guess. I think you're great."

I bit my lip to keep from smiling too much. My cheeks hurt from smiling. "I like you a lot, Adam," I said.

"I like you, too, if that isn't obvious." I could hear the ease in his voice, the relief. "I, um. I do have to go to bed, though."

"Aw, shit." It was almost midnight. Running tomorrow morning was going to be awful. "Me too. Sorry I called so late."

"Don't apologize. I'm glad you did." He yawned. "Good night, Callie."

"Good night. Sleep well."

I hung up the phone. The strangeness of the evening felt like a daydream now, far away, and my whole body thrummed with happiness.

16 MARCO POLO

I woke up to my alarm and a text from Polly: *want to run together this morning?*

The sun hadn't yet crested the horizon, and I wondered if she'd even slept last night. I had been out as soon as I'd gotten off the phone with Adam, and I still felt exhausted.

But Polly had asked, and I needed to run anyway. *sure,* I texted back. *want to meet on the beach in front of the ice cream place?* Too late, I realized that Polly might not know where that was—the exact midpoint between our houses, where I'd always met Cleo when Talia couldn't join us. But she replied, *sounds good, see you in 30.*

I got there before her, having done a few sprints on the way. I wanted to get in some speed practice by myself, because I suspected, though I couldn't say for sure, that Polly was slower than I was. I was pretty fast, and she'd said she wasn't on the track team. Besides, I had never seen her eat more than a few bites at any meal, and food was necessary for runners. For anyone, really, but I didn't know how to talk about that with her.

She jogged up just as the air was starting to get warmer. I gave her a hug automatically and was surprised when I felt her arms around me tight, almost vibrating with energy. As I pulled back, she was smiling widely.

"Last night was so good," she said. "I just wanted to keep moving. Thanks for letting me tag along today."

"No problem," I said. I looked at her carefully. Maybe it was the morning's new sun on her skin, maybe the sweat, but she looked like she was shining from the inside out.

"What's wrong?" she asked, furrowing her brow. "Are you feeling okay?"

"Last night . . ." I trailed off. Polly's eyes lit up with understanding. She grabbed my hand and squeezed.

"We had fun, right?"

I nodded.

"And we didn't hurt anyone, right? And we didn't get hurt ourselves?"

I shook my head. I felt like a child.

"And we gave some kids a great story to take back home to Ohio or wherever, right?"

I laughed. "Right," I said.

"Right," she said, smiling. "We didn't do anything wrong, Callie. You can give yourself permission to have fun sometimes, you know."

"Yeah," I said. "Okay."

And for the first time this morning, I let myself remember— really remember—the exhilaration of prowling around the golf course invisible, the showers of sparks that lit up in my blood when we moved through each other, and I smiled.

"Come on," Polly said, leading me closer to the high dunes. She sat down, looked all up and down the empty beach, and started to disappear.

It happened so fast, and I was so surprised, that she was already halfway gone when I said, "What the fuck?"

She looked up at me, startled. Through the fine lines of her face, I watched a chickadee land, hop a few times, fly away again. "What?" she said.

"We're— We're running," I said.

Now her eyebrows arched a fraction higher. "Are you really telling me you haven't been changing before you run?"

"I— What?"

She laughed, clapping a half-transparent hand over her mouth, and when she met my eyes again, she smiled. I had never seen her look so utterly at ease. "Callie, come on. I promise, you're in for such a treat."

And right before my eyes, she disappeared.

I felt the heat of her hand, transparent, intersect with mine. What could I do? I checked again for people in either direction, then closed my eyes and repeated those now-familiar words. I wanted to be invisible, and then I was.

"Toward Cleo's house or yours?" Polly asked, her voice rich and warm.

"Cleo's, I think," I said. "How will you keep— Um, how will we stick together?"

Polly laughed. "I don't mind if you go faster than I do. I want you to. I'll just yell out if I'm worried about getting too far behind."

"Okay." I had my doubts, but the new, reckless part of me shoved those away. We were on a beach alone; nothing would happen. "I, um, I guess I'm going to go ahead and—"

"Come on!" I heard from many yards ahead of me.

I started running.

For me there has always been a difference between running to get somewhere—jogging after a friend, across a street, to get to class—and running to run. Running to get somewhere is all function, speeding up the natural pace of your body to accomplish a goal. I had done that while invisible before, as recently as last night.

But running to run—that's all beauty, grace, form. I wake up to run every morning for no reason except that I love it. And not since that first night, when we'd all frolicked down the beach feeling the thunder and lightning of this new power inside of us, had I turned invisible and run to run.

Then, I had been too overwhelmed to piece apart the sensations I was feeling. Now I could feel the new lightness of my body, how when my feet pressed off the sand, the same effort propelled me further. I breathed in and it felt like the oxygen had a shorter path from my throat to my lungs to my blood. My heart, invisible though it always was within the cage of my ribs, thumped with joy.

I fixed my eyes on a piece of driftwood in the distance, pushed myself experimentally until I passed it. Fixed on a walkway farther away, pushed a little more. Passed it. Pushed more, and more, and more, and more.

I was so fucking fast.

Cleo had wished for flight.

This was close.

I didn't stop until I heard a faint noise, far behind me. I had almost forgotten about Polly. I looked around; we had gone far past Cleo's house. A tendril of worry snaked into the euphoria as I strained to hear the noise again, and I was about to yell out when I heard Polly shout: "Marco!"

I laughed. "Polo!" I yelled.

We Marco-Polo-ed our way back together like little kids in a swimming pool. When I heard her say, "Marco," right in front of me, I said, "You were right."

"I know," she said. She laughed, and it sounded like the call of a bird. "You're a lot faster than me, huh?"

"Sorry," I said. I felt like I could have run a marathon. Two marathons.

"You're not sorry," she said. I could hear the smile in it. "And you shouldn't be."

———

The magic lasted even after Polly and I left each other and went home, through the shower and as I packed my beach bag and ate lunch and played in the ocean with my friends. We didn't see anyone we knew that day—it was just us, us and a world made new under our command. Somewhere dim in the back of my head, I recognized that this was a giddiness bordering on hysteria, but I couldn't, didn't want to stop to look at it closely. It all felt too good: our jokes sharp and smart; the sea blue and effervescent; our bodies meeting beneath the water, solid, then empty, solid, then sparks; splashing each other with translucent hands and shrieking in delight.

We ordered pizza to work that night, a rare indulgence. By that time, the happiness had faded a little to something warmer and softer. I minded the front desk and watched my friends skating, Janelle Monáe blasting on the speakers. I could've watched them forever.

As Cleo and Polly passed, skating slowly, I stuck out the pizza box. "Have a slice?"

"Absolutely," Cleo said, grabbing one and eating half of it in a huge bite.

"I'm fine," Polly said.

"One slice is not going to kill you," I said.

"Really, I'm good," she said, and I was about to insist, when something caught my eye on the far side of the rink. There were two tall guys, and between them, pressed against the wall, a much smaller girl.

"Can y'all watch the counter?" I asked, and I set down the pizza box and was out through the gate before Cleo could finish asking me what was going on.

I skated directly across the rink, in violation of our clockwise-only policy. It could've been nothing. It probably was nothing, just three friends talking. But one night in the spring, when the rink was only open on the weekend and Talia and I were working alone, a man had started yelling at his girlfriend, and it had gotten scary. The whole rink had grown quiet, and this woman—she was older than me, they were in their twenties—had looked terrified. Fortunately, some of their friends intervened and took the woman home, and he left right after in a different car. Talia and I hadn't done anything. I felt guilty about it for days. I told myself that if anything like that ever happened again, I would stop it. I just wasn't sure exactly how.

Now I reached the corner. "Everything okay with y'all?" I kept my voice light, easy.

The two guys turned, and as they did, I finally caught a glimpse of the girl they were talking to. I recognized her: a rising sophomore, someone I'd seen hanging out with Talia's sister Olivia. She was flattened against the side of the rink, slipping a little on her skates as she tried to keep her balance.

"All good," the taller guy said. He gave me a smile with a little too much charm. Now that I was closer, I knew for sure I didn't recognize them. Tourists. Older, maybe in college. His friend just kept chatting to the girl—I racked my brain for her name. Lana? She couldn't have been older than sixteen. His voice was low and reassuring as I tuned in.

". . . Honestly, it's super chill. It's just me and Johnny here and a couple of our buds, we've got some great tequila and this house is huge, you'd love it. I think a couple other girls are coming over, but no one who can compare to you. I mean, look at you." He made an admiring gesture with his arm, brushing his hand against her hip.

Lana or Lara or Lacey met my eyes. Her fingers gripped the railing behind her.

"Laura," I said. She relaxed a fraction; I had guessed right. I tried to think of an excuse for her to leave. "Um, that's your purse over by the door, right? Your phone keeps ringing. Want me to grab it for you, or . . ."

"I'll come get it," she said quickly. She pushed off from the wall, a little shaky, and the shorter guy reached out. She stopped.

"Let me help you," he said, winding a hand around her waist.

"She's fine, actually." Talia had appeared behind me. "Right, Laura?"

"Yeah. Fine." Laura reached out and Talia grabbed her hand, guiding her to the edge of the rink again, where she started making her way back to the front. In a glance over my shoulder, I saw a cluster of girls spot her and wave. I mentally reminded myself to give them a lecture about keeping better track of their friends.

"What the fuck," said Johnny, with mild indignation.

"She's fifteen," Talia said flatly.

The shorter guy scratched his head and put on a rueful expression. "Can't blame a guy for trying, right?"

"How old are y'all?" Johnny asked with a smirk. His eyes crawled over me, slow. I was wearing running shorts with barely any inseam and a cropped tank, because it was so goddamn hot, but now I wished I were wearing a sweatshirt like Polly. Better yet, I wished he couldn't see me at all. Which was possible—I felt the invisibility pulling at me, in my hamstrings and my shoulders and all the places that had gone tight under his gaze. Then he looked away from me and toward Talia.

That made me finally find my voice. "It's actually time for you to go," I said.

His friend had the audacity to laugh. "Come on. We're just having fun. You heard her, she was good."

"This isn't fun," I said, my voice rising, and I could hear myself sounding younger than I wanted to, like a kid having a tantrum. Johnny slid forward on his skates until he was only inches away from me. He smelled of leftover sunscreen and beer, chemical and sweat.

"We're all fine," he said slowly. "You're certainly fine. Just relax."

I felt frozen.

Because here's the thing—it probably *was* fine, but I didn't know. You can never know, not for sure. Nine out of ten times, maybe ninety-nine out of a hundred, it's nothing. He's bored or he's a jerk or he's drunk or he's insecure, and you throw words at each other, and then you go home safe. That's especially true with tourists, who want to spend a week with their bros and have a fling with a girl with sun-streaked hair. We've all met those guys. We've been ogled and rolled our eyes and turned away.

But sometimes it isn't nothing. Sometimes, those guys have teeth.

"Callie," Talia said, tugging me away. She cocked her head toward the door, where Laura and her friends were leaving and Cleo and Polly were watching with obvious worry. "We've gotta get back."

"But—"

"Enjoy the rink, y'all," Talia called to the two men. The shorter one had the decency to look vaguely guilty. Talia tugged me back toward the front of the rink.

"They should not be here," I protested, but she just shook her head.

"It's not worth it," she said. "You know it's not."

Cleo and Polly asked us what was wrong when we got back. I made a frustrated motion with my hands while Talia explained. "They were just creeps," she said. "Anyway, I'm making a sno-cone, anyone want one?"

"Talia, I don't see how you can just not care!" I burst out. That man had gotten so close to me. I kept hearing how he had said the word *fine* as he looked at me. I had never wanted to be invisible more.

"Of course I care," she said, setting down her paper cup. She took a deep breath, gaze fixed on her hands on the counter. "I just want us to be safe, Callie. We got Laura out of there, and that's good, but there's nothing else we can do. It's not like we have security here. It's not like we can call the fucking cops."

I bit my lip. Focused on the pain of my teeth.

"Maybe we can close early," Polly said timidly. "Just half an hour early."

"Let's do that," Cleo said.

I turned the music up loud.

The two men skated around and around. I watched their skates, the muscles of their legs, and I didn't look up to see if they were looking at me.

Twenty minutes later, Polly got on the intercom. "Hey, y'all, we're gonna have to close early tonight," she said in a singsong voice. "We're getting word that a storm's coming in, and we need everyone to get home safe. Last skate."

I put on Illuminati Hotties. People grumbled and shot looks at the four of us. As the floor was clearing out, a kid frowned at Polly and said, "I didn't know it was supposed to rain."

She shrugged. "Weather's unpredictable down here."

Johnny and his friend left with the rest of the crowd. It was 9:32 when Polly locked the door. The sun had set, and the dark hung in the still air outside like a bruise.

I exhaled. I felt like I had been holding my breath for hours.

Polly flicked off the lights, and without talking, we all changed. It happened so fast, and I wanted it so badly, that I forgot to be freaked out by the sight of my friends disappearing. Then it was dark and empty except for the sparks of the disco ball moving through us, and I felt the heaviness of the man's gaze fall away from me like I was shedding a skin.

I didn't know exactly where the others were, but after a few minutes of skating in circles around the rink, I made my way to the center and stood under the disco ball, looking up at it as it turned. All those hundreds of mirrors, reflecting nothing but light.

"I've been thinking," Cleo said from close beside me. I wasn't surprised; we always gathered in the center, sooner or later. "About what we should do next."

"I'm down for another run at Little Mimi's," Talia said, and I bit my lip, barely feeling the touch of my own teeth.

"No," Cleo said. "I mean, maybe, but that's not what I'm talking about. I think we should make a video."

"What?" Polly said sharply.

"You mean like a music video or something. Unrelated to this. Right, Cleo?" Talia was cautious, and I closed my eyes imagining an alternate world where Cleo had brought a video camera in June and we had spent the summer making an amateur movie. Written scripts. Sewn costumes. No ritual, no power, just a more grown-up version of playing pretend.

A music video was not what she meant.

"You mean like the girls on YouTube," I said slowly.

That night skating home, when we had talked about what we would do with our power. Cleo had been clear with us from the beginning, like she always was. *I'm gonna make my own version of that video. But better . . . Maybe a whole series.* I hadn't taken it seriously, because why would I? I never thought it would happen.

"Yes," Cleo said. "Showing other girls how we did it and how they can do it. There aren't a lot of good instructions out there. And honestly, you saw the girls in the other videos. We're better than them. We're faster. I haven't seen anyone else disappear things outside of themselves. We could film you with the broom, Polly. We could get a lot of views."

"Is that really what you want?" I asked. I was trying to stay open to the idea. "A lot of views? I mean, I understand wanting to help out other girls, but it feels like getting a lot of eyes on us doesn't seem great."

"Not specifically views, I guess, but it'd be nice to get some recognition—"

"No."

Polly's voice cut through the darkness, loud and clear as a bell.

"Polly," Cleo said, and I could hear how startled she was. "Can we at least talk about it? I just think—"

"No," she repeated. I had never heard her sound so firm. Or so cold. I shrank away from it even as I was intrigued—had this girl been inside her all along? "Absolutely not. We're not telling anyone."

"Polly's right," Talia said, and she sounded a little shaken. "We haven't told anyone yet. There's no reason to change that. It's supposed to be a secret. That's important."

We were all quiet for a minute. Then Cleo started to appear before us. She had her arms wrapped around her knees, and she looked more than a little guilty.

"What's wrong?" I asked. She hadn't said anything about changing back. "Are you okay?"

"Yeah, I just— Well— I didn't necessarily think that this was going to be the reaction from y'all, and I have some things that I need to show you, I guess."

She pulled out her phone, and for a second it was like I could see the future. "Cleo," I said, "oh, no."

"Cleo, you didn't," said Polly. She sounded panicked.

Cleo looked up and around, though she couldn't see any of

us, then sighed and started tapping her phone. "I didn't put up any videos," she said.

"Thank God," said Talia fervently.

"I've just been posting on the forums a little, comparing stories and ideas . . ."

"Not with our real names, right?" Polly still sounded sharp, but less worried.

"Of course not!" Cleo shook her head. "But . . . I mean, I wanted to give back. We never would've figured this out without all those posts and videos from the other girls, right? So I wanted to help other girls, like they helped us. And I gave some advice."

Cleo looked up, her eyes pleading. I wanted to be there for her to see. I closed my eyes and evened my breath to change back. Talia followed suit. Polly didn't. "What did you say?" she asked from somewhere to my right.

Cleo shrugged and handed her phone to me. "I told them about the ocean and the dresses. And that we weren't having any trouble with our clothes disappearing, or stuff in our pockets, or our skates. And I talked about being able to disappear other things. But"—her voice rose as Polly started to ask a question—"I didn't say where we were, just that we were at a beach in the Carolinas, and there are no real names."

She had pulled up the pages that showed all her comments on the various forums and YouTube. I scrolled through them, Talia looking over my shoulder. In the comments (coming from madame____C_) she was bubbly, excited, encouraging. It was strange to read her account of what we had both been through. She described the feeling of it coming over her as like stepping under a waterfall.

"Nothing about Little Mimi's?" Polly asked after a moment.

Cleo shrugged uncomfortably. "I posted today and said we played some pranks. I didn't say where. There's nothing identifiable, I promise. And I didn't post any of the videos."

"The videos?" Talia looked up.

"I took a few videos of myself. Only myself," she added quickly. "Just in my bedroom. In the mornings while you were out on your runs, Polly. I was going to post them, but I wanted to show you what I had done. I thought . . . I thought you might like them, and maybe we could make something with all of us. But obviously— You know, obviously I won't post any of them, now." She looked away, then looked back at us. "I still don't get it, though. Why is it such a big deal? I mean, before we did any of this, I said I wanted to make a video. No one had a problem with it then."

I swallowed.

"I didn't think it would work," I said. My voice sounded as small as a child's. As silly as I had thought our plan was in the first place, it felt, now, equally absurd that I had ever failed to believe. That the summer could ever have gone differently.

"Yeah," Cleo sighed, meeting my eyes with a rueful grin. "I know."

"Cleo, I'm so sorry," Polly said. Finally, she came visible again, and she put a hand on Cleo's leg. Cleo startled, looking at Polly's hand as if it were an unexpected animal. "But the secret is part of it," Polly said. "Telling would ruin it. I don't mean what you've done— I mean, I don't love it, but I understand, if you're not using our names and there's nothing that could identify us. That's okay with me. But anything beyond that . . ."

Cleo leaned into Polly's shoulder. "Even if we just put it up without showing our faces?"

"Yes," Polly said, gentler now. "I'm sorry, Cleo, I get it, but we can't."

"I agree," Talia said.

"Callie?"

"We can't tell," I said after a minute. "It would be dangerous."

Cleo exhaled, straightening away from Polly and running a hand through her short hair. She hugged her arms around her waist. "Okay, then."

We all sat there, unmoving, the wooden floor cooling beneath us as the night sank into itself.

"What do you mean by that?" Talia asked after a while. "Dangerous."

"All of this is dangerous," Polly said softly, as though it was obvious, and I didn't know what she meant exactly. I didn't know what I had meant, exactly. All I knew was what the world had taught me and every other girl, over and over again: Anything that felt this good, it also had the power to wound.

We shifted back into invisibility to clean up, and I put on MUNA, and it almost felt like we had never fought. Skating home, invisible still, we saw almost no cars on the road. I felt the wind shift through me and gulped in fresh air, deeper breaths than I'd taken for all the hours I'd spent in the rink. The stars were bright and the air was soft and damp. Polly hadn't lied; there would be rain soon. It felt good to be outside and quiet and together.

When we reached Cleo's house, though, Cleo said, "Hey, Polly, do you mind if I keep going for a bit? I'm just feeling a little restless."

"Yeah, no problem," Polly said, though she sounded surprised. "Do you want me to stay with you?"

"Nah, it's fine. Just, if my grandma wakes up, tell her I'll be back by curfew. I'm just going to skate on with Callie and Talia and then come back."

"Okay, if you're sure," Polly said. A minute later, she walked out from behind a car and waved goodbye.

I expected Cleo to turn back at Talia's house a few minutes later, but no—we saw Talia turn visible again safely, and when I asked, "Are you headed back?" Cleo said, "I think I'll stick with you, if it's okay."

She told me about her grandfather's latest woodworking endeavor and her older sister's college boyfriend drama, and if I hadn't known her for so many years, I might've thought that she really was just restless. But I could tell when she was stalling.

When we got to my house, I lingered at the bottom of the steps as Cleo finished her story about her sister. I laughed at the right places, and then Cleo said, after a pause, "Well, I should probably head back."

"Do you want to sit with me for a bit?" I asked. "Just on the stairs? I can stay outside for a while."

"Oh," she said. "Okay. Sure."

We turned ourselves back in the shadows of my house and sat down on the stairs. A lone car drove by, its headlights lighting up the sandy sidewalk, then drifting away again.

Finally, she said, slowly, "If I tell you a story, will you promise not to tell anyone else?"

"Yes," I said.

"Not even Talia."

"Okay," I said, though I hated knowing things I couldn't tell Talia. "Not even Talia."

"Okay," Cleo said, and she let out a breath. "So I'm sure you've noticed that Polly almost never eats anything."

"I have," I said cautiously. This was not where I expected the conversation to go.

"Yeah, well, a few months before we came here, I tried talking to her about it. I had tried before, but this time I really prepared. I had this eating disorder website pulled up. I had read all these things about how to talk to someone you love about disordered eating. I know how stupid this sounds, but it was supposed to be an intervention."

"How did it go?"

"Not that great." Cleo sighed. "I got upset. At one point, I said she could die, and she said she'd be fine with that."

"Oh."

No one I knew had ever said anything like that to me before.

"And when I said I didn't want her to die," Cleo continued, her voice wavering, "she said she didn't really want to die, she just wanted a break from her body."

"Oh," I said again. Understanding started to dawn on me.

"So after that, I still kept trying to help her, even though I don't think there's much I can do. But I kept trying to encourage her to eat, and just, I don't know, be a good friend to her and make her feel welcome in DC. And I think it helped, but— I mean, I can't do it by myself. Her dad's always gone, and when he's in town he and her mom just fight all the time. Nothing feels certain in that house— Nothing feels stable. I hate going over there. They've never let her live in one place more than three years, did you know that? And her mom always compliments her on how thin she is and complains about how fat she is, she makes her go to these awful weight loss yoga classes with her, and I don't even know if it's about food, in the end, and Polly doesn't have any other friends. Except you and Talia, now."

The words were pouring out of her. Even if I had known what to say, I couldn't have gotten a word in.

"And so while I was doing all this research trying to figure out how to help her, I just started poking around the internet reading sci-fi stories about, like, people uploading their consciousness to the cloud or whatever, just anything about not having a body, and that's how I came across what we're doing now. I thought maybe if she had an escape, it would help."

Cleo finally took a breath.

"So that's why," she said. "Not because I wanted to make a video or a movie. I mean, it's a fucking superpower, and I love it for that reason, too. And I really do like the idea of helping other girls who are trying this, which is why I was posting about it, and I think uploading some videos would be cool, even though I understand why y'all don't. But—" She stopped for a second, and I heard her exhale unsteadily. "It wasn't because I wanted to get internet famous. It was never that. It was for her."

I had no idea what to say. I settled on the obvious. "You," I said, "are such a good friend, Cleo."

She laughed, and I was surprised to hear a touch of bitterness. "A friend," she said. "Yes."

We sat there for a minute, maybe two, as I tried to place what I had heard in her voice.

And then an image sprang into my head—Polly and Cleo at

work a few days earlier, Polly laughing a big, delighted laugh as Cleo tried and failed to juggle six bags of corn chips. Cleo smiling so big as the bags fell to the ground, not at her own joke but at Polly's face, Polly's joy.

"Cleo," I said, "when you told us about Polly, last fall, you said she was a friend."

"Yes." I had never heard her sound so wary, almost scared.

"Well." I cleared my throat, then continued cautiously. "You've told us about girls you have crushes on, too, and it's always— It's different. You say it's a crush, or you say she's hot, but you don't just say she's a friend."

Cleo was quiet for so long I thought she might have gotten angry. But finally, she whispered, "I thought of her as just a friend. At first."

"Oh," I said softly, again.

Cleo shrank away from me in the dark.

I should have known. I sifted through the past year of our friendship, the memories golden and precious. Talia and me talking about Michael and Adam while Cleo listened avidly, asking questions, never talking about girls in DC. The way Cleo had told us about Polly, especially as summer got closer, the champagne bubbles in her voice over the phone. And Cleo now, always by Polly's side.

It was true that Cleo had told us about her crushes before. She had come out to us when we were all fourteen, and she was out at school and with her family, though I knew that— like me—most of her acquaintances in Little Beach assumed she was straight, and she had never corrected them. At home, she had gone on dates with some girls and even had one short-lived sophomore-year relationship with a flute player named Katrina, which ended amicably after a few months of making out and going to movies together.

I knew how she talked about girls she liked. But I don't think I'd ever heard her talk about a girl she loved.

I reached out for her hand, which was wrapped tightly around her leg. She let go, slowly, and allowed me to hold it between both of my own.

"I'm so sorry I didn't know," I said. Cleo exhaled again, and this time it sounded like a sob. "I love you," I repeated, "I'm so sorry I didn't know."

"How could you have known?" she said finally, her voice shaky. "No one knows. Polly doesn't know."

"Oh, Cleo." I scooted closer to her and wrapped my arms around her as she broke out in tears. As long as I'd known her, I'd heard Cleo cry only twice—once when she sprained her wrist falling from her skates, and once over the phone, when her favorite younger brother was in the hospital with pneumonia. This was worse than either of those times, a torrent of crying that poured out of her as if it had been already brimming over, waiting for the moment to release itself. "I'm so sorry," I said. "I'm so sorry."

She rubbed her face and then tucked her head back onto my shoulder. "Please don't tell anyone," she said. Her breathing was starting to steady.

"Of course I won't. But are you sure, with Polly . . . I mean, that she doesn't—"

"I'm positive," she said with conviction. "Honestly, I'm not sure if Polly is interested in dating anyone at all. She said once that because she moved around so much, she tried to never have crushes. But I know she isn't interested in me." She took another long, shuddering breath. "Like, I know she loves me. We're best friends. But I've tried to . . . to give her hints, and just see if she responds, but there's nothing. And I don't want to mess up what we have."

I nodded and gave her shoulders a squeeze. "Okay," I said. "I understand."

She sighed and pulled away from me, wiping her eyes. "Thank you," she said.

"For what?"

"For asking. I wanted to tell you. And Talia, eventually, too. I just . . ." She shrugged. "I was scared. Everything is going so well this summer. Better than I could have ever imagined. I didn't want to mess it up."

I needed the words to explain the ferocity of my love for Cleo, the importance of her, right alongside my mom and my dad and Talia, the certainty that we would always be a part of each other's lives. But I didn't know how.

"There's nothing wrong with wanting more," I said finally, softly. "It's nothing to be ashamed of. And besides, there's nothing you could tell me that would make the slightest bit of difference in our friendship." I touched her hand. "I love you so much."

She laughed. "I love you too," she said. "I'm glad you know. About her and about why I wanted to do . . ." She gestured expansively in the air. "All of this."

"Do you think it worked?" I asked her, and she gave me a look.

"Of course it worked," she said. "Do you think you've been hallucinating for the last few weeks?"

I rolled my eyes. "Not the ritual. Polly. Do you think she's doing better?"

Cleo bit her lip and looked out at the road. She smoothed her hands over her thighs.

"I've never heard her sound happier than when she's invisible," Cleo said.

"That's good," I said.

"Good," Cleo repeated softly. "Yeah."

In the grass beside us, a frog croaked. Out beyond the next row of houses, the sea drew in and out. And Cleo and I breathed, that same in and out, next to each other—until my mother opened the door and asked me to come inside, and I looked for Cleo beside me, and she was gone.

17   LIGHTNING

On Monday, the rain that had held off all week finally broke loose. While I was running that morning, flying invisible down the beach, the sky kept getting darker and deeper, as if night were coming on as soon as it had left. The first drops fell as I was walking in my door. The horizon pulled down lightning from the clouds all day.

Talia and Cleo and Polly came over around eleven, after my parents had gone to work and I had taken a post-run nap, and for a few hours, it was nice. We put on a movie. I made boxed mac 'n' cheese, which Cleo and I split while Talia and Polly ate leftover salad and drank unsweet iced tea. It felt almost like the holidays. I had never spent time with Cleo or Polly in winter.

But by around two in the afternoon, as we were doing a puzzle of a horse, it had stopped being cozy and turned claustrophobic. Talia was flipping channels, lingering on one just long enough to make it jarring when she switched. Cleo, who hated puzzles but also hated giving up on anything, was getting increasingly frustrated at her inability to find a piece in the horse's mane.

And Polly had never looked gloomier. Her shoulders hunched over the coffee table as she put together the puzzle with grim, methodical focus. I had just found the final piece of the horse's rump, when Polly said, "Fuck this horrible fucking puzzle." She sat back and sighed so deeply that I was surprised any air remained in her body.

"What's wrong?" I asked.

"Nothing," she murmured.

"Don't give us that," Talia said, eyes still absently trained on the TV.

"Yeah, what's up?" Cleo scooted away from the table with a sigh of her own. "I mean, this puzzle sucks. But you've been weird all day."

"My parents," Polly said after a minute. "I talked to them this morning, while you were in the shower, Cleo. They're not getting divorced like I thought."

"That's great!" Talia said bracingly.

Polly didn't smile. She said, "They're moving. Or we, I guess. We're moving."

"Wait, what?" Cleo leaned forward, and Talia turned off the TV. Polly had our attention now, and she looked uncomfortable with it, folding her sharp knees up to her chest.

"My dad's work said that he has to be somewhere in Texas. The job in DC was supposed to last two years, but it didn't. So we're leaving. In the middle of September. That's why he and my mom were fighting. Because she wanted to stay. But I guess she lost."

She spoke in a monotone, her jaw set hard and square.

Cleo was drumming her hands on the edge of the table, impatient. She looked past distressed, almost panicked. "But they can't just do that," she said. "They can't just take you away before your senior year. That doesn't make any sense."

Polly laughed joylessly. "They have done it so many times, Cleo. Honestly, I should've expected it."

"You can stay with me," Cleo said, sitting up straight. Her smile sparked to life. "We have enough space. We'd have to share a bedroom." She coughed, waved a hand in the air abstractly. "But that's no big deal, it would be fine."

I glanced at Talia. What would it be like if Talia suddenly had to move? Or if I did? I had started school with her every year for as long as I could remember. She met my eyes, and I knew she was thinking the same thing. I felt a pang of gratitude for her, her constant, steady presence and her love.

"My family adores you," Cleo continued. "My parents think you're great. We could work it out."

Polly shook her head.

"We can," Cleo insisted, and there it was again, that edge of panic.

"Cleo," Polly said sharply. "I can't, okay? My mom is obsessed with keeping the family together. Whatever that means."

Cleo opened her mouth and closed it again, bit her lip. I could see the arguments turning in her head: the phone call to her mom and dad, the promise of Polly helping to babysit her younger siblings, the letter she'd write to Polly's parents. But she didn't say anything else.

"I'm so sorry, Polly," Talia said quietly. Polly inclined her head in Talia's direction, barely an acknowledgment.

I asked, "How can we help?"

Polly looked up from her knees. Her eyes were watery. Outside, the thunder cracked against the windows.

"Can we do it?" she asked. "Now? Out on the beach?"

Talia looked outside, at the wall of water that was the sky.

"What, are we gonna get hit by lightning?" Polly asked, roughness at the edge of her voice, and she had a point. Lightning couldn't strike what wasn't there.

I wasn't afraid. The rain was so dense I could barely see ten feet in front of me; no one was out on the beach. Even the crabs and seagulls had disappeared. We turned ourselves in my entryway, so that even if a neighbor had been watching, all they would have seen was the front door open and close, as if someone had cracked it to go outside and then decided against it.

The air on the beach was sweet and cool—it had been so hot—and the rain falling through us felt extraordinary, disconcerting and sexy, like a full-body shiver. I knew the others felt it, too, and for a while we just sat there in the damp sand, feeling it and watching the waves roil and toss.

"I want to do this more," Talia said eventually.

"What do you mean by that?" I asked. "Sit in the rain?"

"Not that specifically. I . . ." She trailed off, or the rain got louder. "It just feels right, you know?"

"Yes," Cleo said.

Too right, I thought, and said, "Yes."

Polly spoke up, farther down the beach from me. "But ultimately it's useless, right?"

"Don't say that," Cleo said. She was a little in front of me and to the right. The waves washed up almost to my toes, and I thought about how it felt to have the ocean water move through you. I hadn't felt it since that first night. "It's not useless if we like doing it."

"Yeah, but it is, kind of. All day I've been thinking, how can I use this to make my parents let me stay in DC? And the only thing I've come up with is, like, give myself up to the government or something. I'm sure there are more evil scientists in DC than there are in Texas."

The sarcasm in her voice was palpable. When we'd started, that same thought had flickered through my mind, the idea of being discovered and forced to endure an endless series of lab tests. But that was like something out of a movie. Of all the shadowy, incoherent fears I'd had since that first night in the ocean, I had never really worried about government scientists. They didn't give a fuck about four teenagers haunting a mini-golf course in North Carolina.

"You're not going to have to become a lab mouse to stay in DC," said Cleo. "We will figure something out. I promise."

Lightning struck the ocean. The wind swirled and the rain lashed around us, through us. I felt as if it might blow us away.

"I wish we could just stay here," said Polly softly. "That's how I've always felt. Every place I go, I want to stay forever. And I always, always have to leave."

"Polly, I'm so sorry," said Talia. She sounded sadder than I'd heard her in a long time.

"If I always have to leave, what's the point?" Polly continued, as if Talia hadn't said anything. Her voice grew wild, like an animal snarling, at the end of its leash. "What's the fucking point of any of it? It would be easier for my parents if they didn't have to drag me around. If I was just fucking gone, if I—"

"Stop that," said Cleo, sharp. "Stop it right now. You're not going anywhere. You can't." I heard the same desperation from last night, on my steps, and I ached for Cleo—for Cleo and for Polly both, for different reasons. I wanted to hold them in my arms until their pain eased. "You can't," Cleo said again. "You can't."

After a long time, Polly said, "I know. It'll be okay. We'll figure something out."

She sounded tired.

"We'll figure something out," repeated Cleo.

I don't know how long we stayed there without talking. It could have been an hour, or two. It felt like the first night, alone on the beach, surrounded by water. Except that now none of this was new, and the scary thing was also mundane. There would be moving boxes. Tearful goodbyes. A new high school for Polly, a new address for me to mail postcards.

But for now we were invisible, and the air was white noise around us. I lay back in the sand and kept dozing off, waking up afraid that my friends had left me—"Talia?" I said, more than once, and she said beside me, "I'm here," and Polly and Cleo echoed, "Me too," "Me too."

Finally—and this, too, was like the first night—someone sighed and shuffled, and someone else said, "Should we go back?"

"Yes," I said. I had gotten cold. We had all planned to go to the rink that night as usual, but I wasn't scheduled to work, and I thought about staying in. Mom was making Bolognese.

We walked back to my house still invisible, our feet barely making prints and the rain filling the air around us with sound. I had no idea what time it was, but my parents' cars weren't in the driveway, which meant we weren't late for work yet. I opened the door.

"Let's go upstairs," I said, in case my parents came home while we were changing back. I walked through someone accidentally, and if I'd had cheeks to fill with color, I would've blushed. In my room, the door closed on its own. I sat cross-legged with my back against my bed, thinking, *I am visible. See me, see me, see.*

Maybe I was just tired. I hadn't gotten that much sleep, after all, and we had been out on the beach for a long time. Maybe it had taken more out of me than I thought, doing it in public. Or maybe it was Polly's sadness, covering everything, hopeless and heavy. But whatever the reason, turning back was the hardest it had ever been. My body clung to the lack of being. The harder I pushed with my mind, the more deeply I tried to sink into meditation, the more the pleasure of being invisible hummed and danced in my blood. The power inside me sang as I tried to walk away from it.

I focused on my breathing and tried to remember everything I loved about being in my body. The muscles of my calves as I finished a sprint. The bright, heady pain of a scraped knee. My pajamas on my skin, salt on my tongue. Adam's mouth on mine.

That did it, finally. The cool-sheet feeling faded and I exhaled. I kept my eyes closed for a second. My heart was beating fast. It had been getting harder to come back, but never that hard.

When I opened my eyes, the others were still transforming. I looked down. I had seen it before, but it never stopped being weird. Weird like strange—I could literally see their bones—and also weird like intimate, like watching someone change into a swimsuit times a billion. Only when I could hear all of them shifting on the carpet did I look up again.

Polly pulled up her hair. Cleo hugged herself. Talia smoothed her hands down her legs.

"It's getting harder," I said.

"No it isn't," said Cleo.

The rain pounded against the windows, and we sat together in my bedroom, us and our bodies and that lie.

18 SUNRISE

It was five minutes past six in the morning, and Adam was late. I stood on the beach, waiting for him and watching the sky change color in the east. I bent over to stretch my hamstrings and saw the world in reverse: dark sky lightening to the bright line of the horizon, darkening into the ocean again.

I made a deal with myself: I would wait for him for as long as it took to go through my normal stretches twice instead of once. Then I would start running whether he was there or not. I lowered myself into a lunge on the sand, feeling the ache in my calf.

During our most recent late-night phone call, Adam had teased me about not honoring our pact from earlier in the summer. "You know, O'Connell—" I loved it when he called me that. No one else ever called me by my last name. "I seem to remember you offering to run with me one of these mornings. I've been getting faster. You scared?"

"Saturday morning," I shot back. "Six a.m. The beach in front of my house."

"Why do I have to come to you?" he asked, all faux offense. "Also, six a.m.? I've been going in the evenings."

"Sunrise is the best time to run," I said, and even though it was too late and I was so tired, I smiled. "Take it or leave it. I would love to beat you."

"Deal," he said, laughing. "Saturday. Six a.m. You're a maniac."

Now, on the beach, I stood up and pulled my leg into a quad stretch, closing my eyes. A tumbleweed of nervousness danced in my belly. I wasn't worried about keeping up with Adam—if anything, he should've been worried about keeping up with me—but ever since that morning running with Polly, I hadn't run without turning invisible first. I had gotten so used to the lightness of it. I had never timed myself exactly, but I knew that I was faster that way. I felt like a gull skimming over the waves, my feet barely touching the sand.

Now, here, I was all too aware of the heaviness of my sneakers and the damp cotton of my socks. The heat already rising from the dawning sun to settle on top of me.

"I'm sorry I'm late!" I opened my eyes to see him jogging toward me, shirtless. I nearly fell over.

"Don't sneak up on me like that," I said. "I was taking a nap here. Like a flamingo."

"You're the one who set the time." He shook his head and grinned. "You do this every morning? I'm impressed. Also, hi." He wrapped me in a hug, and I lingered in it, only my sports bra between us. Despite how often I had replayed the memory of our date, the sensation of his skin against mine still felt new.

"Hi," I said into his chest.

He pulled away a little. "You okay?"

"Yeah. Just tired." I started to fake a yawn and then yawned for real. I looked up at him and made a split-second decision. "I know I said I wanted to race, but do you think we could maybe save that for another day and just jog a few miles? I woke up feeling kind of off this morning."

He stepped back with an expression of shock. "She's afraid! Oh my God, she's afraid she's going to lose!"

"No," I moaned. "I still want to kick your ass. Just, like, another time."

"Uh-huh. Well, I wasn't planning to admit that I feel terrible because I couldn't fall asleep last night, but if you absolutely insist on a light jog, I'm not going to argue."

"Okay, then." I gestured toward the rising sun. "Shall we?"

He let me set the pace. It was slow, dramatically slower than I had gotten used to—even, alarmingly, slower than a jog would've been for me before the ritual. A part of me worried that Adam was judging me for it. I kept glancing over at him, trying to tell if he seemed bored or annoyed.

But no—he looked fine. Happy, even. He stayed a beat behind me, and I started to enjoy myself. The birdlike, incorporeal speed of my invisible self was like a miracle, and I missed it. But this was good, too. My sneakers on the yielding sand, my sore awakening muscles, the breeze hitting the sweat on my skin. And Adam next to me. I looked at him again, and he looked right back, smiling.

"Is this too slow?" I asked him. Being able to speak comfortably was never a good sign, speed-wise.

"No," he said. "It's good. It's nice. Not everything has to be a race. Especially this early in the morning."

"The temperature is incredible, though, right?"

"Maybe, but at what cost?"

I laughed. "So why couldn't you get to sleep?"

He yawned, nearly tripping over a dead jellyfish, then said, "Jen and I are going to Atlanta tomorrow. To visit my mom for a few days. I was kind of hoping we could go out again, but I guess I'll have to postpone asking you until next weekend."

"Can I pre-accept?" I teased.

"Yes, definitely." He grinned, but there was something off. I waited, tried to keep my breath even, until he said, "She has a boyfriend."

"Oh."

"She wants us to meet him."

I tried to remember exactly when Adam's parents had gotten divorced. It was sometime in middle school, so four years ago? Five?

"Is this the first time you've ever met someone she's dating?"

"Yeah. I mean, as far as I know, it's the first time she's dated anyone. She's never talked about it before."

"That's probably for the best," I said.

"Yeah, I think so. Anyway, this is the first person who's been serious. She says she thinks we'll like him."

I tried to imagine meeting someone one of my parents was dating. It was unfathomable. I had never once worried about my parents getting divorced, which, I realized now after spending so much time with Polly and Adam, was not necessarily common.

"What has she told you?" I asked.

"His name is George. He's a meteorologist."

"Like on TV?"

"No, not like that. He does some other kind of weather science, more lab-based. I don't know. She said he's a cyclist. She said they go for bike rides together on weekends. Oh, and he's divorced, too, and he has a daughter, but she's older. I think she just graduated college."

"So has your mom met his daughter?"

"Not yet."

We ran in silence for a minute, letting another early-morning runner pass us with her dog.

"It's weird," he continued eventually. "To think about her dating someone else. It's not the worst thing. I mean, I want her to be happy, and I never thought that my parents were going to get back together after they got divorced. They made it pretty clear it was final at the time. But now, if it is really serious with this guy . . . I mean, do they get married? And if so, he'll be there when we come for holidays, and maybe my mom changes her name? And I guess Jen and I will have a new sibling." He shook his head. "Anyway, that's why I was up late last night. Falling asleep has never been easy for me, but especially now, I just can't stop thinking about how weird this all is. I'm so jealous of people who can close their eyes and just be out."

"I'm like that most of the time," I admitted. "Though not recently."

"I'm jealous." He swatted me gently on the arm. "Most of the time. What's been happening recently?"

I didn't answer for a while. I was kicking myself for saying anything to indicate that something was wrong. It was just so easy to talk to Adam. He was such a good listener. I wanted to tell him everything, about the invisibility and how it felt sometimes like it was dragging me under, and I knew that I couldn't. But maybe I could tell him something.

"There's this situation," I said, improvising. "With— With a friend." Maybe it would be easier to anonymize if I didn't explain that it was about all four of us. That it was, in some ways, about me, too. "It's not— I mean, I can't totally explain the details. But we're sort of having this argument about something she's doing, which is a good thing sometimes, and maybe sometimes not a hundred percent healthy. I'm worried that she's going to end up getting hurt. And I can see it happening, and I'm telling her I'm seeing it, and she's not stopping. And, I mean— I'm enabling it, too. I know I am and I don't know how to stop."

Adam was quiet next to me as I caught my breath. It had been a lot of speaking to do while running, and beyond that it was strange to speak about at all. I felt like I was talking to him in a different language, both hoping and not hoping that he could understand.

"I think," he said finally, slowly, "I know what you're talking about. Talia, right?"

If I hadn't had the momentum of my legs already carrying me forward, I would've frozen. I swallowed hard and went over my words in my head. I hadn't let anything slip. I would've known, if I had let something slip. I thought about our gatherings on the beach, in the ocean, at work. We had always made sure to speak quietly, or not at all, if anyone else was around. None of the others would've said anything. Finally I glanced down—my limbs were all present and accounted for. So what could Adam possibly know?

He continued without my asking. "I'm really sorry. It's got to be hard, seeing how Michael treats her."

I was so relieved I tripped over a conch shell and nearly fell on my face. "Whoa," Adam said as I stumbled. "You okay?"

"Yeah," I said, and I laughed. Of course he didn't know anything. "Yeah. Shells, right?"

"Uh-huh." He looked a little bemused, but he didn't run away from me, so that was a good sign.

I got my legs back underneath me and tried to breathe deeply as we kept jogging. Maybe he took my silence for reticence, because he said, "We don't have to talk about it if you don't want to."

Talia. Michael. I went back over my words again.

Their relationship, their decaying, infuriating, passive-aggressive relationship—I had worried about it almost from the beginning. But with the exception of Cleo and Polly, no one else had ever seemed to think it was unhealthy. They were just another beautiful couple, laughing on the beach.

"Aren't you friends with Michael?" I asked. Our high school was huge, but it still felt like everybody knew everybody, and Michael and Adam were part of the same group of soccer-guys-slash-swimmers-slash-runners who were represented at every social event, inside or outside of school.

Adam answered that with a sharp laugh. "Michael is a jack-ass," he said. "We're not mortal enemies or anything. Maybe he thinks we're friends, I don't know. But I just . . ." Adam shook his head decisively. "He thinks he's so cool and funny, and he wants everyone else to think he's cool and funny, so he'll make fun of anyone if it gets a rise out of his friends."

"Wow." I had never heard Adam talk shit about anybody. "I didn't know you disliked him that much."

He glanced at me with some surprise. "Do you not?"

"Oh, no, I can't stand him," I said, and Adam laughed. "I mean, Talia can be pretty argumentative, even with people she loves, but they fight all the time. I don't know why anyone would want to be in a relationship where they fight that often. And I wouldn't mind it if it was just that, but he's so mean to her when they fight. Then he ignores her. Then he's so sweet for like a week, and then he's mean to her again, and it starts all over."

"That must be hard to see."

"It's awful." I exhaled. "Every time I get close to telling her to break up with him, she says she doesn't want to talk about it."

We ran in silence for a few minutes. Then Adam said, "Is that all that's bothering you?"

I could have said yes. He probably would have believed me.

But we were the only people on the beach, and he was sweet and good, and for one precarious moment, I wanted to tell him everything. It would have been such a relief. I opened my mouth.

The faces of my friends flashed in front of me, half-transparent and laughing in the firefly light of the disco ball.

I closed my mouth.

He had noticed my silence, though—of course he had—and suddenly I saw an opening for something I had been genuinely wanting to tell him, had not yet figured out how to say. Something honest.

"Not bothering me, exactly," I said. Now that I was actually saying it, this lesser secret, I was having a harder time than I expected. I felt his curiosity, light as his footsteps beside mine.

"I, um. I'm bi. Sexual."

Jesus, why had I said it that way?

"I hope you don't—" I swallowed. "I hope that doesn't change anything."

"Hey." He slowed to a stop, and I slowed to match him. His face was serious, and my stomach turned over.

"Of course it doesn't change anything," he said, reaching out for my hand. My blood pounded, from the running and from the pressure of his hand in mine and from the look in his eyes, so kind, so absolutely unbothered. "Who else knows?"

I shrugged and smiled as the adrenaline started to drain away. The air was already hot, but a breeze swept off the ocean, cooling the sweat on my neck. "My family. Talia and Cleo, obviously, and their parents. Cleo's grandparents. And Polly, now."

"Can I ask why . . ." He hesitated, as if choosing his words carefully. "Why you feel like you need to keep it a secret?"

It was a reasonable question. It wasn't as if our school was completely hostile to queer people; it was a big school, fairly diverse, and there was an LGBTQ student group, albeit not a particularly active one. I had never witnessed any of those kids getting bullied or harassed. Not that I would necessarily know if they had been.

"I don't feel like I *have* to keep it a secret." I squinted at the sun, trying to figure out a way to explain why I kept this part of myself hidden. "I'm not ashamed. And I don't really think anyone would make a big deal about it, at least not to my face. But I've just . . . I've always felt like coming out would be more trouble than it's worth. All that fuss, for what, you know? I mean, I've never liked anyone enough to want to date them, until you."

"You don't tell very many people much about yourself at all, do you?" His voice was gentle.

I shook my head. "I'm sorry, but I'm picky."

He laughed. "Well," he said, "I won't tell anyone. But I'm grateful you trust me enough to tell me."

"Yeah, of course." I squeezed his hand. I was glad I had told him, but it felt strange and new, being this intimate with someone who was not a friend. Not bad, exactly, but new. "Should we turn around?"

"Yeah, let's."

We started jogging back, even slower than before. A few minutes passed, and then he said, "Never liked anyone enough until me, huh?"

I looked at him and laughed at the smile he was trying to hide. "Oh my God."

"Actually, I have been meaning to ask you." He slowed to a stop, and his eyes crinkled. He said, "Callie, would you be interested in being my girlfriend?"

He was sweaty and smiling, his chest bare, hands on his hips, shining in the newly risen sun. He could've stepped out of a dream.

"I would be interested in that, yes," I said.

He kissed me, and we ran home, the light at our backs.

19 RUNAWAY

As I was skating to Talia's before work on Friday, the sun bit into me like a mouth into an apple, and I was tempted again to transform. That week, the air had twisted itself into a hard, bruising heat, the kind of heat that made me seriously question taking a job with no air-conditioning. It would be easy, disappearing. I was so good at it now, I didn't even have to close my eyes. The people in the cars on the road would watch me pass, slipping from the edges in—

I glanced down and nearly fell over. My left hand had started to shimmer.

See me, I told myself firmly, and I skated faster.

I was pouring sweat by the time I got to Talia's. I left my skates and socks at the bottom of the stairs. I gave a perfunctory knock before coming in and called, "Hello?"

"We're eating dinner, Callie," Mrs. Maris said from the kitchen. Her voice was quiet, terse. I could see half of her body, sitting at the head of the table, arms crossed. "Come and join us. We're almost done."

And I knew something was wrong.

They found out is the first thing I thought, which made me want to run. But Talia never would've been so careless. And they had invited me in; I couldn't leave Talia now. I slid into the kitchen, sitting down in the empty place reserved for guests.

"Would you like some pork, Callie?" Mr. Maris asked tightly.

I would. But no one else was eating. "No, thank you."

It was deadly quiet. Talia's eyes were red and her jaw was set, trembling. Her plate was untouched. But looking around the table, it was very clear that this was not about our powers. Her parents looked pissed and disappointed, not shocked or scared. Olivia looked as if she had just been crying. Angelica, tucked into her seat in the corner, eyes darting back and forth, was the only one who seemed unaffected. Mostly, she looked like she just didn't want to be there.

"Olivia," Mrs. Maris said. "Talia. Are we clear?"

Talia crossed her arms.

Olivia muttered, "I didn't even do anything."

"Olivia. Come on."

"Yes, okay, fine," Olivia said with a sigh that could've rattled windows.

"We're going to be late to work," Talia said. "Can I go?"

"That depends," said Mrs. Maris. "Are we clear?"

Talia shoved back her chair. "Personally, I am clear that I'm not going to sit here and be judged for having sex with my boyfriend, which is a normal and fine thing to do because I am seventeen fucking years old. Yes, I am *clear*." She got up, spun around, and ran upstairs.

"Talia!" shrieked Mrs. Maris; "Come back here," yelled Mr. Maris; "This is all her fault!" said Olivia, who burst into tears.

When Talia did not come back, her parents exchanged a look

and followed her upstairs. Olivia, now fully sobbing, slipped through the sliding door to the back deck. Angelica and I were left alone at the kitchen table. We looked at each other.

"How are you?" I asked after a moment.

She shrugged. "Fine."

Upstairs, we heard knocking on a door, Mr. Maris's voice: "Talia! Open up!"

I looked back to Angelica, who had pulled over Talia's untouched plate and was now digging into it. "We were all out today," she explained, like a newscaster. "I was on the beach with my friends and Olivia was at Hazel's. But Hazel had bad PMS so Olivia came back. And she found Talia and Michael, um . . ." Angelica looked uncomfortable for the first time.

"Oh."

"Yeah. So I guess Olivia called Mom and told her, and then Talia got really mad and went through Olivia's stuff and found some condoms. But then Mom got home and asked where Olivia had gotten the condoms, and Olivia said that Talia had given them to her. But Talia said that was bullshit and Olivia admitted she had stolen them. Or, borrowed, she said."

"I assume Michael had left by this point," I said, somewhat distracted by the persistent knocking upstairs.

"Yeah. I guess. I didn't get home until Mom and Dad were already here."

"How, um. How did Olivia find Talia's condoms?" I had helped Talia make her hiding place. It was a hollowed-out hardback edition of *Crime and Punishment* from our sophomore English class. Kind of an ominous place to hide contraceptives, actually, but effective until today, and it had been fun to cut out all the pages.

Angelica shrugged again.

"Also," I said as Mrs. Maris yelled, "Talia, I mean it!" above us, "is Olivia sleeping with her boyfriend? What's his name again?"

"Andrew. And she was going to. I don't know if she is anymore. I mean, she doesn't have any condoms."

"I assume Andrew could supply them."

"I don't know his situation. But Olivia and Talia aren't allowed to go on dates for a month now, so I doubt it would happen anytime soon, anyway." Angelica paused and took a bite, considering. "I really don't like Andrew or Michael, honestly."

I started clearing the dishes from the table. Might as well make myself useful. Through the window by the sink, I could see Olivia sitting on the porch, one hand pressing her phone to her ear, the other gesticulating wildly. Above us, I heard a door open, and Talia's parents called her name again, but this time, it sounded less angry and more confused. Then alarmed. Their footsteps moved into the other upstairs rooms. "Talia, where are you?" Mrs. Maris called, and just as I set down the stack of dishes, Talia whispered from beside me, "Don't be mad."

I spun around. There was no one there.

Angelica gave me a weird look and said, "You okay?"

"Yeah," I said, trying to sound like I wasn't about to pass out. Angelica went back to eating.

"Chill," Talia said very quietly, right next to my ear.

"Sorry, Angelica," I said. "It's just that your sister is my best friend, but sometimes I want to absolutely murder her."

"Same," Angelica said.

"Open the back door," Talia whispered.

"What are you up to this evening?" I said from between

gritted teeth. Above us, closet doors were opening, Talia's parents' yells getting louder, more worried.

"I was going to go over to my friend's house, but now Mom and Dad probably won't let me," said Angelica, sounding unhappy for the first time. "So I guess I'll just see if Olivia wants to watch TV with me."

"I'm going to go outside and get my fucking skates and go to work," Talia whispered.

"That's a terrible idea," I said.

"You think so?" Angelica looked outside, where Olivia was still on the phone. "I guess she's probably still too upset."

"Do it," Talia hissed.

I crossed the kitchen to the back door and opened it, stepping out onto the porch. Olivia turned around and looked at me. Her face was red and teary. "What?" she said.

"Are you okay?"

"I'm fine." She turned away from me and spoke into her phone. "Sorry, that's just Callie . . ."

I closed the door again, trusting that Talia had been able to get out. In the same moment, her parents came back into the kitchen, looking around. "Is Talia down here?"

"Nope," said Angelica. She finished the last bite of Talia's dinner.

"I don't know where she went," Mr. Maris said, crossing his arms again. His expression was changing from confusion to real worry, and I couldn't blame him. His daughter had disappeared from underneath his nose.

"Let me check outside," I said.

"Did you hear her come downstairs?"

211

"No, but maybe we just missed it. Angelica and I were talking." I was trembling from anger, from trying not to show it. "Maybe she's just getting her skates on for work."

"Oh, yes, I guess you're going to be late." Mrs. Maris ran her hands through her hair. "I'm sorry, Callie, I didn't mean this to take so much of your time. I— Goodness."

"It's no problem," I reassured her. I went past them, out the front door, and ran down the steps. Talia was nowhere. But I opened the little storage closet underneath the house, and there she was—almost all the way visible, but not quite.

"Close the door," she snapped. Her body shimmered, slipped. "I have to focus."

I closed the door and dug my fingernails into my upper arm. She emerged a minute later, looking tired, skates in hand.

"Talia—" I started.

"Let's just go."

We put on our skates in silence. As we were standing up, the front door opened and Mrs. Maris called, "Callie, did you find her?"

"Yeah, she was getting her skates," I called back, though Talia was glaring at me in a way that I was pretty sure meant shut up. "We do have to go," I added. I wasn't a complete traitor.

"Talia? How did you get down there?" Mrs. Maris sounded mystified.

"I walked," Talia shouted. "We're going."

"We still need to talk," her mom called back, but Talia was already racing down the street with long, decisive strokes, her hair dancing in the wind. I shot Mrs. Maris an apologetic look and followed.

Talia was going so fast that it took me a couple of minutes

to catch up, and by the time I did, I was breathing heavily, my quads feeling the ache of the sprints I'd run a few days ago.

"What the hell," I panted.

"I should be asking you the same thing." She threw the words over her shoulder at me. The road was busier than normal, and we had to skate single file, so she was still a little ahead of me. I couldn't see her face.

"I didn't do anything!"

"You told my mom where I was."

"I wasn't going to lie, you were right there. What were you going to do, disappear on them again? And also, by the way, what the fuck was that?"

"Are you seriously judging me for using my power for something that harmless?" She shot me a look over her shoulder. The disgust in it shook me.

"Your parents were worried," I said. "And besides, they could've seen you. They could've found out."

"First, they were being huge assholes and deserved it, and second, they were never going to find out, Callie. I'm fast. I'm good at this."

"I know, but—"

"Jesus!" She moved onto the sidewalk, even though it was supposed to be reserved for pedestrians, and turned to start skating backward. I slowed to match her pace. She narrowed her eyes. "I assume Angelica told you what happened? That Olivia fucking tattled on me for having sex in my own bed? And then it turns out she's also been stealing my condoms?"

"She did tell me that."

"And that I'm grounded from dates with Michael for basically the entire last month of summer?"

I nodded.

"Then you can see why I had to leave that conversation, and in fact the entire house, as quickly as possible."

I nodded again. "But, Talia," I started, "maybe it isn't that bad not to see Michael for a while. I mean, lately, he's been—"

"God, not you too."

"I'm not judging you for having sex with him! That's fine! I'm just saying—"

"I know what you're fucking saying," she snapped, and I noticed too late that the sidewalk panel behind her was uneven, a little higher than the others, just enough that when the back of her skate hit it, it tripped her up, sent her feet catapulting forward and her body back. Her eyes widened as she fell through the air and slammed into the concrete. She knew how to fall safely—we all did—and I was sure, even as I veered off into the sand at the edge of the sidewalk to stop myself, that she wasn't really injured. But I also knew how those bruises would feel in the morning. Lying on the ground on her side, she burst into tears.

"Oh, Talia," I said helplessly. I knelt beside her and helped her sit up. She leaned into me and cried into my shoulder. We sat there for minutes while she sobbed and I shot glares at passersby to make them cross the street.

"I'm sorry," she said finally, her voice shaky. Her crying was starting to taper off. "It's just, things with Michael were already bad, and now he's going to be really, really mad because of this, and my parents are mad at me because of Michael, and Olivia's mad at me because she messed up, and Angelica—"

"Angelica's not mad at you."

"I guess not, but Angelica will probably find a reason to be mad at me tomorrow." She sniffed and wiped her nose. "It feels like you and Cleo and Polly and this thing we do are the only good things in my life right now. I don't know, I shouldn't have done it at home. I know I shouldn't have. But I was so frustrated, and I panicked, and it just—" She pulled away. "It was almost like I didn't choose to. Like it just happened. A reaction. Has that ever happened to you?"

"No, but I understand." I could imagine, storming away from a fight, how it could feel like the only option.

"Anyway, and then I thought you were mad at me, too, and everything—everything felt bad." She pulled me into a sloppy sideways hug. "I'm sorry."

"It's okay," I said.

Holding her there on the sidewalk, feeling the knots of her spine and the sweaty tangle of her hair, I wanted to mean it. And in some ways I did: *It's okay* is a two-word translation of *I forgive you,* and *I'm not angry,* and *you're still my best friend in the world.* All of those things were true.

But *it's okay* also meant that it, all of this, everything around us, was fine. And that was increasingly hard to believe. More and more I felt that we were moving toward a breaking.

20 TOO MUCH

We were late to work, of course, by nearly forty minutes. It was busy, with a particularly difficult crowd. Before we'd even arrived, Polly had cleaned up a massive soda spill and Cleo had dealt with a man insisting that the last time he'd visited, socks had been free. (In the nearly fifty-year history of the Little Beach Skating Rink, socks had never been free.) We had to kick out a group of older folks who were drinking—it took both me and Talia repeatedly referencing our NO ALCOHOL signage—and calm a panicked child whose mother had gone outside for a cigarette.

At the end of the night, Cleo said wearily, "Callie, Talia, I'm not mad that y'all were late." I had filled her and Polly in during the two-minute breaks between crises. "But since we set up on our own, can you clean?"

We had little choice. Cleo and Polly went home, and Talia and I listened to Lizzo and cleaned up quietly, not even bothering to become invisible. I wanted to, but I didn't want to be the first to do it. And Talia didn't bring it up—just passed me the broom and started cleaning skates. Later, after dropping off Talia at her house, I did disappear myself, just for a few minutes, just for the rest of the skate home.

Things were better the next day. We met up in front of my house, and the water was calm and cool. It was easy to float. Cleo and Polly had gotten some sleep and forgotten about the injustice of the night before, and even Talia seemed okay.

"I called Michael last night after work," she told me. "He was pissed at me."

She didn't sound upset, and I said, "And you are . . . all right with that?"

"Oh, I cried a ton," she said, her tone matter-of-fact. "Eventually he apologized. And, I mean, we are still going to see each other during the day and stuff. And if it's okay with you guys, I might skip cleanup some nights to hang out with him. We just can't go on normal dates."

I met Cleo's eyes and she shrugged. *We can't make them break up,* she seemed to be saying, and she was right. I sighed and ducked my head under the water.

When I came back up, Polly was in the middle of a sentence: ". . . happened? I still don't totally get it."

Talia explained. "I think after the initial shock of the whole situation, my mom was more upset about my disappearing on them than anything else. Not that she saw anything," she added quickly. "Just, you know, I think it freaked her out. My dad, too."

"I mean, yeah," Cleo said. "I'm not surprised."

"Come on," Talia said, defensiveness starting to creep in around the edges of her voice. "I know I shouldn't have done it. I don't need more judgment."

"I'm not judging," said Polly. "I would've done the same thing, I think."

We floated in silence. The sun disappeared behind a cloud, a breeze swept through, and I shivered. Then the cloud moved and warmth fell on my skin again.

"How often are you guys doing it these days?" I asked.

A minute or two passed.

"Well, when we clean up after work," Cleo said eventually, a little reluctance slowing her voice. I knew this already. Last night had been an exception: We had made a habit of disappearing after the rink closed almost every night. "And sometimes in the mornings, when Polly and I are skating down to your house or Talia's for the day."

"Mostly the same for me," said Talia. "And, I guess, in the shower after work. It reminds me of that time we went out in the rain."

Polly nodded. "Yeah. And sometimes when I run in the mornings."

"Yeah, me too," I said, although for me, it wasn't sometimes. It was every morning. I knew that Polly was lying, too, that it was every morning for her, because at least two or three mornings out of the week, we were running together. "It feels like you're . . ."

"Lighter," Polly finished. "Faster."

"Yeah."

The current was slowly drifting us down the beach. Far in the distance, in the direction we were floating, was a group of people in the water and another on the beach who could've been kids from school. Or it might have been just more tourists, out enjoying the ocean on another normal summer day.

"Do you think we're doing it too much?" I asked.

No one answered for a long time. Long enough that we floated past the house in front of us, and past another and another, until finally we were within shouting distance of the groups I had seen from down the shore. It turns out they were people we knew. Michael and some of his friends were in the water, and Adam was with a big group on the sand, throwing a Frisbee.

"I'm gonna go talk to Michael," Talia said. She bit her lip and smiled, and I wished she didn't sound so excited.

"Isn't that your boyfriend?" Polly asked me, inclining her head toward Adam.

"I suppose it is." I smiled, too. "I might go say hi."

"Come on, Polly, let's do the rounds," Cleo said, swimming toward slightly shallower waters so she could walk. Talia paddled toward Michael; Polly followed. I started wading in past the breakers.

"Callie," Cleo called. I turned. Polly and Talia were with the group of guys farther out in the water. Cleo was standing, the waves bobbing up and down around her. Now I could see her torso, now only her head, now the tops of her thighs.

"Yeah?" I called back.

She said, "Maybe."

We didn't talk about it anymore that day. Talia and Michael made up and disappeared somewhere for a few hours. And Adam split away from his friends and hung out with me and Cleo and Polly. In the water, he put his hands on my waist and kissed me, tossed me in the air and caught me when I shrieked, and I felt like I was watching a movie about teenage happiness. Cleo and Polly kept catching my eye and grinning. I was embarrassed, but in a good way.

I stayed out on the beach with him for ages, after the others had all gone home to get ready for work. The tourists packed up their tents and chairs and dragged them inside to nap or prepare dinner. Adam and I sat in the sand at the edge of the ocean, making a drip castle.

"So . . ." We hadn't had any late-night phone calls since he'd gotten back from Atlanta on Wednesday. "How did the visit go? Did you meet the meteorologist?"

He made a face. "We met the meteorologist."

"Not good?"

"He was fine. It was just . . ." He exhaled heavily. "It was just weird, you know? We all went out to dinner together. He was really friendly with the waiter, joking with him and stuff, and my mom was laughing at it." He held his closed fist above the pile of sand we had made and opened it a little, letting the wet sand fall and crystallize on impact.

"That sounds . . . not too bad," I said cautiously. Talia's mom always joked with waiters. I had never thought it was a big deal as long as you tipped well and weren't a jerk about it, but maybe I was missing something.

"Yeah, it's objectively fine, but it's the kind of thing Mom wouldn't have laughed at when she was with my dad, you know? And then he was asking about track and school and Jen's marching band stuff, and trying so hard to be pleasant, and I get it, but it sucked." Adam looked at me and laughed a little. "It sucked, actually."

"I think that's understandable," I said.

He smoothed his hand over the edge of the castle, shoring up its sides with wet sand. I picked up another handful and dripped it onto the top of the castle. It was almost as high as my chin now, sitting down as we were.

"It feels good to say that, I guess," he continued. "I've been trying to convince myself to like him."

"I don't think you have to like him. As long as you're polite and you don't think he's hurting your mom."

"No, she's really happy. That's what's weirdest. It's been a long time since I've seen her this happy." He shook his head and smiled a little. "It's all okay. I don't want you to feel bad for me. It just feels like in this one small way, the basic foundation of my life is shifting. And I'm having trouble finding my footing." He looked over at me. "Does that make any sense at all?"

"Yes," I said softly. The sound carried out into the sea. I looked at the castle, at all the nooks and crannies that the sand had created as it stiffened. Adam inclined his head. He hadn't heard me.

"Yes, it makes sense. And I do feel a little bad for you," I said gently. He laughed, leaning back on his elbows. My eyes lingered on the lines of his torso. "But it's not like that's the only thing I feel for you."

"Oh yeah?" He raised an eyebrow. "What else do you feel for me?"

I meant to sit up fully, kneel, and turn to face him, so both of us were on the same side of the sandcastle. But as I put my foot down and pushed into the sand, it yielded into a sinkhole, and I lost my balance. I smashed into the sandcastle and fell, inelegantly, right on top of Adam.

"Fuck!" I shrieked. Wet brown sand covered both of us. Half

my body was on top of half of him. My right hand had landed on his stomach, perilously close to the top of his swim trunks, my left hand trapped in the wreckage of our castle.

I tried to sit up, but my hand just sank farther into the sand. "Oh my God— I'm sorry—"

He started laughing, big belly laughs that shook his stomach, and he reached an arm out and pulled me closer, sandy though I was. He lay back, taking me with him, and I started laughing, too. I propped my arm on his chest and looked at him. His face was close to mine, and I was aware suddenly of all the places where we were touching. I was practically on top of him, right there on the beach. It felt simultaneously goofy and sexy. I was so new to sexy as a real-life concept that I didn't know what to do with it.

"You were saying?" He smiled.

"I wasn't saying anything," I said. "I was falling over my own ass."

"Oh, no, you must be mistaken, I think you were about to say something very romantic."

I laughed and inched up his body, bringing my face closer to his. "Something romantic?"

"Yeah. I'm waiting." Underneath the smile and the strong arm holding me close was vulnerability, and I drank it in. His eyelashes and his cheekbones, his skin and his bones, his soft and his hard.

"I like you very much, Adam Liu," I whispered, and I kissed him. Between our two mouths, there was no sand, there was nothing at all.

I drifted through work that night. Drifted through disappearing after we shut the door behind the last family. Drifted invisible down the road on my skates when we were done cleaning. I had made out with Adam Liu on the beach. Me, making out with Adam Liu. When Cleo asked me what Adam and I had done after she and Polly had left, I made a face and said, "Nothing," and she immediately said, "Oh my God, you hooked up, didn't you?" Talia shrieked; Polly clapped. I laughed. I drifted on that happiness. The invisibility made it easier, like it made everything easier.

I turned myself back just long enough to take off my skates and go upstairs when I got home. I was so distracted from the memory of Adam that it took a few minutes of focus, sitting in the darkened living room, and even then I didn't quite make it all the way. If my parents had woken up and turned on the light, they could've seen through me.

I slipped back under to shower, feeling the heat of the water inside me, wondering absently, underneath the happiness, whether I was getting clean without any soap. I concluded that I probably wasn't. Thinking about the sensation of falling asleep on sandy hair—one I knew well—was what finally made me come back to myself. I don't know how long I stood in the shower, repeating, I am visible, see me, see, before I finally felt my own skin under my hands.

I looked down at my naked self under the water, clumsy and soft and angled all over, the crevices on my knees and my knobby toes. A body was such a strange thing. I closed my eyes while I washed my hair and chided myself a little for staying invisible so long. Just today I had asked my friends if we did it too much, and here I was, doing it too much.

The house was dark and quiet as I toweled my hair dry and put on my sleep shirt. I curled up under the covers and listened to the ocean. *Tomorrow*, I thought, *we can talk about how to taper off. Tomorrow we can figure it out. Tomorrow, I can be better.*

My alarm rang at five-thirty, waking me up for my sunrise run. I snoozed for ten minutes and then got out of bed. I had dreamed of making out with Adam while invisible, feeling my body bleed into his, the heat of him at the middle of me. The dream clung to me as I stumbled to my dresser to hunt for a clean sports bra. My lips were chapped from the dryness of the air in my room, but it felt as if it might have been from kissing. The arousal that had come over me, persistent and unfamiliar, wouldn't go away no matter how much I tried to shove it down. And the cool-sheet feeling of the invisibility was still with me, too. In my right foot, of all places, traveling up my shin to my knee.

I bent down to pull a pair of shorts from the pile of clean laundry on the floor and nearly fell over.

My leg.

Everything below my knee was invisible.

"Shit," I said, too loud. I froze, waiting for the sound of my parents' door opening, but I hadn't woken them up. I looked back down at my absent leg. I was breathing fast. "Shit," I said again.

I shut myself in my closet, just in case my parents had woken up without my realizing it, and sat in the dark. "I am visible," I whispered aloud. "See me."

I repeated it over and over, wrapping my arms underneath

my thighs to hold myself together, and very slowly, almost reluctantly, I thought I could feel the invisibility inching away. I was so used to the feeling by now that I wasn't absolutely sure. I kept chanting, tamping down my frantic breath with the familiar words. And then, tentative, terrified, I slid my right hand down my leg to see if I was solid again.

21 RUNNING ON SAND

In through the nose. One, two, three, four.

Out through the mouth. One, two, three, four, five, six.

My coach had taught me these breathing exercises for pre-meet jitters. Sunny days when my legs were itching with pent-up energy, waiting to go, go, go. Now, in the dark of my closet, I sat and touched my right leg and foot with tentative fingers as I counted over and over. My calf had a few days of stubble and my big toenail was a little jagged. I ran my finger over it until I had memorized its shape.

Only when my breathing had gotten back to normal did I step out of the closet and look down. My leg was there. I was whole. Shaking, but whole.

I laced my shoes, put on my running gear, crossed the road to the beach, and set off at a sprint toward Cleo's house. It was still too early for Talia to be awake, or Cleo for that matter, but I knew Polly would be out on her run. I could catch her on her way back.

After flying down the beach invisible, running normally felt too difficult. The rub of my socks was a distraction, the breath in my lungs a nuisance. But it was comforting, too. I pushed myself hard for the two miles down to Cleo's. When I got to the beach in front of her house, I was seeing stars. I put my hands on my knees, gasping, and watched the circles of light dance in my vision.

There was no one on the beach. I yelled, "Polly?"

No response. I walked a little farther and called her name again.

This time I heard her voice, faintly. "Callie?"

"Where are you?"

"In the water," she said. I kicked off my shoes and socks, peeled off my shorts, and waded in. It was low tide, calm and glassy, and I was in up to my waist when she said, "What's up?" Her voice was close and clear. I could have reached out and brushed my hand through her. "Is everything okay?"

"Turn back," I said through gritted teeth.

"What? Why?"

"Just, please, do it."

"Someone could see." She sounded nervous.

"Get down in the water. So just your head is poking up. I'll stand in front of you. No one's out here anyway."

I turned around to give her privacy and looked at the flat, quiet beach, the wind ruffling the dunes. I tried that breathing exercise again. In for four, out for six, calming my frantic heart. My legs started to ache from the hard run and the effort of keeping myself planted in the sand. I had cut myself shaving a few days ago, and it stung. I counted to forty before Polly said, "Okay."

I turned and sank into the water beside her. She was pale, with dark circles underneath her eyes, and looking at me with a wariness that she usually reserved for rowdy groups at the rink. "So?" she said. "What's going on?"

"When I woke up this morning, half my leg was missing," I said. Polly's expression didn't change. "Not on purpose," I clarified. "Like, it happened while I was sleeping. And then it was hard to turn it back. Really hard."

Polly blinked. "That's what's wrong?"

"Yes!" I heard my voice come out too loud, and I slipped farther into the water, digging my feet into the powdery sand. "It was terrifying. It felt like it was out of my control."

"Oh." She looked down at her hands floating in front of her.

"Wouldn't that be scary to you?"

She shrugged, a tiny movement. "Well, it's been happening to me for a while now. Kind of in a bigger way. Like, my whole leg one time. And one time both my arms."

Now it was my turn to blink.

"I didn't think it was a big deal," she continued. "I thought it made sense, you know? Like a reflex, like the way people talk in their sleep, or twitch."

"But was it hard to turn back when you woke up?"

She shifted. "Well, usually after I put on my clothes, I just turn myself invisible entirely. I like running better that way. You know that."

I swallowed. "Has it been hard to turn back?"

"Yes," she said simply.

"And that doesn't alarm you?"

We looked at each other for a long time. She didn't answer.

Finally, she started wading back to shore. "Want to come in?" she said over her shoulder. "Talk to Cleo?"

"Yeah," I said. I felt as if Polly were on the other side of a long bridge I couldn't cross.

I sat on the steps of Cleo's house, feeling too jittery to go inside, as Polly went to wake her up. They emerged a few minutes later. Cleo was bleary-eyed and yawning, wearing an oversize T-shirt and sleep shorts.

"What's up?" she asked as she sat down beside me. "My grandparents want you to come in and have some breakfast."

"I told them you were upset and didn't want to stay long," Polly said.

"Well. That is actually true." I couldn't stop touching my right ankle.

I told Cleo what I'd told Polly. She sat up a little straighter, but she looked guilty.

"So it's been happening to you too," I said, trying not to sound accusatory.

"I wouldn't say *been* happening," she said. "It's happened twice. Not as bad as what you're describing. Last week a couple fingers. And then a few days ago, just the bottom of my foot. I wouldn't even have noticed but I thought I had stepped on something and I reached down to brush it off, and . . ." She pressed her lips together, squinting into the horizon. She looked older, sadder, than she had all summer. "And yeah, it's been harder to turn back recently. Not as much for me in those two cases, maybe because it was so little space, but, well." She looked right at me, and all traces of sleepiness were gone from her eyes. "I think it's a problem."

I tapped my finger on my ankle, on the layers of it. Skin, blood, bone.

I ran home after that. "I just want to shower," I told Cleo and Polly, trying to sound normal—like I wasn't freaking out and desperate to be back in my familiar bedroom, back in the house I grew up in. Cleo said she'd call Talia in a few hours and ask her if she'd woken up invisible, too, then meet me at the beach in front of my house. I felt a little bad about not being the one to talk to Talia. But I didn't want to have the same conversation for a third time that day.

Besides, at that point, I knew. Of course it had happened to her. The only question was how bad it had gotten. And, I guess, whether she thought it was an issue at all. At home, I put on Hiss Golden Messenger and turned the shower as hot as it would go, until guitars and steam had wiped my mind clean.

I came downstairs braced for my parents to notice that something was off. But Mom was stressed about the unusual number of bike repairs they were dealing with, and Dad was trying to calm her down. I made us omelets with sausage and peppers and thick slices of leftover garlic bread. By the time they left for work and I pulled together my beach bag, I felt a little better. There is no cure like good eggs.

On the beach, Cleo, Polly, and Talia were waiting for me on a blanket. As soon as I sat down, Cleo pulled out her notebook.

"At last we can begin," she said, businesslike.

"Sorry for eating breakfast."

"Your apology is accepted." She winked before opening the

notebook. Her normal cheer was back, and I wondered how she had talked herself into happiness. "Okay. So. I did some research, on those blogs and forums? I had stopped checking them as often since, you know. We decided that I wouldn't be posting any videos." She coughed, then took a breath and continued. "Some of them have gotten taken down in the last few weeks, but a lot are still up, and a few of the girls have posted updates. There's good news and bad news."

"I still don't know if this is that big a deal," Talia began, but Cleo shot her a look.

"The bad news," Cleo continued, "is that we're not the only ones having this problem. Someone posted a video, and someone else wrote about it—" She pulled up a screenshot on her phone and passed it to me. I had to squint to see it in the sun. I scanned the text: *seems like it's happening without my even realizing it, woke up and everything below my waist, anyone have ideas???* I passed it to Polly, who plucked it from me delicately, like it was dirty laundry. "So it's not uncommon. And in fact, it seems like a lot of people have it worse than us. Which is kind of good news because it means we're not total freaks."

"I feel like the situation we're in would actually not support that claim," I pointed out, but Talia sighed, Polly rolled her eyes, and Cleo ignored me.

"The better news is that there's a cure."

Now I leaned forward. Even Talia and Polly sat up a little straighter.

"A cure?" Polly asked, guarded.

"Yes," Cleo said. "But you're not going to like it."

Talia hugged her knees. "Is it going to be painful?"

Cleo shook her head. "Not painful. Just final."

"The cure is death?!" I said, much louder than I intended. Cleo laughed.

"Jesus, Callie, no." She took a breath and smiled, but the laughter was gone. "I just mean that we can stop ourselves from changing without meaning to, but once we stop, that's it. It's gone. For good. We won't be able to do it anymore."

Silence. A wave crashed, a child shrieked. The edges of a song from someone's speaker filtered through the wind to us, then disappeared.

"It's not that bad," said Polly. She pulled out her ponytail holder and started combing her fingers through her long blond hair. "Changing without meaning to. We've all noticed as soon as we've woken up, right? And then we change back. No big deal."

"Seriously?" Now I laughed. "It doesn't scare you at all that this thing that we used to be able to control has just started happening? I mean, what if it happens when we're awake? What if we go back to school and it happens in the middle of class?"

"We can still control it when we're awake," Talia said, though she sounded less than certain.

"That did actually happen to one girl," said Cleo. She tapped her phone a few times and read aloud: " 'My grandpa died a few days ago and today was his funeral. We were really close, and it's been hard. During the service, I started crying, and I realized most of my left hand was gone. I had to leave the church to collect myself.' " Cleo looked up at us. "So for her, it was strong emotion. Grief."

"So we're fine as long as no one around us dies," Polly said. "I mean, everyone's families are in good health, right?"

I stared at her. It felt like for weeks, she had been reshaping herself in front of us, from the reserved girl I'd met in June into something wild. She glanced up and met my eyes, then looked away.

"Polly, come on," Cleo said, and I was grateful I hadn't had to say it. Grateful there was someone on my side. "You have to admit this is a problem."

"It's only happened a few times," Talia protested, and at the same time, Polly said, a little hysterical, "It's not a problem!"

"It is a problem for me," I said.

"And for me," said Cleo.

Talia drew a circle in the sand with her finger. Polly kept messing with her hair.

Cleo wordlessly reached into her tote and passed me a bag of chips, then pulled out an apple for herself. We sat there and ate and I tried to figure out an argument that would make Talia and Polly change their minds. After minutes of silence, I went into the ocean. Cleo followed.

Once we were far away from shore, I said, "We have to stop. Right?"

Cleo looked at the horizon, and I looked at her. She was so beautiful; her skin shone in the sun. She had gone looking for magic and found it. She had led us into it by sheer force of will, by the strength in her belief that we, four girls of no particular consequence, could do the impossible. And now I was asking her to turn her back on it. To undo the greatest summer project of them all.

"Yes," she said. "We have to stop."

We didn't convince Talia and Polly that day. They came out into the ocean eventually and Talia started telling us about another fight she'd had with Michael, how he thought she'd been flirting with one of his friends. Polly said her parents were firming up their moving plans. We talked about those awful, everyday woes. And we didn't talk about anything else.

22 MIAMI PARTY

"Are you absolutely sure we can't go home?"

Polly fidgeted with the spaghetti strap of her dress. The four of us stood at the base of the stairs to Alexis's house. Above us was the thump of music and the high, frantic buzz of girls laughing at unfunny boys.

Part of me wanted to go home, too. A familiar pain pounded in my head. It had been there almost constantly since the day, one week ago, that Cleo and I had decided to stop. I didn't know for sure whether Cleo had stopped as completely as I had. But I hadn't turned myself invisible since then, not even once, even though my body wanted me to.

I hadn't realized how much I'd been doing it until I stopped. Talia and Polly still did it after work; they took the front area and the office while Cleo and I silently swept the rink and picked up trash with our graceless, heavy hands. I was tired. Irritable. Running slower.

I felt as I had every day for the past week, off-kilter and feverish, slightly nauseated. But I wasn't going to spend the last few weeks of my summer moping in bed. And every time I came close to falling back into invisibility, I remembered the terror I'd felt in my closet, that horrible numbness so far beyond my control, and I pulled myself together.

"We came all this way. We got dressed up," Talia said. She finished changing out of her skates and tucked them with the rest of our skates behind a large potted plant at the bottom of the stairs before pulling a pair of flats from her purse.

"It'll be fun," Cleo coaxed. "The only party we've been to this whole entire summer was the Fourth of July, and it was with my grandparents."

"You wanted a Miami party," I reminded Polly. "This is probably as close as you're gonna get."

I was overselling it. This party was unlikely to be much more than loud music and gossip, with a smattering of whatever low-quality alcohol people had managed to smuggle from their parents or buy from their older siblings. But Alexis's parents wouldn't be back from their dinner in Wilmington until midnight at the earliest. And for once we had a Saturday night off from work: There had been an abrupt but robust infestation of sugar ants at the rink, and Miss Abby was bringing in an exterminator. When I'd told Adam, he'd invited me on Alexis's behalf and, by extension, Talia, Cleo, and Polly.

"I never said I *wanted* a Miami party," Polly muttered.

Cleo rolled her eyes, grabbed Polly's hand, and proceeded up the stairs.

I trailed behind the two of them and Talia. I had gotten us into this, but I was nervous, too. I wasn't sure who knew that Adam and I were dating. I wasn't used to being a subject of gossip. Part of me wanted him to drape his arm around me as we stood in a circle of people chatting, kiss me and bring me a soda, and have everyone raise their eyebrows. Another part of me wanted to keep him to myself: an absolute secret, the warmth in his voice and hands only rising toward me when we were on the phone or alone together.

But in a town this small, we were never going to keep things quiet. And, as I kept having to remind myself, there was no reason to. It wasn't like the secret I had with Talia and Cleo and Polly. Dating someone was normal.

It took three knocks from Cleo before the door opened. Parker, Alexis's boyfriend, smiled broadly when he saw us.

"You came!" he said. "Adam said you would!"

"We came," Cleo said. "How are you?"

We followed her in as Parker explained some inane argument between him and Alexis. I closed the door behind us.

Inside, all the lights were off, except in the kitchen, which shone fluorescent to the left. There was an old action movie on mute on the TV, and the dining room table had been turned into a beer pong table, except—I snuck a peek as I wandered past—it was water in the cups. Even shitty beer was too precious to waste, apparently.

Talia spotted Michael in the kitchen, gave my arm a tug, and gestured toward him. I waved at her to go on as I lingered in a corner, looking for Adam. Polly's eyes flickered between me and Cleo.

"Go ahead with Cleo," I shouted to Polly—we were standing by a big speaker. Cleo was greeting a group of people on the couch, giggling at something I couldn't hear. "I'll catch up."

"Are you sure you'll be okay?" Polly looked terrified.

"These are all people I know, Polly. I will be fine." I squeezed her hand. "So will you. Go with Cleo, just stick with her and laugh at jokes and it'll be nice."

She mouthed *thank you* and turned to step around a cluster of girls.

I leaned against the wall and scanned the party. Like a lot of the newer, nicer beach houses, the whole floor was basically one room, with the kitchen tucked into a corner and doors that led into bedrooms. Adam wasn't playing not–beer pong, wasn't on either of the two big couches, wasn't with the group playing cards at the dining room table.

I felt a flicker of nervousness. I had imagined a variety of unlikely, upsetting scenarios for this evening: Adam ignoring me, people openly laughing when Adam and I kissed, the cops arriving and arresting everyone in the house for underage drinking. But I had never imagined that Adam just wouldn't come. Not after he had invited me specifically.

I headed toward the kitchen—Talia would help me find him—and as I rounded the corner, there he was. He was engaged in vigorous debate with Jonah, a guy we ran cross-country with, and his back was to me. Talia caught my eye, glanced at Adam, and nodded at him.

I tapped Adam on the shoulder, interrupting him mid-sentence.

"But even if a shark had the *ability* to walk, don't you think—"

He spun to see me and his eyes lit up. He flung his arms around me in a big bear hug.

"You came!" he said. "You're here! Do you want a drink?"

I hadn't been around that many drunk people, but I didn't need much experience with alcohol to know he was drunk. He leaned down and kissed me messily before I had a chance to kiss him back. His breath smelled stale and yeasty, and he had never been this bold with me around other people.

"Hi, no, I'm okay," I said.

Jonah started laughing, and my stomach swooped. That laughter. That's what I'd been afraid of.

Adam pulled away and swung us both back to face Jonah. "Jonah, meet my girlfriend, Callie," he said happily. "She's my girlfriend."

Jonah laughed harder.

I thought about excusing myself to the bathroom and then moving to Pluto.

"Adam, we've been on the same cross-country team for three years now," Jonah said, wiping his eyes. "I think we've met. Hi, Callie. How did this asshole convince you to date him? I thought you were better than this."

I started laughing myself. All that nervousness fell away, and I felt buoyant. I looked up at Adam fondly, and he squeezed me close. "I have no idea," I said. "Just lucky, I guess."

Jonah gestured to Adam. "We were just talking about who would win in a race between a shark and a very fast runner."

"So the shark is swimming and the person is running?"

"Well, that's the question, isn't it?"

I leaned against Adam as he and Jonah started up their argument again. It was loud and unfamiliar, but I could feel Adam's voice resonating in his chest, and from the living room I could hear the edge of Cleo's voice telling a story.

On the other side of the kitchen, Talia and Michael stood in a separate circle, but neither of them were speaking. Talia's smile was wide and fake, brittle at the corners. Michael's arm was locked around her waist too tight.

I tried to catch her eye, but she was staring into space. Michael inclined his head toward her and said a few things, too quiet for me to catch. She said something back without looking at him. His grip on her tightened.

So they were fighting again. How could they have found something to fight about? We had just gotten to the party. The usual suspects—she was flirting with someone else, he was ignoring her, she forgot something important, or he said something shitty—we'd barely had time to cover.

A tiny, unfair part of me thought, *Why should I do anything?* I had listened to Talia cry over Michael more times than I could count; I had coaxed, cajoled, suggested, said every way I could, *You should break up with him.* I had celebrated with her when they made up, which they always did. I had stood beside her through every part of the cycle that she and Michael repeated over and over again. Including in the middle, right now: My role was to rescue her.

I looked away.

Maybe it wasn't a real fight. Sometimes there were just these long moments of tension between them that led into nothing, the argument dissipating as quickly as it had formed. I would check back in a minute, and if Talia still looked upset, I would ask her to come help me find the bathroom.

Jonah said, "Okay, man, but hear me out—"

"No," Adam interrupted, "we're not talking about if the person has fins, that's completely beside the point!"

I relaxed into him, pushing Talia and Michael away from

my thoughts. This was nice. It felt good. No one around was laughing at us. Well, there were a few people laughing at Adam, but only because he was so animated. I was laughing, too. Jonah leaned against the kitchen counter while he debated; behind him were empty cups and unlabeled glass bottles and the dark of the night sky through the window, and all of it felt incandescently adult, so different from my normal. These people, who I saw all the time during the school year, were new in this context. This house, like a hundred other beach houses lined up along the shoreline, was new without parents.

I closed my eyes briefly and imagined myself at college, in a year and change, at a party like this. Maybe somewhere different. Maybe somewhere with snow.

"I think we should see what other people think." Adam's delighted voice brought me back. He addressed the group next to me. "Okay, guys, so here's the situation . . ."

I glanced over to Talia and Michael.

They were gone.

That was probably fine.

They were probably finding a private moment to talk, or they had decided to go hang out in the living room instead of the kitchen.

Talia probably wasn't crying alone somewhere while Michael talked shit about her to his friends.

I disentangled myself from Adam's arm and kissed his shoulder in a movement so automatic and natural that it startled me after I did it. "I'm gonna go find Talia. Be right back."

Adam caught my hand as I turned to go. "Please come back," he said, and he smiled such a sweet, drunk smile that I seriously considered leaving Talia to her drama and throwing myself into his arms.

Instead, I told him, "Of course I will," and pushed out of the kitchen into the living room.

Cleo had settled on the couch and was holding court there, saying something that involved a lot of hand movements. Polly was squeezed between her and the edge of the couch cushion and looked miserable, like a dog forced to take a bath. Talia wasn't with them. I checked the bathroom: no Talia. I checked the porch. Nothing. The only places left were outside—maybe they had gone for a walk or were sitting underneath the house—or upstairs, where, presumably, Alexis's and her parents' bedrooms were. *where are you??* I texted her, but I didn't get a response.

I tried to think like Talia. Angry, upset, maybe hurt, but rarely a cliché and never stupid. She wouldn't take Michael to an empty room with a bed if she was mad at him. And even if I had dramatically misinterpreted her expression and they were seeking alone time for a very different reason, she wouldn't be caught dead having sex in Alexis's parents' bedroom. I went outside, down the stairs.

But they weren't there. I walked around the bottom of the house in its entirety: just stucco and sand and deflated boogie boards.

"Talia?" I called half-heartedly into the night. There was no response.

If I had seen Michael without her, I would've been worried about her turning herself invisible. But they were both gone, and she never would have done that with him. I went back up the stairs and opened the door without knocking.

And almost hit Michael in the back.

"—doesn't excuse the fact that you fucking cheated on me," Talia was yelling. Her face was red and pin-striped with tears, and her hair was coming loose from her ponytail in strands around her face.

"First of all, I didn't cheat on you, and second of all, I wouldn't have had to if you weren't so fucking uptight," he screamed back.

"Whoa," I said. But they took no notice of me, despite the fact that I was less than a foot away from both of them.

"Excuse me for not wanting to get pregnant!" Talia shrieked.

Other people were noticing them. Adam and Jonah stood in the kitchen, mouths hanging open. On the other side of the room, Cleo was attempting to extract herself from the crowded couch. Polly, beside her, looked ill.

Michael reached up, pushed back his hair, then—with a quickness that shocked me—balled up his fist and slammed it into the wall beside him. When his hand fell back to his side, there was a dent. I could see it clearly. It was only a few feet from my head.

On the porch outside, kids were still talking and laughing, but inside, everything but the music had gone quiet.

Michael had never stopped looking at Talia. "You're such a bitch," he said.

Cleo and I locked eyes across the room.

"Okay," I said, "we're going. Talia, come on."

Michael looked at me as if seeing me for the first time; far behind him, Adam snapped alert, closed his mouth, and started making his way through the crowd to the front door. Talia had broken into tears. I wrapped an arm around her as Cleo and Polly reached us. Some friend of Michael's was grabbing his shoulder, saying something into his ear as he stretched out an arm for Talia. I heard Adam say, "Michael, man, that was out of line," and then we were out the door.

Talia's sobs were loud and scary in the silent night air. I coaxed her down the stairs while Cleo, behind us, said, "Talia, it's okay, let's go home. It's fine, it's okay, let's just go home." Her voice was calm and even, and if I hadn't known her for so many years I might not have noticed the tremor underneath.

"No," Talia said between gasps.

"No, I know, it's not okay, I know," I said.

"No, I don't want to go home," she said viciously, and then broke down again. We had reached the bottom of the stairs, and she leaned against the banister. She took a deep breath, steadied herself, and looked at each of us in turn. "I want to go to the beach."

She said it slowly, deliberately, her face wet and furious, and I knew what she meant.

My eyes met Cleo's. *We have to,* she said to me silently.

We can't, I said to her silently.

We looked at each other for what felt like a long time.

It was Polly, finally, who said, "Okay, let's go."

23 HUMMINGBIRD

Alexis's house was right on the water. We left our shoes and our skates at the bottom of the stairs and padded in our bare feet up the splintered wooden walkway to the beach. Polly went first, walking quickly, followed by Talia, then Cleo, then me. The lights from the party stretched onto the sand, but Polly led us to the left, where it was darker. She and Talia tossed their purses onto the ground and melted into the night. I heard both of them sigh in relief. Talia laughed in a tiny hiccup—the way she always laughed when she was starting to feel better—and I wanted to reach out and hug her. Of course she wasn't there.

I sat down at the edge of the water. I was suddenly and completely exhausted. I thought of Adam, drunk and bewildered, back at the party. Maybe he was mad at me for leaving. Irrationally, I was sort of mad at him for not being there with me when I'd run into Michael opening the door, even though I had never asked him to come look for Talia with me. I fought the urge to stand up and go back for him. The waves in front of me rustled and moved unnaturally; Polly and Talia were wading in.

Cleo sat down next to me and twined her fingers with mine

in the sand. Her dress was rumpled, one strap sliding off her shoulder. She bit her lip and looked out at the ocean. The sound of laughter filtered back to us, as if through the inside of a seashell.

"How did it start?" I asked eventually.

Cleo released a long, tired sigh. "I don't know. I saw them come down from upstairs, and it looked like they were going to leave. Or maybe just Talia was going to leave. But Michael grabbed her, and when she turned around, she looked pissed. That's when I knew something was wrong."

I thought of Michael's hand on her shoulder, her waist, encircling her small wrist, and felt sick. "What were they talking about?"

"I couldn't hear. They stood there for a few minutes and I could tell they were arguing, but they weren't making a scene or anything. Talia started shouting just as you walked in."

"Great." I lay back and looked up at the sky. Dark clouds drifted like flocks of birds; a half-moon shone down on us. The sand crunched in my hair, pressed cold and wet into my thighs. It would've been so easy to disintegrate. To become part of the air, light as a breath and just as soft.

I said, "So he cheated on her, then."

"I guess so."

"With who?"

"I don't know. I didn't hear. I was looking around the room after she said that, and that blonde with the weird-looking eyebrows— What's her name?"

"Mackenzie. I think she draws them on."

A cheerleader. How predictable. How depressingly, infuriatingly obvious.

"Yeah, Mackenzie, she looked really uncomfortable. But I don't know if that means anything. I mean, Polly was uncomfortable, and I'm pretty sure Michael didn't cheat on Talia with her."

That made me smile. But the smile faded fast. Everyone had watched that fight. Everyone. The freedom I had felt earlier in the night, that glimpse into the future, narrowed into nothing. People would talk about Talia and Michael. They would stare at her at the rink. And, yeah, maybe some people would be nice, maybe there would be girls who would hug her and whisper, "He's a jerk." But most people wouldn't be nice.

"I wish we had stayed home," I murmured.

"Even with Adam there?"

"Seeing him wasn't worth that." Was he waiting for me? Or would he just go home? I checked my phone—there were misspelled texts from him, asking me where I was, and two missed calls. I texted, *taking care of talia, we're good but I can't talk, I'll text you tomorrow?* Then I put my phone back in my purse. He couldn't come out here, couldn't be a part of this, and I couldn't leave.

Cleo sighed again. "Yeah. Not a great night."

We sat there in silence for a minute, listening to the waves and the wind and the occasional, imperceptible murmurs that came from out in the water.

Cleo tucked her legs up to her chest and rested her chin on her knee. "I know why we stopped," she said softly. "But right now, I kind of wish we hadn't."

"Yeah." I could feel the riptide of the power inside my chest, tugging at me, ready to pull me out to sea. "You've stopped completely, too, right? You haven't been . . ."

"Alone? No. Well . . ." Cleo glanced at me, looking a little guilty. The gold of her earrings glinted in the moonlight. "I mean— Right after we agreed, I did do it one more time that day. In the shower. I thought maybe if it was for just a little while, it would be okay. But then I woke up the next morning and my leg was gone up to, like, midthigh, and I haven't done it since."

"I don't blame you," I said, and I didn't. I felt so tired. "I've been tempted. But it's dangerous."

"That's the thing, though," Cleo said, turning more toward me, her legs falling into a crisscross. "It always felt so safe to me. When I come down here for the summers—" She broke off, shook her head. "Never mind."

"No, what?" I turned toward her, too. I kept listening to the ocean, but judging from the faraway sound of their laughter, Talia and Polly were in the same place as they had been.

"I always feel like I have to be a little on guard here," Cleo said after a second. She was looking down at the sand, tracing patterns. "I mean, you aren't out to the rest of your school, either, so I know you sort of get it. But like— Do you know how many Confederate flags we pass on the drive from the airport to here?"

"I do." On the back roads, they hung from front porches and on homemade billboards, as present as the Stars and Stripes.

"It's not like I'm the only Black girl on the beach, and no one has ever said anything terrible to me. But there have been some little offhand comments—not about me, but just in conversation—that are definitely, absolutely racist." She took a deep breath. "I don't go anywhere alone here, you know? I'm careful. Careful in a way I have to be at home, too, sure, but not even remotely to the same extent. And when I was invisible, all of that was just . . ." She picked up a handful of sand, let it fall through her fingers. "Gone. I didn't have to worry about anyone looking at me, what they might think. What they might do."

"Safe," I said, echoing her word. I thought of the men at Little Mimi's, how they had looked right through me, how my blood had sung with the freedom of it. But that was only a small fraction of what she was saying.

"Yes," she said. "Safe."

Cleo lifted her hand again to let sand drop through, and I put my hand below to catch it.

"I wish there were a better way," I whispered. "I wish it could be there when you needed it. Only when you needed it, and not causing any harm."

"Me too," she said. "But I can't just lose myself in it. Even if that sounds awfully nice sometimes."

She looked so tired and so small, the two of us alone on the beach in the light of the half-moon.

Back in the direction of Alexis's house, voices carried, not loud enough to be comprehensible but loud enough to tell it was a fight. I looked at Cleo. She sat up straight, eyes alert.

"Should we go farther down the beach?" I asked her.

"Yeah, maybe," she said, squinting out into the water. "But I don't want to lose track of Polly and Talia. Maybe—"

We heard a loud, clear "Fuck you!" from the house; a moment later, the slam of a car door; a moment after that, a big truck revving up and peeling away.

"Do you think that was Michael's truck?" Cleo asked, and I relaxed a little.

"That would make sense," I said. Michael did drive a truck, and it was just like him to leave a fight and drive drunk.

"Actually," Cleo said, standing up, "I think I'm wrong.

Remember, his truck wasn't starting right? Because Talia was late the other day, and she said—"

She stopped talking, because a figure had just stepped off the walkway and was running out onto the beach, yelling, "Talia, come the fuck on! Talia, what the fuck?"

Michael.

"Cleo, lie down, come on," I whispered, tugging at her hand. Maybe if we were flat on the sand, he wouldn't see us.

Cleo started to bend down, moving slowly, but she was still standing when he turned and saw her. I could see the moment it happened, his spine straightening, shoulders lifting and falling, and then he started jogging toward us.

I scrambled up. For a second, I squeezed my eyes shut and used all the best-friend mind-reading power I had accumulated over the last fourteen years to send out a message to Talia: Stay quiet; stay invisible; don't do anything to tell him you're here.

Then I opened my eyes, and he was in front of us.

He was slightly out of breath, pupils dilated in the moonlight, and he seemed enormous. His muscles were thick and his chest was broad and I was aware, so aware, that I might've been taller and faster, but Cleo was shorter and slower, and he was much stronger than either of us. He slouched his weight onto one leg, as if he was trying to seem relaxed.

"Hey, Callie, hey, Cleo," he said. "Do you, uh, do you know where Talia is?"

"She went home," Cleo said. Her voice was pitched a degree higher than usual, like she, too, was feigning calm.

"Huh," Michael said. He reached up to scratch his head, and I could see some of the veins standing out in his arms, branching lines in the night. "She left her purse?"

"She forgot it," I said. "We grabbed it for her."

"And her shoes and skates, too?"

He had seen them. At the end of the walkway. I swallowed. We could have hidden them anywhere. In the dunes. Beneath a car. Anywhere, anywhere, but we had just left them for him to find. Such a basic mistake.

"She wanted to walk home," Cleo said. I was thankful, because I wasn't sure my vocal cords would have worked correctly. "On the beach. Polly went with her. She just didn't want to carry her stuff such a long way."

It was about as smart a lie as we could have come up with. Talia did like walking on the beach, and her house was about three miles east, far enough to make a walk improbable but not impossible. Michael turned to look down the beach, the way she would have gone, maybe calculating how much time had passed, if he could catch her if he ran. I wanted him to try. To sprint as fast as he could down the beach away from us.

As he turned back around, Cleo slipped her hand into mine.

We were standing close enough that it wasn't a big motion, but what startled me, what made me suppress a gasp, was the heat in her hand. Not the heat of skin or of fear but of invisibility, the heat I had not felt in so many days, that I had thought about and dreamed about every time I let my focus lapse. It was only a little, just about half of her thumb, but I knew what it was saying. That if Michael came any closer, we could just slip away. He would see us do it, of course, and that would present more problems than I could possibly imagine, but who would believe him? And he couldn't hurt us. Safe, safe, safe. Only a breath away.

"I'm sorry, guys, but I don't believe you," he said. His voice was louder and colder. "I need to talk to my fucking girlfriend. Is she, like, up in the dunes? Is she fucking hiding from me? That's messed up."

Cleo's palm was hot now, the rest of her thumb, her ring finger. But I found my voice. "Michael," I said, and I couldn't meet his eyes, but I focused on the tip of his nose. "She really did go home. She's not here. You can look all around, but she wanted to walk home, and Cleo and I wanted to sit and talk for a while. That's all."

He looked at me hard for what felt like a long time, and I kept looking at the tip of his nose, focusing on that point and feeling the heat in Cleo's hand stall and tremble.

"Fuck," he said, finally. "Okay. Fuck!" The last word came out as a yell, and I jumped a little, but he just shook his head. "Thanks for the help. I'll figure it out. See y'all later."

He turned and stomped away through the sand, looking like a toddler. I didn't let go of Cleo's hand until he disappeared down the walkway.

The ocean in front of us splashed a little—movement that could've been fish or our friends. "Talia?" I said to the air. My voice came out shaky. I took a deep breath, another.

"Yeah," she said. "I'm here."

"Me too," said Polly.

"Let's go farther down," Cleo said. I couldn't have agreed more. She and I set out at a jog. By the movements in the sand beside us, Talia and Polly were running, too. We ran until the walkway had disappeared into the dark, hearing just the sounds of each other's breathing and the waves coming in and out, and then Cleo and I sat down.

It was difficult to focus on anything. I felt askew. Standing in the kitchen with Adam, watching Talia and Michael fight, talking with Cleo, and lying to Michael on the sand—it was too much emotion, all at once, and all in the darkness. I wished I could see Talia. But Cleo spoke up first.

"That was really scary, Talia," she said quietly.

"I know," said Talia. Her voice came from right beside us. She sounded miserable. "I'm sorry. I couldn't think of anything to do. I thought about—about splashing him, maybe, or trying to draw him away with my voice, but—"

"Staying quiet was the best thing you could have done," I said with conviction, and Cleo murmured her agreement.

"He's not usually like that," she said, but even she didn't sound convinced.

"What even happened?" Cleo asked. "It seemed like a normal party and then suddenly y'all were yelling at each other."

"He's been wanting to stop using condoms," Talia said.

"I assume you shut that down," said Polly, some alarm in her voice.

"I did," said Talia softly.

She didn't say anything else for a long time, and I started to think she might have gotten up and walked back into the water, but then she spoke again. "He was talking to her when we got there tonight."

"Mackenzie?" Polly asked.

"Yeah. Honestly, they *were* just talking. But I found him and gave him a hug and he came with me to the kitchen, and I kind of teased him, you know, like, 'Having a good time with Mac?' " She sighed. "And he just wildly overreacted. Got super defensive. He would barely even talk to me. I told him I didn't mean anything by it, and he said he was sorry for talking to her but he didn't sound like it, and then I apologized for teasing him, but that ended up just making me more angry.

"Finally he was being so weird that I dragged him upstairs where there weren't any people—just in the hallway, there—and I had gone back to apologizing, I said something like, 'I shouldn't have even said anything, it's not like you cheated on me with her.' And then . . ." Her voice had grown soft and bitter. "The look on his face. I just knew."

"How long has it been going on?" Cleo asked.

"You know, I asked him that question."

"Did he actually have sex with her?" Polly wanted to know.

"I also asked that. I'm guessing yes."

"So are we going to have to have him drowned?" I asked tightly.

Talia laughed sharply beside me. "That sounds right, yeah." She moved her hand through my hand briefly: I felt the heady, intoxicating warmth of it, there and gone again. Holding hands with Cleo, and then this, my body screamed for more. I took a breath, in, out.

"You know, a part of me would love that," Talia said, and she laughed, a real laugh this time. "God. I still can't believe it. I mean, Mackenzie, of all people!"

"I didn't think they had ever said two words to each other."

"Me neither. But I guess we were wrong. Anyway, I followed him downstairs and he was trying to tell me that we'd talk about it later, that I was overreacting, but I wouldn't stop asking him about it, obviously, and, Callie, that's about when you came in."

I reached out automatically and felt sparks as my arm moved through her. We watched the moonlight skip and shiver against the waves.

"What are you gonna do?" Polly asked eventually.

"Break up with him, I hope," Cleo said.

"That's a problem for tomorrow." Talia exhaled, and my stomach twisted. She wasn't going to break up with him. "I think for now I just want to go home. Pol, let's change back."

I closed my eyes. I didn't want to watch them change back; it freaked me out, still, the sight of their pale skeletons sketching themselves into the air. I focused on my own breathing instead. I was tired, and I had almost fallen asleep when Talia said, "Guys?" Her voice had a serrated edge that made me open my eyes.

She was seated on the ground, halfway visible. Everything above her waist was solid, but below that, her legs still shimmered like a shadow. Her face was white as bone.

"What's wrong?" It was like a switch turned on: I had never been more alert.

"I can't feel my legs." She cleared her throat.

Cleo was up now, too. "You mean like you can't change back?"

"No. I mean, yes, no, I can't change back, but it's— I can't feel them at all." She was starting to panic, her voice growing louder, her eyes getting bigger. "I don't know how I didn't notice, I was fine when I sat down, and then— I thought it was just something strange about changing back, but I can't—"

"Polly?" Cleo said, worry creeping into her voice, too, and I twisted to my left. At first I thought she was fine, safe and whole. Then I saw: Everything below her elbows was gone. As if her arms had been sliced off at the joint.

"My hands," she said. And she didn't sound panicked at all. She sounded far away, as if she were speaking about someone else's body, telling a story from a different time. "It's like they're gone."

"Guys," Talia said. She was breathing fast, scared. "Guys, what do I do?"

"Don't panic," I said automatically. It felt both totally useless and like the only viable thing to say. "You're trying to turn back, right?"

"Yes I'm fucking trying," she spit out.

Polly, on the other side of Cleo, had lain back in the sand and was reaching her arms over her head, swaying them slowly. "Amazing," she murmured. "They're not even there."

The humid air felt tight and heavy against my skin. I grabbed Cleo's hand. She squeezed.

"Maybe the water will help," she said. Her voice shook, just a little. "Polly, come on. Get up."

I didn't question it at all. The water always helped. I tugged off my shorts and T-shirt and turned to Talia. "I can't stand," she said. Her eyes were huge in the darkness, pupils like wishing wells.

"I'll hold you," I said, as Cleo helped Polly to her feet.

It was awkward to pick up Talia. I wanted to try putting my hand where her thighs shimmered, but I wasn't sure whether my palm would slip through, and anyway I was afraid of hurting her, even though moving through something had never hurt any of us before. In the end I had to hold her in front of me, as if I were carrying a big box, one hand under her hips and the other around her back. She clung to my neck like a baby animal. Her weight lessened as I waded into the ocean, and I thanked God that the ocean was calm.

I stopped when the water brushed against the bottom of my bra. Talia's breath was hot and quick in my ear. "I'm scared," she whispered.

I sank down in the water and loosened my hold on her. A few yards away, Cleo and Polly were facing each other, whispering, too.

"I know," I said to Talia. "Me too. Just feel the water and focus."

"Easy for you to say," she said. She was crying again, silently, her eyes red and salt water everywhere.

"You can do it," I said. "Come on. Hold on to me and focus. Remember the meditation? Breathe in and out. Slowly."

I tried to do it myself: in, out, in. After a minute, she closed her eyes and took one deep breath. Another minute later, she could have been asleep but for the focused press of her lips. My arms, even under the water, ached from holding her up, but I didn't let go.

Then I felt something brush my calf under the water. My first thought wasn't a thought at all—it was just fear, that ancient, original terror of an animal with teeth in the depths. We were out in the ocean at night, after all, and sharks were more active at night than in the daytime. My second thought was that it was just a fish or a piece of kelp and I was a coward who, incidentally, had lived her whole life by the ocean and regularly made fun of people who were afraid of sharks.

But Talia opened her eyes and smiled wide, loosening herself from my arms. It had been her foot, solid again.

"Thank God," she said. "I was starting to worry. That was—"

"Shh." I nodded behind her. Over her shoulder, Cleo and Polly were still quiet, eyes closed. Their foreheads were touching; Cleo's hands rested on Polly's shoulders. We watched them breathe together. I thought: *How could I possibly not have known?* Finally, Polly reached out of the water to embrace Cleo, her hands thin and opaque. She smiled and opened her eyes.

"That took ages," she said. "How weird."

Relief flooded me as sharp and strong as adrenaline, made the moonlight on the water shine like a knife. Then just as quickly, anger rushed in. Incoherent, unfair anger, toddler-tantrum rage: at Michael for cheating on Talia and threatening us on the beach, at Talia for arguing with him and pulling me away from Adam, at Adam for not helping more, at Talia and Polly for refusing to let go of the invisibility when they knew it was hurting them, at Polly for not caring about being hurt. I wanted to scream.

"Let's go home," I said, trying to hide the tightness in my voice. I dove under the water to swim the short way back to shore. The salt, bitter in my eyes, helped.

We had no towels, obviously. My shorts and tank top stuck to me as I tugged them back on. The others hadn't taken off their dresses, and the fabric stuck to them in a significantly more suggestive way. The four of us stood in a circle, looking at each other and starting to shiver.

I thought about calling home and asking my parents to pick us up. Years ago, my mom had told me that if I ever needed her to come get me from a bad situation, all I had to do was call and say a special code word—hummingbird—and she wouldn't be mad. She'd take me home, no questions asked, no consequences. A get-out-of-jail-free card for a day, or a night, when I looked around and didn't like where my actions had led me.

I had never used the code word. I had never needed to.

I trusted what she'd said. That she wouldn't be angry, that she wouldn't ask what happened.

But she would worry. And I didn't want her to worry, especially not when we could get home just fine on our own. Yes, we'd have to walk back to where we'd left our purses and pick up our skates, and we might have to talk to someone who had seen the fight tonight. We'd have to skate back in our wet clothes, with the cool breeze chilling us, and probably we'd get honked at by at least two assholes in pickup trucks. But all that was worth it, if when my dad looked at me and said, "Callie, what happened?" I could answer simply, with chattering teeth, "We went skinny-dipping."

Polly dug her toes into the sand. Talia redid her ponytail. Cleo crossed her arms tightly across her chest. Everyone waiting.

I turned away and made my way back down the beach—toward our skates, toward the road, homeward—and the others followed.

24 POURING RAIN

Sunday, it rained. Not the raucous thunderstorm of a few weeks ago or an on-and-off drizzle, but a constant, quiet downpour, like God had turned on a shower with bad water pressure. I woke up way later than usual—almost nine; I hadn't slept for that long in ages—and ran anyway, three slow miles on the damp, empty sidewalk. All the tourist families were shut inside their rental homes, grumbling at their cousins about a bad start to the week. When I got home, Mom looked up from the newspaper. "Good run?" she asked. "It's pretty gross out there."

"Yeah, it was kind of nice. Chill." I looked around the entryway for a towel and, not finding one, went to the laundry room. I stripped off my soaked running clothes and traded them for the load of clean towels in the dryer, wrapped myself in one, and started to fold the others. "Why aren't you at work?" I called back to her.

"Oh, you know. Rain means it'll be a slow day. I was just taking a late morning." She came into the laundry room and leaned against the door, looking at me. "Are you doing okay?"

"I'm very damp."

She rolled her eyes. "Yeah, but I mean generally, Callie. Is everything all right?"

"Yeah, I'm good."

She didn't step away. I could feel her looking at me, feel the pressure of her worry like a hand on my shoulder. When I had come in last night soaking wet and told my parents the lie I'd planned, Dad had laughed and said, "Attagirl. The summer you're seventeen isn't complete without at least one post-work skinny-dip." I had almost forgotten—they hadn't even known the rink was closed. I felt miles away from them.

"It's just that Talia and Polly are having a hard time," I said. I glanced at Mom briefly to meet her eyes and made a face that I hoped struck a balance between sympathetic and exasperated. "You know how Talia is with her family, and Michael's being especially terrible, and apparently Polly's going to have to move again. They just moved to DC last year, but her dad got a job somewhere else. Cleo's upset about it, too."

"Oh, that's awful." Mom sighed, but that heaviness lifted off me a little. "Those poor girls."

"Yeah. They're just really struggling and I want to be there for them but, you know . . ."

"You also want to have a nice summer," Mom said. "I get it. It's hard to be a good friend sometimes."

She gave me a big hug. "Yeah," I said into her shoulder. I hugged her back as tightly as I could while not letting my towel fall. I swallowed hard.

I thought if I stayed there for too long, I would start crying. I pulled away and kissed her on the cheek. "I'm gonna shower," I said. "Are you going to work?"

She made a face. "I guess I should. Hey, maybe I could bring you and your friends some takeout at work tonight?"

"Oh my God, yes, please," I said. She laughed.

"Okay. See you later. Have a good day, okay?"

"You too."

I went upstairs and started the shower. I looked at the water pooling in the tub, slipping down the drain, and remembered the light, empty feeling of Talia's half-gone body in my arms. I shivered. Stepped into the heat.

It was one of the first days all summer that I didn't see the others. After I got out of the shower, I called Talia. She didn't pick up, just texted back, *feeling gross, napping, see you later.* Cleo texted me that she and Polly were staying in with her grandparents. I thought about going over there; I hadn't seen her grandparents in a while. But we would all be at work tonight, the extermination or fumigation or whatever it was having been completed, and we could talk then.

I made a bag of popcorn and wandered around the house with it. This was good, I thought as I tried to avoid getting buttered handprints on the stair railing, to have some time apart. For months, we had rarely been out of each other's sight for longer than the time we spent asleep. One day alone was not a big deal. It was great, actually. Totally fine.

I texted Adam, *how's work/your hangover?*

He didn't respond.

I tried to watch TV but couldn't find anything I wanted to

see. I cleaned the kitchen. I did a hundred push-ups, just for the heck of it.

And then it was two p.m., not even close to time to leave for work. It was still raining, and I was still alone.

I laced up my skates and set off toward Cappuccino by the Sound.

It is dangerous to skate in the rain. I'm almost as comfortable skating as I am running, and even I try to avoid it. Everything's slippery, and the puddles make it so that you can't spot uneven places in the road or the sidewalk, and it's harder to see drivers, who aren't usually at their best in the rain, either. But I wanted dangerous. I felt restless and jumpy, as if I were prowling back and forth inside the electrified cage of my body.

And besides, Cappuccino by the Sound was too far away to run to, even for me.

I arrived, soaked but intact, and pushed open the door. Adam was there behind the counter, perched on a stool and reading a thick paperback. He looked up at the sound of the bell and saw me. His eyebrows shot upward.

"Hi," I said.

"Hi," he said.

I was suddenly, acutely aware that I was still in my skates and dripping water all over the floor, and we were not the only people in the shop. Cappuccino by the Sound is basically just one room, but it's big enough to fit seven or eight two-tops and a couple of booths, and much of the seating was occupied.

Adam came out from behind the counter and pulled out a chair for me at an empty table. "Are you okay?" he asked quietly. "Not the greatest day for skating. And I was worried about you last night."

"I texted you a couple hours ago," I said as I sat down and unlaced my skates, pulling my flip-flops out of my backpack. It sounded accusatory. I didn't want to be that way, but I couldn't help it.

"Ah," he said, blushing. "I was, uh. Really absorbed in my book. It's the third book in this fantasy series I've been reading, and the politics of the alien court are just so intricate, the prime minister's daughter is just starting to— Well, not daughter really, they don't have gender in the same way we do, but . . ." He looked at me. "You do not care about this."

"I would love to hear about it later," I said truthfully. I looked around. No one was staring at us, but I felt exposed. "Is there maybe somewhere I could dry off? I did not think this through." On the way over, I had envisioned showing up to Adam alone in the shop, the two of us spending the afternoon in a private coffee-scented cocoon. Instead, we were surrounded by strangers eating muffins and looking at spreadsheets on laptops.

"Yes, for sure." He tucked my skates beside the door and led me behind the counter. He paused to set a small bell next to a prewritten sign saying, RING BELL FOR SERVICE, with the addendum (ONLY ONE PERSON IS WORKING HERE RIGHT NOW AND SOMETIMES THEY HAVE TO USE THE BATHROOM, THANK YOU FOR YOUR PATIENCE).

The door led to a stockroom, with stacks of cups and ten-pound bags of coffee beans. It was blessedly quiet and empty. I sagged against the wall. "Hi," I said to him again.

He smiled and handed me an oversize apron. "This is about as close as we have to a bath towel."

"Thanks." I started wiping down my face and arms. My clothes were a lost cause. "How're you doing?"

"I've had about six cups of coffee today, so I'm okay." He winced. "I'm so sorry about last night. I almost never drink at all, but then I got to the party really early and everyone was trying this horrible apple whiskey, and I hadn't really had dinner, and—"

"It's okay," I interrupted. "I'm not mad at you."

He smiled wryly. "That makes one of us. But hey, what's up with you? Are you okay? That whole thing with Michael and Talia . . ." He shook his head. "I should've come and helped earlier. Fucking apple whiskey."

"It happened fast." I sighed. Last night felt like a bad dream, too bright and blurry at the edges even though I hadn't had anything to drink. "You know after we left, he came after us?"

"What?" Adam straightened, looking alarmed. "What happened?"

"Nothing." I shrugged. It hadn't felt like nothing, but I didn't know how to explain it. "Polly and Talia had left to walk home on the beach, and Cleo and I had stayed just to talk and decompress a little." I disliked the lying, but there was no alternative. "And then Michael came and was looking for Talia and he was drunk . . ."

"Did he do anything?" There was a hard note in his voice that I had never heard before, and even though there was nothing, absolutely nothing, he could do, it comforted me.

"No," I said. "But it was still scary."

Adam leaned against the wall and shook his head. "I'm so sorry. After y'all left, Jonah and I and a couple other guys were trying to calm Michael down and stop him from going after Talia. And he did leave, but he swore he wasn't going to look for her. He said he was just going to take a walk."

"Well, he didn't find her."

"I'm so sorry," Adam said again. He took a step closer and wrapped his arms around me, and some of the buzzing, anxious energy that had filled me up started to slip away. He smelled like coffee grounds and cinnamon. "Is that why you came? To tell me?"

I shook my head. "I don't know why I came." My voice was muffled in his shoulder. "I just didn't want to be alone."

"You're not alone," he said softly.

I raised my head, and he kissed me.

It could have been a comforting kiss, something soft and sweet to pull me in out of the rain. But all of a sudden I wanted more. I touched his cheek, the back of his head, and kissed him more deeply, and it was as if he had only been waiting for my signal. He pressed me against the wall. His hands were on my hips, on my arms, on my waist skimming up to the bottom of my bra strap and then back down again, to my bare, rain-soaked thighs. I felt his teeth, his tongue, the silk of his skin beneath his thin cotton T-shirt. I had never been kissed like this and I never wanted it to end, there was no Michael in the dark and no dent in the wall and the only heat I felt was the heat right here between our bodies, this—

The bell rang.

For service.

"Shit," I whispered.

He stepped back. I blinked. He straightened his apron.

The bell rang again, and we both started laughing.

"Okay," Adam said, "um, I am going to go get coffee for that person, and you just— You come out when you're ready, and, you know, we'll, uh—"

"To be continued," I said.

"Yes." He laughed again, and I was so glad I was here and not at home. "To be continued."

I spent the rest of the afternoon at Cappuccino by the Sound, drinking a latte and reading a mystery novel Adam had given me from the lost and found, which ended up being absorbing enough to get me out of my head for a few hours. At the end of his shift, Adam drove me to work. He kissed me before I left the car, and I almost asked him to pull the car around back and park for a few minutes. But he had to get home to dinner, and I had to do my job.

I was the first one there. I unlocked the door and set about my preopening routine. The exterminator's chemicals still lingered in the air, and I propped the doors open with a pair of broken skates we kept around for just that purpose. With San Fermin blasting on the speakers and the sound of the rain behind it, I felt better. I knew how to do this: start up the sno-cone machine, check we had enough change in the register, sweep the floor even though we had already swept it on Friday. The others would be here soon, and we could talk.

I had to turn away only one pair of hopeful preteens before Cleo and Polly arrived. Cleo looked like I felt, pale and nervous. Polly, on the other hand, looked great. Her hair was smooth despite the rain, her eyes bright and alert and calm. She was always beautiful, but that night especially so.

"We thought we'd be the first ones," Cleo said by way of greeting.

"I was going nuts stuck inside."

"Yeah, us too."

"I had a nice day," Polly said, and Cleo shot her a look I couldn't read.

"I'm going to sweep," Cleo said. I didn't tell her it would be the third time. Outside, thunder cracked. The rain was turning into a storm. Part of me hoped it got bad. On drizzly nights, we were busy, but when the rain and wind were really heavy, no one wanted to leave the house. I wasn't particularly interested in seeing customers tonight.

Polly joined me behind the register. "What's left to do?" she asked.

"Not much. I got here a little while ago."

She nodded and sat down on the stool. "I like this song," she said after a minute.

"What's up with you guys?" I wasn't sure if I was mad at Polly or not. I kept seeing her in my head, sitting there on the beach with her arms empty below the elbows, looking like there was nothing in the world to concern her.

"Cleo is upset," she said without elaboration. "Should I wipe down the shelves?"

"Be my guest."

We never, ever wiped down the shelves. This place had dust dating back decades. But if she needed something to do with her hands, I wasn't going to stop her.

Talia got there as Cleo was finishing her last pass with the broom. "Hi," she called out. She shook the rain out of her curls and looked at all of us, Cleo drawn and quiet, Polly lustrous, me looking . . . however I looked. "I know," she said. "I'm late."

"It's no big deal that you're late," I said. "But—"

"We need to talk," she interrupted. "Hi, Callie, yes, I know that, too. Hi, Cleo, hi, Polly. Yes, we all need to talk."

She flipped the cardboard sign in the window to OPEN and joined me and Polly behind the desk. Cleo came, too, approaching slowly. Her apprehension was not without reason. Talia was wearing lip gloss and eyeliner and no other makeup, which for her was practically the same as going to the grocery store with an acne patch on. Her arms were crossed tightly and her fingers were pressing a pattern into them, a nervous holdover from years of piano lessons.

My eyes met Cleo's. *You or me?* I asked silently.

She inclined her head a millimeter.

Me.

"After last night," I began, careful to keep my tone even, "I feel even more strongly that we need to stop disappearing. All of us. Permanently."

No one said anything.

"I agree," Cleo said. "Last night was scary."

I looked at Talia, and her eyes met mine. In them was sadness and fear and something unreadable. Silently, I tried to say: *You know this.* I tried to say: *Please.* Her gaze slipped away.

"Talia? Polly?" Cleo said tentatively.

"I just don't see the harm in it," Talia said, looking at the ground. "We're fine, you know? I mean, sure, it was freaky for a minute, but we're here. It was no big deal."

"Talia, come *on!*"

Without my meaning to, it came out as a yell. The others turned to me. Their eyes were wide, like startled cats. But I was suddenly so angry. It was too much. I had nearly watched Talia disappear in front of me. She didn't see the harm?

"I know you don't want to do this," I said. I tried to take a breath, but I was shaking. "I know it's important to you. This summer has been . . ."

"Magic," Cleo said.

"Magic." My voice broke on the echo. Talia looked at me. She ran her hand slowly through her hair, more rain falling on her shoulders. "But it's starting to hurt us. You get that, right?"

Talia bit her lip.

A minute passed.

Cleo said tentatively, "Polly? What do you think?"

I looked at Polly, and out of nowhere, it was like looking directly into the sun, a fire so bright it hurt. I would've taken a step back if I hadn't been already leaning on the counter. Her hands were in fists at her side, and her eyes were wide, ferocious. She shook her head sharply.

"No," she said.

I sagged against the counter. I'd had so much nervous energy when I got here, and now I felt like I could collapse.

"Polly," Cleo said. She wasn't angry, like I had been; instead, there was a touch of weariness there. It struck me that maybe this wasn't the first time they'd had this argument. That maybe, as I'd been wandering around my house and watching TV, they'd been having this argument all day. "It's not safe. We don't know what—"

"No," Polly repeated. She looked like she was ready to cry or scream, her cheeks sunburn red, her hair white gold and blazing around her face. "I won't. You can, but I won't. I can't."

I tried to jump in. "Polly—"

"No!" She whipped around to me. "This is all I have. Do you get it? In a few weeks I'm going back to the only place I've ever really felt at home and then I'm going to turn around and leave."

She practically snarled the last word, and I shrank away from her. "Talia, Callie, you guys have each other. Cleo, you have so many friends. I have no one. I'll be away and you will forget about me and it'll be just like it used to be, I'll be alone, and this will be it. This will be all."

"Polly," Cleo said, her voice shaky, but Polly shot her a vicious look. Cleo closed her mouth.

The room was silent. Polly's chest was rising and falling quickly, and after a moment, she fell back against the shelves and ran her hands through her hair. Her eyes were wet. "I can't," she repeated weakly.

Cleo crossed the few feet to her and wrapped an arm around her waist, leaning her head against Polly's shoulder. "We don't know what's going to happen if we keep doing it," Cleo said. "It's already going wrong. It's getting worse. There's so much good ahead of you, Pol. In a year you get to leave your parents. In a year you can be wherever you want. We can go to college together, like we talked about. Remember? You can't do any of that if you're sick or . . . or what? We don't know what happens. If you're just gone."

Polly was full-on crying now. She shook her head.

"I'm not going to forget about you," Cleo said softly.

"None of us are," I said. I could hear the desperation in the words, that they had come out too loud, and I pressed my lips together.

Polly looked down at Cleo, her face white and shining. "Promise?"

"Promise," said Cleo.

"Promise," said Talia. It was the first word she'd spoken in ages.

"Talia?" I said. She looked miserable. She wouldn't meet my eyes.

"How would we do it?" she asked quietly. "Would it hurt?"

"No," Cleo said, relief flooding into her voice. "No, not at all. I've done all this research, I've exchanged DMs with some of the girls who have done it, and it'll be just the same as the first time. Just at the full moon instead. You disappear, and then you turn back like we normally do, but you have to hold the intention of giving it up. Words like *forever*. *Always*. That's what you have to think. But it doesn't hurt. No one said it hurt."

Talia sniffled, nodded.

"I'll do it," she said finally. "I fucking hate it. But if that's what needs to happen, fine."

I reached out to her. She took my hand and squeezed. I took a deep breath in and out: We hadn't broken anything that couldn't be repaired. She was staring at the ground now, her fingers tapping again on her arm.

"I promise," I said. "I promise this is right."

The four of us stood still for a long minute. Polly was crying silently, holding Cleo close. Then—one tiny, final movement—she nodded.

"Okay," she said. She let go of Cleo, tied her hair back in a ponytail. "We stop."

We stayed in a circle, looking at each other. We had stood in this same formation eighteen hours ago, on the beach in the moonlight, and that strange magic was gone. Surrounded by socks and skates and dust, the fluorescents buzzing relentlessly over us, I felt splintered.

"Hello?" A tentative voice came from behind us. I turned to see a woman standing just inside the doorway with two little kids, one on either side of her, all of them dripping rainwater. "Are y'all open?"

It took me a second to remember we were at work; my first instinct was to tell her that she shouldn't be here, she wasn't a part of this. By the time I had gathered my wits, Cleo had already said, "Yes, hi, come in!" and Talia had called out, "What size skates will you be needing?" The woman gave a relieved smile and hustled her kids up to the counter.

Polly ducked into the bathroom. I plugged in my phone and thumbed through my playlists. The rain pounded outside and emotion still lingered heavy as a storm cloud around us; I wanted to lean into it and put on something slow and sad, Phoebe Bridgers or Lucy Dacus. But that wasn't skating music for moms. I switched to a throwback pop playlist that Talia had made me. Britney Spears blasted into the empty air like a plane crash, and I took a steadying breath.

25 THE BIRTH OF VENUS

The end of the summer had snuck up on us. On me, at least, but Cleo, as always, was prepared. Before I called my dad to pick us up from work later that night—the rain had only gotten worse—she said, "Friday. That's when we'll do it."

Polly, her eyes still red from crying, bit her lip. "Does it have to be then? Can't we wait until the last minute? Saturday night?"

"We're leaving in exactly one week," Cleo said briskly, finishing her sweep of the seating area at the front of the rink. The calendar hit me all of a sudden, making me dizzy: School started in ten days. "So this is pretty damn close to the last minute. And besides, Friday is the full moon."

Talia furrowed her brow. "But why does it have to be at the full moon?"

"The new moon helped us disappear," I said. "The full moon is the opposite. It makes sense."

"But—"

"Friday," Cleo interrupted. Her voice was harsh and final.

"Fine," sighed Talia, and Polly didn't speak again.

Less than two weeks left in the summer, less than one week until we permanently ended the world's weirdest group project: I expected to spend every spare second with my friends, soaking in the gift of being together.

So I was surprised when Talia, as we skated to the beach on Tuesday, said, "Hey, let's skip work tomorrow."

"Why? To do what?"

"A double date." She twisted, skating backward, her hair blowing in her face, and gave me her most charming smile. I kept my face carefully neutral.

Cleo had assumed that Talia and Michael were done after the fight at the party. Not me. I had learned not to hope. On Monday, we were out on the beach, when Michael and his friends appeared down the shore, kicking around a soccer ball and blasting staticky music. Talia jumped up and adjusted her swimsuit, saying, "I'm gonna go say hi to Michael."

Cleo looked genuinely shocked. "Why?"

"He's my boyfriend," Talia said, as if it were obvious, and flounced off. Cleo looked at me and said, "What?" while Polly took a minuscule bite of a peach.

"If they ever break up," I said, weary, "we'll know. Until then . . ."

Later that night, before we opened, Talia said, unprompted, "He apologized, you know. He's really sorry."

No one said anything.

Talia and I had made up quickly after I yelled at her at the rink. Sisters fight; we'd raised our voices before and would again, and we knew how to be gentle with each other afterward. But I was still worried about her, about how much it had taken for her and Polly to agree to stop what we'd been doing. In the meantime, I had been mentally putting off the Michael question. A double date made that a little more difficult.

"You're not allowed to go on dates with Michael," I said. "Right?"

Talia waved a hand dismissively. "Yeah, but my parents have my work schedule, and I'm scheduled to work Wednesday. I'll just swap with Polly. It's not like they're going to come check on me."

Of course. "I don't know if Adam's available," I tried.

"What else is he gonna be doing on a Wednesday?"

I shrugged.

"You and I have never been on a double date, you know," she said.

"I've never had a boyfriend."

"And now you do."

I couldn't help smiling a little. "We only have a few nights left with Cleo and Polly, though."

Talia spun around, graceful as a falling leaf, and skated beside me again.

"He really did apologize, you know," she said after a minute. "For Mackenzie. He said it was only once. They didn't plan it or anything, she was just at his friend's house when he was over, and they were drinking, and they went for a walk, and it just happened. Not sex. Just making out. He feels terrible about it, Callie. He cried when we talked on Sunday."

I didn't say anything.

"I love him," she said, so softly I almost didn't hear it against the wind. "I want it to work."

I couldn't tell you exactly why it was important to the continued functioning of their relationship that Adam and I sat
with them across a booth for a night. But I guessed it had
something to do with feeling normal. Her boyfriend, her best
friend, two couples eating dinner together, Mackenzie and the
party and his presence on the beach forgotten. And maybe,
on top of that, she wanted my blessing. I liked to think that
mattered.

"Okay," I said. "If Adam's free. And if we can go to Island
Italian."

She grabbed my hand. "I wouldn't have it any other way."
She squeezed. Her palm felt tender in mine.

———————

I wanted that final week to be good.

To be perfect.

I wanted it more, maybe, than I had ever wanted anything.
More than I had wanted the invisibility to work or—later—not
to work, more than I wanted Talia to break up with Michael,
more than I wanted Adam. More than making any grade, win-
ning any meet. I wanted to sit with Cleo and Talia and Polly on
the beach and feel the crystalline, otherworldly blessing of our
friendship cranked up to a thousand. Every word, every glance,
every joke in its right place. I wanted to look at them and have
them feel the full force of my love screaming out of my chest,
a love strong enough to part the tides, and feel it reflected back
at me. Because that was how I felt about them. I would've done
anything.

But we had pushed our luck too far, and at the end, it ran out.

Monday, Tuesday, and Wednesday were awful.

Not all of it. There were moments. Polly tossed a football back to some guys who had lost it on the beach and accidentally threw way too hard, clocking one of them in the nose. We all struggled not to collapse from laughter as he attempted to turn his bruised ego into a date with her. Cleo made up a new skate-dance routine.

But the rest of those days was bad. Polly and Talia were going through withdrawal, as I had come to think of it, and they were slow and irritable. Talia complained about the sun. Polly snapped at me when I offered her a sandwich at lunch. I tried commiserating: "I know how bad this feels—" but she cut me off with a cold, "No you don't."

I shut up, even though it felt unfair.

Talia sighed, and Polly sat silently looking at the ocean through her sunglasses, and Cleo held a book in her hands and looked at Polly. Being around them was difficult. I knew the others could feel it, too, that all of us wanted to give up and go back to our separate homes and fall asleep.

But we didn't. Invisible ropes had tied us together. They might have been fraying, but they held true. We had tied the knots too tight.

———

When Wednesday night came around, I was happy to have some time away from the group. And to be with Adam. He had come by work to say hello on Monday and brought me lunch on the beach on Tuesday, but that wasn't the same as a date. I showered and put on a tank top and shorts, then changed into a dress, then back into nicer shorts and a nicer top. I put on mascara, smudged it, and wiped it off. I tried to forget about the fact that, in addition to spending time with my boyfriend and my best friend, I'd have to sit across the table from a cheating scumbag of whom I was a little afraid.

"A double date," Adam mused as he pulled out of my driveway. "Whose idea was that?"

"Talia's. Before her, some Greek philosopher, probably." I looked at him, at his face in profile, trying to figure out if he was upset. But he shot me a rueful look, meeting my eyes for a second before returning his gaze to the street.

"Don't get me wrong. I like Talia a lot, even if selfishly I'd rather spend the night with just you. It's just, you know, with Michael, after the scene on Saturday . . ."

I rolled down the window. Humid air, scent of salt.

"I know," I said. "Believe me, I know. Thank you for coming."

He reached across the dash and put his hand on my leg. He had such good hands.

"It'll be good," he said. "I'll burn my mouth on hot cheese. You'll look gorgeous while also burning your mouth on hot cheese. It'll be great."

I put one hand on his and let the other fall out the window, feeling the air shift between my fingers, the velvet drag of it like water.

———

Talia and Michael were already there when we walked into the restaurant, sitting on one side of a booth under a faded poster of

The Birth of Venus. When she spotted us, Talia waved excitedly—like she hadn't seen me three hours before—and jumped up.

"Hi, hi, you look amazing," she gushed, hugging me tightly. Michael gave Adam an awkward nod, and Adam raised a hand in greeting, equally awkward. Talia didn't see it. She turned to Adam next. "Hi, Adam, so good to see you, I'm glad you could come!"

She hugged him, and Michael, apparently taking her cue, put one arm lightly around me. "What's up, Callie," he said.

Yet another reason I hated Michael. He was a terrible hugger. Not that I wanted him to touch me at all, really, but it was the principle of the thing.

"Hello," I said. I couldn't meet his eyes.

We sat. Across the table, Talia mouthed *Thank you* at me. The booth was small, and Adam and I were squeezed together cozily. So, yes, okay, I could handle this. I looked over the menu, as if I didn't already know that I would be getting breadsticks and spinach artichoke ravioli.

"So, Michael, how are you feeling about tryouts next week?" Adam asked. As a senior on the varsity soccer team, Michael didn't have to actually try out, but he did have to be on the fields all day the week before school started, watching freshmen run drills and attempt to not pass out.

"God, they suck. But it'll be good to see the new guys."

If there was any safe ground with Michael, it was soccer. Talia's shoulders relaxed.

We ordered, and the conversation segued from soccer into running, from running into the beach and the slow erosion of the dunes, from the dunes into the new condos that were coming up a few miles down toward the pier. It wasn't exactly titillating subject matter, but it was fine.

When thirty minutes had passed since our order, and the breadstick basket was empty, Michael got up and said, "I'm going to the bathroom. Isn't that supposed to make the food come?"

He walked away and Talia leaned across the table, grinning. "This is nice, right?"

"I want my ravioli, but yeah, this is pretty nice," I admitted. "I'm allowed to still be mad at him, though."

"Yeah," she said, and her smile faltered a little. Her eyes flickered to Adam. "Have you told him what happened with Mackenzie?"

I shook my head. He hadn't asked. I hadn't volunteered. He raised an eyebrow at us, and I sighed.

"Coincidence, drinking, just once, not sex, he's sorry. Is that right, Talia?"

"That's the shape of it," she said. "Seriously, though, he apologized like a billion times. God, I'm hungry."

"I'm sorry, Talia," Adam said quietly.

Talia blinked.

"Thanks," she said. She looked back and forth between us. "I really do think things will be better now."

Michael chose that moment to return from the bathroom, and Talia straightened. I desperately wanted another breadstick, both because I was hungry and because it would've been something to do with my hands. Adam coughed. Talia started to slide out from the booth to let Michael in.

"No, no, don't get up," Michael said, grinning. "I can slide in over you."

She shrank back against the seat, pulling her legs to the side so he could shuffle in, his butt closer to her face than I would've preferred to see in the middle of an Italian restaurant. It required some contorting. Something fell to the ground.

"Ah shit," he said, pausing while half standing over Talia. "That phone is brand-new."

"I'll grab it, Jesus, just sit down," Talia said with a bite of impatience.

Michael slid into his seat. "Still no food, really?" he asked, relaxing. As Talia reached down to the floor, I heard a small metallic buzz. It was barely there, just two soft bursts of static, and I might've thought it was all in my head if not for what happened next.

She picked up the phone and held it in her hand, her brow furrowed. Michael was leaning across the table, saying something to Adam about wind sprints, but I was looking at Talia. Her jaw clenched. Her knuckles around the phone grew white. Adam was talking about the difference between sprints and long-distance running. Talia slid the strap of her bag over her shoulder and stood up. Only then did Michael notice her.

"Talia, babe, what's up?"

"We're done."

I had never heard her sound so angry.

Even as my stomach dropped in fury and concern, a weight fell away. I had told Cleo: *If they ever break up, we'll know.* Finally, I knew.

She held out the phone to face him, so he could see whatever was on the screen. His cheeks flushed. He snatched at it, rattling the table, but she took a step back.

"Come on, this is such bullshit," he said. He was trying to get up. I shoved the table at him to make it more difficult. Maybe a little childish, but whatever. Without breaking eye contact with him, Talia passed his phone to Adam, who glanced at it, shook his head, and gave it to me.

"Adam, come on," Michael entreated. "She's crazy, man. Give me my fucking phone."

I heard Adam say, "You really fucked up, you know that?" But my eyes were on the phone. It was a text. From Mackenzie. *still coming over tonight? gunna have some fun* ☺

I believe firmly that Michael cheating on Talia was Michael's fault first. Mackenzie wasn't blameless, obviously, but it was Michael I was really angry at, Michael who was in a relationship, Michael who had a responsibility to my best friend. Michael who lied.

But God, I hated girls who spelled *gunna* with a u.

"Talia, you want this back?" I asked.

She shook her head.

Michael, looking at me for the first time since we had arrived at the restaurant, held out his hand. And rolled his eyes. I dropped his phone in my glass of water.

"What the hell?" he yelled.

The place wasn't that full on a Wednesday night, but people were starting to look at us. Our waitress was frozen a few yards away, holding a tray full of food.

"We're fucking done," Talia said, a little louder now. "Get the fuck out."

Michael stared at her, then looked at Adam. His face was red.

"You heard her," Adam said.

Michael sat there for a second longer, then plucked his ruined phone from the water glass. Talia stepped aside to let him out of the booth. He got up, looming over her, and for a second I was afraid he was going to hit her. Adam tensed, and I rose halfway out of my seat.

But Talia stood her ground, and after a second, Michael turned and stormed out of the restaurant.

I let out the breath I had been holding. Talia's eyes fluttered shut.

Our waitress, who had found an empty table to set her tray on, said, "Um, do you want me to put all this in to-go boxes?"

"I think that would be good," I said, but at the same time, Talia said, "No."

The waitress looked between us.

"You sure?" I asked Talia.

"Yes." She sighed and pulled her hair up in a ponytail. "I wanted to have a nice dinner out. I'm not gonna go home and sulk on my couch."

"Up to you," I said.

We sat back down and the waitress laid out the plates. After she left, Talia pushed aside her garden salad and took a slice of Michael's mushroom-and-sausage deep-dish pizza. She took a huge bite, swallowed. "I'll say this about my horrible boyfriend," she said. "He has great taste in pizza."

Adam and I were absolutely silent for a moment.

I cleared my throat. I said, more timidly than I would have liked: "Maybe we could call him your ex-boyfriend?"

Talia froze, mouth full of pizza, and then started laughing. "Ex," she said. "Ex-boyfriend. Yeah. Okay. God."

"Am I allowed to say it's about time?" Adam asked, starting to laugh as well.

"Yes," she said. "Yes. God. Wow, okay, ex."

I shook my head and smiled, digging into my ravioli. "You deserve better," I said. "You always have."

She nodded. "Yes," she said. "I do."

———

It was a good night. We lingered over dinner and then Adam drove us to the rink, where Talia greeted our friends by saying, "It turns out Michael was still cheating on me so I dumped him!" Cleo shrieked; Polly grinned and clapped. I had a strict no-country rule for the rink's music, but I made an exception so we could blast "Before He Cheats" and let Talia take a victory lap. Adam laughed and sang along and wrapped his arm around me, and even though it was Talia's moment, having him there made it sweeter.

He dropped off Talia first. When he got to my house, the lights were off, and there were still twenty minutes until my curfew. "Pull in under the house," I said—where my parents couldn't see his car. He did, and then he turned off the car and looked at me.

"Well," he said. I kissed him.

We made out for nineteen minutes. We didn't go any further than kissing, but still—his hands on my waist, slipping under my shirt to touch my back, warm on my skin, his lips and his tongue, his hair slipping through my fingers, a gasp, a smile, my legs straddling him in the driver's seat. When I slipped in the door at exactly ten o'clock, I was buzzing all the way down to my core, my lips numb. I thought that my body had never known any greater pleasure than disappearing. I had been right, until now.

In two days and two hours, we would go into the ocean and give it all up for good. I was worried about Talia. About Polly. Even, a little, about Cleo. It was a lot to sacrifice, this power that had brought us together, that had let us slip away so easily. But I wasn't worried about myself. I was only beginning to learn what this body could do. I was ready.

26 THE END

Thursday night I slept deeply and for a long time. I dreamed of disappearing, fading in and out of myself like a desert mirage, falling through the ground and finding myself in new rooms, new worlds. Sometimes I saw Talia or Cleo or Polly for a second before they flickered out. Every time I opened my mouth to scream out to them, I made no sound—just gulped air like I had come up from a dive. In the dream logic, I was looking for something I couldn't find. When I woke up in the morning, it was with a shout. I lay there, breathing hard. The sun filtered in through the shades, warm on my face. The wind pushed and shoved against the window like a joyful dancer. It was going to be a beautiful day.

I told myself I shouldn't be scared. There was so much less to be afraid of this time. We had told our parents that we'd be having a sleepover at Cleo's house, and in fact that was the plan; after the ritual, we'd go back to her place and eat popcorn. We had already snuck out to the beach at midnight once and gotten away with it, and if we got caught this time, so what? School started next week. Cleo and Polly would leave. Getting grounded for a few weeks was no problem.

And besides, unlike the last time we had done this, I believed it would work. Cleo had shown us the accounts she'd read from girls who had successfully reversed the process. They had stepped into their salt baths at home, turned themselves invisible, repeated an incantation, and turned back for good, the last time, full stop. Sure, I was a little anxious about turning ourselves invisible in the first place; I hadn't done it in a while. But that part was a nervous excitement. I would get to have that feeling one last time, which in itself was a blessing.

I told myself all this, and it was all the truth.

But a part of me, still, was terrified. I kept thinking of Talia, quiet on the beach. I thought of how thin she'd gotten. Both her and Polly. I didn't know what exactly scared me—did I expect us to fight again? For Talia to refuse when the moment came, and for me to have to pull her back out into the waves in another month, on another full moon? I tried to pin down my fear, but it fluttered away from me, pressing its wings against my chest, a warning sign.

We had all decided. We had all agreed. This was the right thing to do. When I ran that morning, I ran fast, even against the wind.

On the beach: pretzels, peanut butter sandwiches, chocolate chip cookies, salt and vinegar chips, apples with crisp red skin. Lemonade. Soda. "I have a theory," Cleo said, "that if we have a really good day today, you know, physically, in our bodies, it'll help tonight. So eat up."

"Thanks, Cleo!" Talia grabbed two cookies. The way she was eating now, it was like she hadn't seen food for a year. A part of me wondered if it was some kind of last hurrah, before— What? But no. She looked happy, really happy. When I came by her house this morning on the way to the beach, she had run downstairs with no makeup on, not even eyeliner. It was strange and wonderful to see her like this, bare face tipped up to the sun and shining with nothing but sunscreen and delight.

"You too, Polly," Cleo admonished. Polly turned an apple over and over in her hands.

Before today, Polly hadn't been looking good. Her beauty had turned a corner into something exhausted and mean, deep blue shadows under her eyes and hair so pale it sometimes looked as if it weren't even there. The last few days, she had snapped at me when I asked if she was all right. She had been even more withdrawn than usual.

But today, she was different. I couldn't put my finger on it. There was color in her cheeks; strands of hair framed her face in just the right way. She looked serene. Not happy like Talia was; graceful, like a ballerina or something out of a painting.

"You excited for tonight?" I asked Polly. She smiled at me, meeting my eyes, and I had never seen her look so beautiful. Or so at peace.

"Absolutely," she said. She took a bite of the apple.

"Wow, this is delicious," she said, sounding surprised, and I laughed aloud, grabbing a handful of chips from the bag. Talia grinned as she licked chocolate from the corner of her mouth. Cleo raised her hands above her head.

"She speaks!" Cleo hollered, and Polly rolled her eyes. I dug my toes into the sand. God, I loved the taste of salt.

At the rink, I played my favorites. MUNA, Kishi Bashi, Sylvan Esso, the spangled, grieving wails of Florence + the Machine. We had a rush at the beginning and then the flow of people slowed, so Polly and Talia put on their skates and joined the group on the floor. Cleo and I ate popcorn and laughed, watching them. Polly lifted her leg back like an ice-skater and slid around the floor in a wide arc. Talia skated backward effortlessly, barely even looking where she was going, her legs crossing and uncrossing as if she were stitching something into the air. A few people clapped. Near the end of the night, they got roped into teaching an impromptu skating class for some preteens who were just young enough to not be embarrassed to ask. Talia led, shimmying with the joy and confidence of a little kid. We had worn our white dresses from the first night to work, half as an inside joke and half seriously, and doing those coordinated movements together, they looked like dancers in a music video.

It was the best night all summer. Perfect. All the strings connecting us were stretched taut, singing at the strongest, most resonant frequency. I knew as it was happening that it was a night I would come back to. A memory to keep.

And all that was separate from what we were doing after work. I was barely even thinking about the ritual. It was a part of the night, the shimmering end, but no more important than Cleo's smile or Polly's giggles or Talia's hair in her face as she picked up speed on the floor. All my worries fell away, and I knew we could do it. I knew we'd be fine. It would be easy, and then it would be over.

———

After we had kicked out the last group of giggling kids fifteen minutes past closing, after we had closed the doors and switched off the neon OPEN sign, the silence between us was sudden and complete. Cleo looked at the clock on the wall. "An hour and forty-five minutes," she said. "Let the countdown begin."

"I don't want to clean up," Polly said. "It feels wrong. Like we should be doing something more important with our time."

"What else are we going to do?" At the look on her face, I felt guilty. But— "I mean, we're not going home, and there's nothing else happening now." We had gotten bolder since the first time. All our parents were asleep. There was no need to even pretend to go to bed.

"We could go to the beach early," Talia countered. "I'm with Polly. This should feel momentous."

I tensed up just a little, but she was right. It was a big deal. It should feel that way.

"Let's compromise," Cleo proposed. "Callie and I will sweep, and, Talia, Polly, y'all can do nothing, or you can choose one thing to clean. We'll be glad tomorrow."

Talia shrugged, not unhappily, and Polly silently started relacing skates. I switched off the lights, switched on the disco ball and Metric, and grabbed the broom that Cleo passed me.

At the far end of the rink, Emily Haines blaring in the air, Cleo paused beside me.

"We're doing the right thing," she said. "Right?"

"Yes, we are," I said.

Mirrored light flickered over her face. She looked older in that silvered moment—like I was seeing her in ten years, a twenty-seven-year-old woman, someone with a girlfriend, a career, an apartment with art on the walls. It made me wonder for the first time if we would believe our own memories, later.

"Right," she repeated. "Right." She exhaled, started pushing the broom again. "Then let's do it."

So we got to the beach early. With all four of us in our white dresses, we looked as if we were in costume for some kind of performance, and we had to skate from the rink to the beach in front of Cleo's house. Cars honked several times.

It had been a hot day, classic August, but the wind had started strong that morning and stayed strong all day, and the sand was cold on our bare feet. It whipped like shards of glass around our ankles. The tide was right between low and high, going out, and the waves were restless. Not big, not scary, but constantly in motion. Clouds moved fast overhead.

"These are not ideal conditions," said Cleo, gazing at the ocean. "But it's not like we have a whole lot of options."

"We could wait until tomorrow," Polly said, but no one acknowledged it. The moon cast a shadow on her cheeks, then disappeared again. When it was visible between the clouds, it was a perfect white circle, a pearl in the sky.

We got to the edge of the soft sand, where the waves

stretched their fingers, and I sat down. I curled my knees tight against my body. The water felt warmer than the air. The others looked at me.

"What?" I said. "It's not time yet, right?"

Cleo looked at her watch, took it off. "I guess not. We have almost half an hour."

She sat down beside me. Talia and Polly followed suit.

It was only a minute before Polly said, "We have to do it one last time, right? Before we end it?"

"That's right," I said. I sounded only slightly terse.

"Then let's do it now."

I squeezed my legs tighter.

"Fine by me," Talia said. A little too eager, a little too quick. I wondered if they had talked about this before. Not that it mattered.

"I guess so," Cleo said slowly. "But only if Callie wants to. Callie?"

I wanted to. That was the thing. I wanted to, despite myself, one last time. I had told myself that I would wait until the last moment, that I would barely feel it at all before turning it off altogether, but now that Polly had presented it, the idea of a whole thirty minutes in that unearthly state—all the desire flooded back into me.

"Yeah," I said. I tried to keep my voice light. "Why not?"

Polly sighed as if she had been holding her breath. Talia laughed. Cleo squeezed my hand. I closed my eyes. And I let myself slip away.

I didn't expect it to be difficult, exactly. But I figured I'd be rusty. That it might take me a minute to get the hang of the meditation, after a few weeks away.

But it wasn't like that at all. It was as fast and simple as jumping off a cliff. One step, one thought—*I want to be invisible*—and I was gone. I breathed in and that strange, gorgeous coolness came into my lungs, my heart, my legs as if it had only been waiting for permission. It was the easiest it had ever been. I gasped in pleasure and surprise and heard the others beside me, high happy noises that felt too intimate, and when I reached out for them—my eyes still closed—I felt their blood and mine entangled in the air, warm and sweet as honey.

I opened my eyes. They were gone.

"Are you still there?" I asked. My voice was shaky.

It came back to me in a chorus of echoes: "Here," "Here," "Here." Cleo unsteady like me, Talia happy, Polly triumphant. The wind picked up and blew through me like a kiss.

"Let's go in," Polly said. The joy in her voice was so strong, it was infectious. I remembered her at the beginning of the summer, pale and timid, dipping one foot in the water. Three months later, look at her. Or rather, don't.

I got up a little too fast, unused to the new lightness of my body, and waded out into the water. It was still warm from the sun. The current was fast and tricky, not a riptide but not exactly safe. But it was hard not to borrow the recklessness of my friends. Who's to say what would happen if we got carried away? That if we breathed in water, it wouldn't just make us more powerful?

"I've been thinking," Cleo said softly, "about this year. Flights from Houston to DC aren't that expensive. And you have your license now, Talia, right? So you could all come stay at my house for a weekend. I could take you to see the monuments. We could go to the National Gallery. And there's this sushi place . . ."

All summer the future had felt as distant and unreachable as a boat on the horizon, something with which we would never intersect. But it was here. The beginning of it, anyway. New lockers and new classes and college applications. Adam's arm around me in the hallways, off-campus lunch privileges instead of the spaghetti-and-disinfectant smell of the cafeteria. My last high school cross-country and track seasons. Prom.

". . . or come down to Raleigh. Stay with Talia's aunt. There's a train I could take if I skipped a day of school. Y'all could drive up, and Polly could fly in. I know you've been wanting to take us to the Cat's Cradle, Callie, and if there's a show you want to go to on a Saturday, we could plan it around that. We could say it's college visits. You're applying to Chapel Hill, right? I am. I hear the arboretum there . . ."

After that, another summer here, another three months of nights at the rink and days on the beach, and then something new entirely. I couldn't see the shape of it yet, but it was there in the distance, blurry and bright. A new bed. A new home. New friends. Maybe some of us would end up at the same place, but maybe not, and it would be okay either way. We'd have this summer always, a shimmering secret no one else would ever know.

". . . and I've never been to Texas. Have you, Polly? Do you like barbecue? I think that's the thing to do there. I wonder what it's like in the desert? Isn't it supposed to be a dry heat? Well, whatever, you're going to have to show us your house and introduce us to all your friends. They'll probably be so much cooler than us. You won't miss us at all. Maybe we can go to the Gulf of Mexico and dip our toes in the water . . ."

Polly didn't say anything. She hadn't talked about the move in a while, at least not to me. I imagined myself flying with Talia into Texas to visit her, seeing Cleo in the airport, looking out at a flat red expanse as Polly drove us to a mansion in the middle of nowhere. It was sweet of Cleo to try to make her feel better, and you had to try, right? But I knew Polly would not make friends. She would get through it and get out, someplace she chose that would keep her for four years and hold her like she deserved to be held.

She'd be okay. We all would.

Cleo's voice trailed into a whisper and then nothing. We treaded water and floated under the strong, pale moon and were quiet together. The current was drifting us farther down the beach, slowly but surely; we would have to walk back.

The moon slipped behind a cloud again, a big one, and someone gasped so close behind me that it could've been my own breath.

"What's wrong?" I said, too loud, righting myself.

"Nothing's wrong," said Talia. "Just, look."

I looked up first, then back at the beach and out at the black horizon, and I didn't look down until Cleo laughed and Polly whispered, "Oh my God." Which meant I was the last to see it.

Glitter. But better than glitter. Green-gold-turquoise sparks of light in the water, appearing where I moved, settling into nothingness where the water was still. I brushed my hands through the water, and it lit up like Christmas. I started laughing.

"Amazing," I said.

"What is it?" Polly, a little in front of me. I could see where she was now, swirling in the water from the light around her.

"Bioluminescence," said Cleo. "It's algae, right?"

"Something like that," Talia said. "It's the same thing that makes fireflies light up. That's the only thing I remember." She laughed, too. "I've only ever seen it a few times before. And now tonight of all nights."

"Tonight of all nights," I repeated.

The moon appeared again. The light made it harder to see the glimmer in the water. "It's a sign," Cleo said. "It's time."

"Are you sure?" Polly asked. She sounded nervous again. "We might have a few more minutes. Should we go check your watch?"

"It'd take ages to get back there," I said. "Cleo's right. Let's do it now."

Talia, still close to me, took a deep breath. "I'll miss it," she said.

"Me too," I said quietly, and Cleo said, "Me too."

Polly was silent.

"Remember," Cleo said, "it's the same as turning back normally, but it has to be final. Permanent. When you do your meditation, think words like *always, forever*. Okay?"

I had rehearsed it in my head every night leading up to today. "Okay," I said. Talia echoed me.

Polly was silent, still.

"Polly?"

"I understand," she said softly.

"Okay. Then let's do it."

I shut my eyes.

I want to be visible, I thought. *Always.*

Something tumbled in my stomach. My limbs felt restless. Rebellious.

I want to be visible always. I want to be here for forever. I want to be seen from miles away. I want to be unmissable.

300

I willed the moonlight inside me. Tried to take that reflected, refracted sunlight and infuse it into my very bones, bleed the light from the bioluminescence and make myself a firefly, glowing in the dark. I thought about skin and the places on my body where it had been scraped into blood. The razor burns that stung in the salt, the tangles in my hair, the way it felt when I stepped into a hot shower or lost my breath sprinting or kissed Adam. I wanted all of it, and it wasn't a meditation. I wasn't trying to trick myself into anything. It was real. I wanted it all.

When I opened my eyes, my hands were there in the water, palms up, facing me like two old friends. It was dark: The moon was behind a cloud again. I felt like I had run twenty miles. I could've fallen asleep right there in the ocean.

But the power was gone. I knew it as clearly as I had known the morning I woke up with my first period or the day I broke my wrist falling from a tree. Something was different about my body, something final. My wrist had healed, but there was still a line in the bone where it had snapped. I still bled every month. And I would never be invisible again.

A hand reached out and touched me, and I followed it up to Cleo. There were dark circles under her eyes, but she was smiling.

"It worked," she said. "It's done."

I smiled back at her, but my eyes moved past her to Talia. She was almost opaque, shimmering at the edges. She frowned in concentration. She looked sad and sweet, as if she were asleep in the middle of a nightmare. I moved closer to her.

"Come on, Talia," I said softly. "It's gonna be okay."

She opened her eyes, and I could see through them, into the dark of the night.

"Do you promise?" she asked.

"I promise," I said, and I meant it.

Talia sighed, nodded, and reached out a hand to me.

When she solidified for good, I felt it, like a live electrical current suddenly pulled from a wall. I tugged her closer to me. She sighed and fell into my arms. She felt exactly the same as always, this girl I had hugged for most of the days of my life, my sister, and I was so relieved I laughed. She said into my shoulder, "You better be right. I'm really going to miss being a superhero."

"Me too," I said. I pulled away from her. Together we looked to Cleo.

Cleo was staring behind us, lips parted.

I turned, and there was Polly.

She wasn't finished. She wasn't nearly as far along as Talia had been a few minutes ago. It looked as if she'd barely started, really. We could see the outline of her features and the white gleam of her skeleton, and that was all. Her eyes were open, and her smile twisted down a little at the edges.

Cleo said, "Polly, you can do it."

But Polly shook her head.

She was standing in the water. She must have found a place where the sand was a little higher, because most of her torso was exposed. The waves moved gently around and through her like the air around a fire, rich with sparks of light. Cleo's eyes cut over to me, and that was when I started to understand what was happening.

"Polly, please," Cleo said, and she sounded terrified. Polly shook her head again, and Talia's eyes widened.

All of us saw the train now, coming at us predestined and certain, unstoppable.

"I can do anything like this," Polly said. For the first time in weeks, she sounded happy. "I know you don't understand, but I promise, this is what I want. It's okay."

"Polly!" Cleo was almost screaming. She reached out for Polly; her arms went straight through as if she'd tried to catch a cloud.

Polly drifted closer. What we could see of her glowed.

"Tell them I drowned," Polly said. When she dissolved, it was into us.

THREE GIRLS.

Three girls under a high, bright moon.

Three girls, hand in hand. Cold soft dress. Wet white dress. Seaweed wound round our ankles, like needy fish. Hair tangled in the seawater. Flickering green lights flashing at every splash. Three girls screaming. Three girls crying. Noise dampened and flattened by wind into the water, into the thick, shifting dunes. No kitchen lights switched on, no one stepping outside to inquire about the noise.

Three girls, three bodies, four souls.

Fourth girl somewhere, nowhere, breathing, missing, gone.

Sinking realization, bone-tired, half-walking, half-floating. Current, tide, waves.

Starlight crystallizing on skin. Sea licking shivered feet. Three girls together, lowering ourselves blindly onto the shore, hyperventilating into the breath of the wind. Three girls like ghosts, pale and terrified, alone in the night.

Sand below us, hand in hand, high bright moon above.

27 THE END, PART II

There was no funeral.

It wasn't that easy.

We were in front of a commercial stretch of beach when she disappeared, having floated down the shoreline, and all the windows were dark, no one in houses to hear our panicked screams. The wind helped, too. It had picked up even harder, and it moaned and whispered around us.

I couldn't do anything. My mind was a clean white sheet. I stood in the ocean looking at where Polly had been for minutes, while Cleo sobbed beside me and Talia tried to calm her down. Much later, in my first premed class in college, when I learned about shock, I remembered this night and ticked off the bullets in my textbook one by one. Shaking, cold, inability to speak or act.

Talia kept her head on straight. She was the only one of us. Dramatic, impulsive, volatile Talia dragged me and Cleo out of the ocean and made us repeat after her. "We went swimming after work," she said, and after some minutes, Cleo and I echoed her like two ghosts: *We went swimming after work.* "When we were

done, Polly said she wanted to sit out on the beach for a while."
She wanted to sit on the beach for a while. "She said not to wait up." *She said not to.* "We went home to Cleo's house for our sleepover." *Home. Sleepover.* "We were exhausted and we fell right asleep." *Exhausted.* "Cleo, tomorrow we have to tell your grandparents this, okay? And then we just have to be ready to repeat it. Okay? Okay?"

Cleo nodded.

And that's what we did.

I know this part is important, and I wish I could tell it better. But the weeks afterward are just stills from a movie; as many times as I sort through them, I can't remember how they connect to each other. Two cops at my kitchen table. A search and rescue boat on the horizon. Polly's junior-year school portrait on the front page of the paper. Her mom, beautiful even with bloodshot eyes, in my doorway, mouth moving and silence coming out. Vomit on the beach after I had run only half a mile. Shit like that.

I didn't know, and still don't, how much people bought our story. For months afterward, sometimes I would catch my parents looking at me like they wanted to ask me something, and then they wouldn't say anything at all. But I repeated it so much that I almost started to believe it. It was easy to turn that memory of Polly at the end into a dream, to pretend I'd imagined all of it, this miraculous summer and its disastrous end. I repeated it to myself as I went to sleep. *We went swimming after work. Polly wanted to sit on the beach for a while.*

It was good enough, in the end. I felt sick for a month, but none of us were interrogated or anything like that, or at least not interrogations like I had seen on TV, in scary metal rooms. Everyone treated us kindly. They believed us enough to declare her missing, presumed dead. The ocean, after all, is merciless and deep.

And then life moved on.

Cleo went back to DC. She stayed here longer than she'd planned—of course she did; she was a witness—but then she was gone. We talked on the phone every day. At first, all she did was cry. I would pick up the phone to her crying and listen to her crying, helplessly, for hours.

But then a few weeks after she left, before the crying started, she told me about her new AP history class, how interested in it she thought Polly would have been. The next week, we had a whole conversation about the relative merits of fresh versus frozen garlic bread before she broke down. I don't know when it happened, and it wasn't linear, but one night we said, "Sleep well," and hung up, and both of us were laughing.

Talia and I went back to school. She cried a lot, too, mostly about Polly and sometimes about Michael; she told me about the sweet things I had never known he did, how he tucked love notes into her locker on Fridays, folded sheets of notebook paper with a heart drawn in Sharpie on the outside. I told her she would find someone better. Someone amazing. She always said, "Maybe." But they didn't get back together.

The rink shifted to its autumn hours, and we only worked Wednesday through Saturday. I started going to bed earlier and lingering over my morning runs, taking my time on the beach. I had a finite number of days like this left. Adam and I went on dates. In October, on Halloween, we had sex for the first time in the back of his car; it hurt and then it didn't. I took the SAT. Wrote college applications.

After the police stopped calling, after Cleo started to sound more like herself, I found it surprisingly easy to focus. I felt sharpened and clarified and sometimes really happy.

I couldn't explain why, not completely. One of my best friends was gone. I should have been a disaster. But by the time the air started to crisp at the edges, I wasn't sad when I thought of her. I didn't even think of her as gone. Instead, before I went to sleep, I remembered the look on her face in that last shining moment. The moonlight on her lips, curved and joyful, like the half second just before a laugh.

28 AFTER

It's been two years, but the rink is exactly the same. The girl across the counter from me is texting, even though we've been standing there for almost a minute, and I bite my lip to try not to smile. When she finally looks up and asks me what size, I tell her eight and a half, Talia and Cleo say seven, Lauren says ten, and another girl plunks four pairs on the counter.

"Y'all need socks?" the first girl asks.

"We brought our own," I say. Lauren fishes hers out of her purse, holding them up as an example. Cleo rolls her eyes and leans her head on Lauren's shoulder with a smile. This is the first time we have met Cleo's girlfriend, and I already like her so much.

"Twenty dollars," the girl behind the counter says. "Cash only."

I pass her a bill and she tucks it neatly into the cash register. "No inflation," I comment. "Nice." She glances up at me and I can see her debating whether to engage and ask me what I mean. But then a family comes in behind us, and she gives me a big, sweet smile, as practiced as the bow at the end of a play.

"Have a good skate," she chirps. We move away.

"I wish we had our own skates," Talia says, looking with distaste at the beat-up pair in her hands.

"Then we would've had to check bags, and we're only here for a week," Cleo reminds her. She looks at her own pair, the laces frayed. "These will be . . . fine."

"I have never been skating in my life," says Lauren cheerfully, "so I think these will be just great for me."

One week. Just seven days to be not only with each other but with our families, too—Cleo's parents and her younger siblings are visiting her grandparents, who are also meeting Lauren for the first time. After that, Talia will return to Asheville for summer session classes, Cleo and Lauren to DC for internships, and me back to Boston for a job in a research lab. Sometimes it is hard to believe we used to have whole summers, long, lazy months melting together in the heat of the sun. Now, even a week feels like a gift.

After graduation last year, we scattered. We never said it to each other, not directly, but all of us wanted to put distance between ourselves and what had happened. Talia, who had always had a soft spot for UNC Wilmington, went instead to UNC Asheville, six hours across the state. Cleo chose NYU from among many acceptances, arriving three months after one of her older sisters graduated with honors.

I ended up at Boston University. I had applied there on a whim, one of two big stretch schools in big cities, and when I'd not only gotten in but also gotten the financial aid I'd needed, I had accepted without ever even visiting. It was lonely at first. Adam stayed in North Carolina, at NC State, and the ease between us tightened over the distance until it fell apart. It was even lonelier after Adam and I broke up over Thanksgiving. We still text, though. I hope we're always friendly.

Even after being there for a year, I'm still not quite used to Boston, how loud and tall and cold it is. But I like it. I like jogging along the Charles, and I like the warmth and friendliness of my dorms, and I even like the impossibly difficult classes I'm taking on the premed track. There's a girl I like, too. Eleanor. We've been on two dates. After the second, I told her she was the first girl I've ever kissed.

"So?" She shrugged and smiled. She has such a good smile. "You're the tallest girl I've ever kissed."

Life there could not be more different from Little Beach. Sometimes I miss home with a ferocity I feel in my marrow. Other times, the difference is the best part.

"Come on," Talia says. "Let's show these tourists what real skating looks like."

"Don't have to ask me twice," I say. We step onto the rink together.

It's a Friday in May and the rink isn't that busy, but we still move a little closer to the center, where there are fewer people. Taylor Swift is on the speakers, turned up plenty loud. I pull my hair out of my ponytail and take long strides, stretching out my legs. The rented skates are awkward, but they carry me forward smooth and fast. All the rest is exactly how it used to be: the solid, dusty heat of this room and the sound of the wood under the wheels. The kid crying in a corner, the faded signs on the wall. I could close my eyes and be seventeen again.

"This feels good," Cleo sighs, the thin cotton of her dress rippling in the air behind her.

I remember how it felt to skate invisible, as breathless and weightless as light itself.

"It does," I say. I push off the floor again, propelling myself faster.

On the other side of the rink, Lauren is half walking, half skating, her lanky limbs awkward on wheels. She gives a thumbs-up and calls out to Cleo, "Doing great!" Cleo laughs, skating over to help her. I've known Lauren for a day and already I can tell: She sets Cleo alight with happiness.

We're at the rink only about a half hour before we have to leave and walk the few blocks to the restaurant. It's new as of last year, a white-tablecloth seafood place nicer than anywhere I ever went growing up. The food is legitimately great, though I still would've preferred good old Island Italian. When we walk in, our families are already seated at the longest table in the restaurant, siblings and parents and grandparents alike. Angelica is about to enter high school. She still looks like a baby to me, but she'll be taking AP classes next year.

"Our guests of honor!" Dad cheers as we sit down.

"So, girls. Tell us everything," says Talia's mom. It's a little bit silly, because I know that she and Talia actually talk on the phone every week, and even more surprising, Talia was the one to instigate the conversations. "How were classes this semester? How are your grades? Do you know where you're living next year? Lauren, what are you majoring in? How did you and Cleo meet?"

Appetizers appear—pimento cheese, deviled eggs, hush puppies—and we talk. I dutifully update the table on my classes. Talia tells us that she's decided to major in art history, and Cleo attempts to explain how collegiate moot court works. Lauren seems to be just trying to keep up.

"Well," Mom says, leaning in with a gleam in her eye. "We have news, too."

"I got my license!" Olivia shrieks with the excitement of someone who has been waiting many minutes to share this news.

"I was actually going to say a movie theater came in down in Sunrise Beach, but this is much more exciting, of course," Mom says as the table applauds. And though I clap, too, a movie theater that close by really is kind of a big deal. Mom also tells me that Cappuccino by the Sound shut down, while a new donut shop opened up. The town is growing, slow and steady, reshaping itself.

We linger over dinner and caramel cake. Cleo's family is the first to leave, her grandmother claiming that it's past her curfew. We hug tightly and promise to meet on the beach tomorrow morning, just like old times. Talia's sisters are next; Olivia apparently insisted on driving separately to the restaurant, and she now demands to drive her sisters back. Some alchemy occurred when Talia left home, and the three of them get along now like—well, like they're sisters. I squeeze Talia's hand and savor how good it feels to say, "See you tomorrow."

I'm tired, but I don't want to go home. I touch my mom's arm when my dad has gone to the bathroom.

"Would you mind if I stayed out for a while?"

Her brows knit together. "Sure, but why?"

I look out the window. This place is right on the sound, and there's nothing but blackness outside. That familiar restlessness sends sparks through my legs. "I don't know. It's just nice to be back, is all. I want to soak it in."

She smooths back the frizz in my hair. "Do you promise no swimming?"

After it happened, my and Talia's parents got a lot more anxious about us staying out late and swimming by ourselves. We weren't allowed on the beach on rainy days anymore, and Talia's dad started setting an alarm for her curfew on nights she was working or out with friends, waking up and checking to see if she'd made it home. She always did. We didn't break the rules that year, not even once.

"I promise, Mom," I say, and I mean it.

"Okay. Your dad and I will get a ride with Talia's parents, so you can have the car, and— No, take the car, you are not running home after dark," she adds as I open my mouth. I shut it again. She smiles ruefully. "I guess you don't technically have a curfew, but will you be back by eleven?"

"Yes," I say with a laugh. "Of course."

When we leave the restaurant, I sit in the car for a minute while my parents and Talia's pile into their car and pull out of the parking lot. I think about driving down to the pier, or maybe over to my old high school track. I think about texting Talia and Cleo to come back.

Then I get out and walk down the block alone.

The windows of the rink are dark and quiet. The girls are long gone. I circle behind the building and crouch to feel under the bottom stair. Sure enough, the spare key is tucked into a notch in the wood, exactly where it was two years ago. I take it and walk up the stairs, unlock the door.

I step in and I could be stepping back in time. It's different now, empty and quiet, from how it was full of people a few hours ago. The smell is what gets me: leather and dust and wood and heat and cleaning products, the same brands we used to use. The big, soft broom leans against the wall, waiting for the girls to put it away tomorrow. I slip off my sandals and pad across the floor in my bare feet. I flip the switch for the disco ball. It starts to turn with a soft mechanical whir, throwing rectangles of silver over everything: moonlight on restless water.

I watch the rink for a minute, nothing moving but light and dust. I don't know what I came here to do.

I walk back onto the floor and sit under the disco ball, then lie down looking up at it, feeling the smooth old wood under my back. I pull my phone and headphones out from my purse, put on an old song about being rotten, wearing makeup, dreaming, and leaving. I listened to this song a lot after Polly disappeared, nights when I couldn't sleep.

I lie there and let the song repeat once before I start talking to her. I'm speaking to the empty room, to no one and nothing, and it should feel so stupid, but it doesn't. It feels like I'm writing a letter or etching a message into a tree trunk, letting a balloon float away over the ocean, putting something into the world that I trust will reach its destination and say what I need it to say.

I tell her about me and Eleanor, how it felt to kiss her. I tell her about the friends I've made in Boston, laughing in our narrow dorm rooms with the snow falling outside. I tell her about Cleo and how happy she looks when we walk through Central Park, about her plans for law school, about Lauren. I tell her about Talia's house in Asheville with the green door and the five roommates and the Blue Ridge Mountains rising in the background. I tell her I miss her. I tell her everything.

The song ends for the twelfth time, and my voice feels soft and scratchy. I get up off the floor and switch off the disco ball. It stops turning, and the room goes dark again. I pull my headphones out of my ears, put on my shoes, and listen to the night sounds around me. Frogs, birds, the great white noise of the ocean. There's nothing here.

But when I open the door, something moves through me. And then it's gone again, but I know it was there. I know it as certain as I know the beat of my own heart. I felt it inside me like a living memory. Something familiar and intimate, fast and laughing. Something free. A flash of warmth.

CALLIE'S SUMMER PLAYLIST

PLAY

"FERRIS WHEEL"	Sylvan Esso
"MANCHESTER"	Kishi Bashi
"TAKE ME THERE"	Delta Rae
"REJOICE"	Julien Baker
"HOME TEAM"	Indigo De Souza
"AGNES"	Glass Animals
"MAROON"	Taylor Swift
"MR. BRIGHTSIDE"	The Killers
"BITTER RIVALS"	Sleigh Bells
"STILL"	Seinabo Sey
"AFRAID OF NOTHING"	Sharon Van Etten
"GOLD"	Chet Faker
"PARADE"	Jacob Banks
"TAKING UP SPACE"	Jetty Bones
"MAKE ME FEEL"	Janelle Monae
"POOL HOPPING"	Illuminati Hotties
"SILK CHIFFON"	MUNA feat. Phoebe Bridgers
"GOOD AS HELL"	Lizzo
"BILOXI"	Hiss Golden Messenger
"NO DEVIL"	San Fermin
"TOXIC"	Britney Spears
"BEFORE HE CHEATS"	Carrie Underwood
"FREE"	Florence + the Machine
"BREATHING UNDERWATER"	Metric
"ANTHEMS FOR A SEVENTEEN-YEAR-OLD GIRL"	Broken Social Scene

ACKNOWLEDGMENTS

This book was the creative project that carried me through the first year of the pandemic, and for that I am grateful, frankly, to the book itself. But I am more grateful to everyone who supported me, encouraged me, and listened to me complain during its writing, not to mention everyone who helped to take it from a Word document to an actual book. These acknowledgments are longer than any I've ever written, because I have never felt luckier for my community than I have since March 2020.

Hannah Hill at Delacorte Press, who edited this book and in doing so made it so, so much better and more interesting: Thank you so much for your perceptive edits and kind words and for always seeing and believing in exactly what I was trying to do. The process of editing this book was one of the most exciting, difficult, and rewarding writing experiences I've ever had, and all of that is because of you.

Thank you to every person at Delacorte who touched this book in big and small ways: Colleen Fellingham, Tamar Schwartz, Natalia Dextre, Megan Mitchell, Stephania Villar, Katie Halata, and Lili Feinberg, among others. Special thanks to Liz Byer, for copyediting; Diane Joao, for proofing; Megan Shortt, for interior design; and Hokyoung Kim and Trisha Previte, who illustrated and designed the cover, respectively. I've never been so excited about a cover in my life! It takes so much work from so many different people to publish and market a book, and I am grateful to everyone who had any part in it.

Thank you to Maria Bell, my exceptional agent at Sterling

Lord Literistic, for your incredible support, interest, edits, and communication. Every time I get a long email from you, I feel a small thrill in my heart. (Not a joke; as we have discussed, I truly love long emails.) I'm so glad and grateful to be on the same team as you. Thank you also to Nell Pierce, who connected me with Maria, and to Holly Hilliard, who connected me with Nell. I am indebted to all three of you.

Thank you to Julie Jolicoeur and every person at the Lemon Tree House, staff and resident alike. This book would not exist without you and the space you created. Looking out at the mountains from my little green desk, having nothing to do but come up with an idea I liked, typing things like "Greek muses" and "skating rink" and "things start getting weird"—God, that was a great two weeks. Thank you, as well, to Principled Technologies for giving me the sabbatical that allowed me to attend Lemon Tree at all.

Normally I like to list all the places where I worked on a book, something my dad always does at the end of his books. Thanks to COVID-19, that list is a lot shorter than it usually is! But I am still grateful to all the places where I worked, even if there are fewer of them than normal: Charlotte, Hendersonville, Asheville, and Pittsboro, North Carolina; Huntington, West Virgina; Myrtle Beach, South Carolina; Camporsevoli, Italy; Washington, DC; and New York City. Extra special thanks to Topsail Island and Holden Beach, North Carolina, the two towns on which Little Beach is based, and to Durham, the location of my favorite place on earth (my house).

Thank you to Duke Young Writers' Camp, where I learned to write and to devote myself ferociously to my friends, and to everyone who taught me those things, especially Barry, Julia, and MK.

Thank you to Professor Madeleine Lucille Turner, who has

been my friend since before we even had the idea of writing terrible poetry, through the era of terrible poetry, and still now, and who is always and forever a phone call away. We are both slightly better writers today, I think.

Dogpark: Alissa, Jaret, Mitzi, Miller, Alex, Allie, Elsie, Hettie, Clare, Carter, Chloe, Xander, and Lionel, not to mention the reasons we're all here (Tig, Wooster, Penny, Fionna, Louise, and ol' Toaster). I'm so happy to be in your lives every day. Nathan, Chloe, Melissa, and Bethany: When I sat down and started trying to come up with ideas for a third book, the one thing I knew I wanted to write about was how it feels to be together with you. Honestly, I don't think I even got close, but I did my best. I hope I made you proud.

Thank you to Don, Janice, and Kym Azevedo, in-laws so wonderful and kind that they don't even deserve the title of in-laws. And thank you to my family: Mom, Dad, Allyn, and Scott. Your wit, humor, thoughtfulness, generosity, and extreme weirdness have been a blessing every day of my life.

I always thank Ben, my husband, for his unwavering support and care in every aspect of our lives together, creative and otherwise. But I have been particularly grateful to him this time around. I dislike talking about my writing, but I talked about this book with him, most notably when I was really stuck around the thirty-thousand-word mark. (A cursed time for any writer, as far as I can tell.) He listened, made a few thoughtful suggestions, and didn't get annoyed when I immediately discarded them. Ultimately, talking to him let me think through what I really wanted to do and helped me figure out how to get started again. Thank you, my shnug, for being so good.

And thank you to my little yam, for everything you have already given me.

ABOUT THE AUTHOR

Sarah Van Name grew up in Raleigh, North Carolina, and now lives and works in Durham with her family and dog. She is the author of two young adult novels, *The Goodbye Summer*, a Junior Library Guild Selection, and *Any Place But Here*.

SARAHVANNAME.COM